Fire Prayer

Also by Deborah Turrell Atkinson

Primitive Secrets

The Green Room

Fire Prayer

Deborah Turrell Atkinson

Poisoned Pen Press

First Edition 2007

10 9 8 7 6 5 4 3 2 1

Library of Congress Catalog Card Number: 2006940936

ISBN: 978-1-59058-402-6 Hardcover

Poisoned Pen Press
6962 E. First Ave., Ste. 103
Scottsdale, AZ 85251
www.poisonedpenpress.com
info@poisonedpenpress.com

Printed in the United States of America

To Robert, Egen, and Andrew

To mourn a mischief that is past and gone
Is the next way to draw new mischief on.

—William Shakespeare, *Othello*, I, iii, 204

Acknowledgments

I am grateful to Bishop Press for permission to quote Hawaiian proverbs from *Ōlelo No 'eau, Hawaiian Proverbs & Poetical Sayings*, by Mary Kawena Pukui, Bishop Museum Press, 1983 (Honolulu, Hawaii).

My thanks go out to the many people who helped me with this novel, which would be an unfulfilled fantasy without the expertise of Barbara Peters, Rob Rosenwald, and Jane Chelius. Big hugs to Michael Chapman, Karen Huffman, Michelle Calabro-Hubbard, Egen Atkinson, and Honey Pavel, who critiqued, supported, and encouraged.

Claudia Turrell and Patricia NaPier contributed much-appreciated legal points of view. Robert E. Atkinson, M.D., supplied the symptoms, treatments, and side-effects of all the injuries my characters sustain. Officer Mace Minakawa of the Honolulu Police Department shared his knowledge of firearms, while HPD Officer Kevin Kobayashi took me in his patrol car to give me a firsthand view of police procedure. Sergeant Keith Kawano of the Maui Police Department added details as to how the Moloka'i police operate. Patricia Johnson, an investigator with the City and County of Honolulu's Medical Examiner's office, provided procedural details. Dr. William Goodhue, City and County of Honolulu's First Deputy Medical Examiner, imparted a wealth of scientific and forensic information. Tom Chun and Malia DeCourcy helped with important details about life on Moloka'i, such as where cell phones stop operating.

Any mistakes in the story are my own and are probably due to the questions I didn't know enough to ask.

All characters and incidents in *Fire Prayer* are products of my imagination. While it is true that Moloka'i was the home of the most powerful Hawaiian sorcerers, I don't know any of them. In 1995, protesters burned a building on Moloka'i Ranch, but no one died.

Some readers may suspect that I exaggerate when it comes to the small town atmosphere of a state with over a million and a quarter people, but I've probably understated it. For example, when I called the Honolulu Medical Examiner's office to find out what a body would look like after it had lain in a Moloka'i forest for two weeks, Dr. William Goodhue not only shared his expertise, he revealed that he's part of the Meyer family of Meyer Sugar Mill in Kalae, near Kualapu'u, Moloka'i. His ancestor, Rudolf Meyer, came from Germany and married a Hawaiian princess. Dr. Goodhue's great grandfather was a physician at Kalaupapa, the famed colony for sufferers of Hansen's Disease, from 1902 until 1925.

Chapter One

Jenny Williams sucked in a lungful of smoke. Her eyes followed the woman down the front walk, but her thoughts were still on Tanner. His hands had been steady because he wasn't taking his medicine. Which was also why his eyes wouldn't meet hers. And the damned fool told her he had himself under control. Yeah, yeah. She'd heard that story for the past ten years.

His intelligence was an electrical short circuit that could fry them both. Too bad he wasn't in a downswing; he was so much easier to deal with when he hated himself. Angry tears stung Jenny's eyes. His illness was a curse, and everyone he came in contact with suffered from it. He might not like to take the drugs because they slowed his mind down, made him gain weight, even made his hands shake, but he was *lolo* without it. Looney Tunes.

The depressions were easier to handle than his manic swings. Hyper, he was like a meth head, twitching and buzzing with confidence and crazy ideas that peaked, then tapered into paranoia. Not only did he rearrange magazines, books, napkins, eating utensils, or anything else in the house so that lines only he saw were parallel (or at right angles, whatever his obsession that day), he often answered the people in his head before he responded to the ones who stood right in front of him. The invisible conversationalists were former professors and folks he'd admired over the last decade or so and still guided his life. Forget about the wife and kid.

Jenny set her jaw. She'd known when she went to answer the woman's knock, he'd slip out the back door. No way he would stand still long enough to wait. Well, good riddance.

Part of her was a little worried he'd think up some reason to barge back in. Not even a stranger would inhibit him when he was hyped, and there was no way she could keep up with the intricacies of his arguments. Such a sad goddammed waste. All she could do was shut him down. If he'd stayed one more second, they would have had a full-on screamathon. Again.

She heard a soft noise behind her and shouted, with a quick glance over her shoulder, "Get back in your room." She knew it wasn't Tanner because he wouldn't creep, he'd blow in like a tropical storm. Knock over a few things on the way.

At the door, Jenny's voice broke. She cleared it, then coughed a few times. Maybe the visitor would think she was fighting a cold. Right. Still, it wouldn't help to show any weakness, or any distress. The woman was an old high school friend of Tanner's, after all. And God knew giving other people a view of her troubles hadn't done her any good in the past and wasn't about to now.

The woman, a Honolulu attorney, seemed nice enough, and asked how well Jenny knew Lambert Poele and Brock Liu. Jenny was happy to relate that Brock was mostly an asshole with some redeeming qualities and Lambert was a recluse who was hardly ever seen. She hoped Liu was the one in trouble. She figured someone was if a lawyer was asking around, and Brock wasn't very popular around here.

The part about Poele was only a tiny fib, and that by omission. She'd seen him a few days ago for the first time in a while. A smile loosened the grim set of her lips. If she hadn't been so mad at Tanner, she would have blushed at the memory.

Jenny watched the visitor drive away, and turned to the beer she'd left on the coffee table. It had been hard to get past the anguish over Tanner's visit and talk to the woman. Christ, these encounters sucked the energy out of her worse than night shift at the hospital. She drained the long-neck and listened for Luke.

If he'd been peeking down the hall a few minutes ago, he'd been smart enough to lie low. "Luke?" she called.

No answer. She wandered into the kitchen and opened the refrigerator door. She needed another beer. "Luke?" she yelled again as she popped the top. "We need to talk."

Storm Kayama looked good, really good. She had the same dark, liquid eyes that he'd always admired, but her solid athletic frame had an ease she hadn't shown in high school. Fifteen years ago Storm had been a pissed-off sixteen-year-old with spiked purple hair. Now strands of her shoulder-length mahogany hair escaped from her thick French braid and wisped softly around her high, wide cheekbones. She tucked one lock, then another, behind her ears, only to have them work free during the conversation with Jenny. Her voice was soft and low and the big brown eyes he remembered met Jenny's with humor and empathy.

He tore at a hangnail and thought back on himself in those days. A skinny high school senior with acne and no friends. He'd been on the verge of his disease then, and his family doctor, the over-worked family practitioner in Kaunakakai, was the only medical person who believed him. Everyone else thought he was stressing over school work, his perfectionism, the drive to go to a good college on the mainland. Whatever it was, the other students picked on him like a pack of mynahs shredding a ripe mango.

Except for Storm, who actually talked and listened to him. She, too, was a misfit. Rumors drifted behind her like smoke. They said someone powerful had kept her from getting shipped off to the Hawai'i Youth Correctional Facility. A big time Honolulu lawyer, with the clout to get her out of Pa'auilo and the trouble brewing there, took her into his family in the Hawaiian way, made her a *hanai* daughter. The black leather jacket she wore like a uniform only confirmed her bad-girl persona. No one picked fights with her. They left her alone, and she acted like that was just fine.

Tanner had tutored Storm in her sophomore biology class. When she arrived on O'ahu, she didn't have much background in the sciences and was at a disadvantage at the new school. But he detected aptitude, a quick mind, and a toughness he admired. Some of the students at their exclusive school were cruel manipulators, and he'd seen her face them down on a number of occasions. One time, she did it for him.

And here she was, taller, smoother, and a lot more peaceful.

Tanner would have liked to tune out and let his mind wander, especially with the pleasant distraction of watching his old friend Storm make her way up the front walk. He did that sometimes—kind of like staying underwater. But Jenny, with her back to the door, kept poking and punching his arms and chest while she alternated between pleading with him to take his medications and blasting a gut-twisting inventory of how he'd screwed up, how he'd ruined Luke's life and hers.

Right then he wished he could hold Jenny underwater. She'd played the Luke card again, and he couldn't ignore the palpable stab of guilt. My son, he thought, the last remaining love of my life, is the weapon she uses to bludgeon me. He's her silver stake. She wants to pound every one of my failures into the atomic structure of my cells, the submolecular tangle of every neuron and dendrite snaking through my nervous system. She likes to see me twitch.

But he wouldn't let her. Take a deep breath, he told himself. Let the electricity run through your body to your fingers and out into the universe, away from your fractured mind. Look at something tranquil. Storm, who now stood at the door, would do. Though he saw her wince at the sound of their angry voices.

Tanner backed up. Coming on an impulse had been a big mistake. He should have stopped by Skelly's first and asked his friend to give him another haircut. He'd had one last week, but maybe another would have smoothed his rough edges. He also might have borrowed a razor, and scraped the afternoon shadow from his chin.

Hell, Jenny would have ranted anyway. She didn't notice his efforts any more. All the resentment she carried around had stained the sunny glow of compassion that had once been part of her. And, he admitted, some of that was his fault. But her bitterness was taking its toll on all of them, especially Luke.

Storm had decided to go ahead and knock on the door, which distracted Jenny, thank God. When his ex wheeled away, Tanner lingered a couple seconds longer to get another look at this woman from his past, whom he still counted among his friends.

Right then Luke peered around the corner with an expression of pain on his face that sent a surge of remorse and anger coursing through Tanner. The dark circles under the boy's eyes nearly tore him in half.

Luke was the reason he'd gone there in the first place. Tanner tiptoed to his son, ruffled his hair, and whispered that he would help him. Then he slipped out the back door.

He could still hear Jenny's fake cordiality as he crossed through the banana trees bordering the back property line. His property line. His house, for what it was worth. The trees were overgrown, and their heavy leaves and ponderous flowers still dripped with last night's rainfall. He could stand there without being seen.

He couldn't see Jenny, but her voice sliced the still air. What had happened to her, to them? When had her blue eyes flattened to veined granite, her voice changed from a lover's caress to a shrill buzz of destruction? When had her golden hair turned to straw and her willowy stature toughened to sinews of decay?

She would poison Luke. Contaminate him with the venom of her bitterness and desperation. He was still an innocent, like others Tanner had known who'd been destroyed at a young age. But he shoved those memories aside quickly.

Moloka'i can be a rough place; few live here in the style of a university professor or business executive. That kind of job rarely exists on this island, which was why Jenny stewed in her misery. She couldn't see that people could be happy and comfortable if they supported each another, when they relished the crystal seas, the embrace of soft breezes, and the fertile bounty of the earth. Jenny couldn't see past the size of a paycheck and a job with status.

Luke was the best part of Tanner's life, the most important accomplishment of his thirty-three years. He had to do something to mitigate his estranged wife's fury and preserve his son's still unspoiled outlook. Out there under the trees, Tanner's eyes burned and his throat ached. He needed to find a way to prevent Luke from being caught in the same crossfire of hatred and rancor he'd seen ten years ago.

Chapter Two

The brisk trade winds nearly tore the duffel out of Storm's hand. She preceded her partner and lover, Ian Hamlin, down the steps from the thirty-passenger Turbo-prop—Moloka'i Airport didn't bother with jet ways—and looked back at him. "Did you actually meet this guy?"

"Briefly," Hamlin said, and jammed a cowboy hat over his sandy hair. It looked good with his bushy moustache. "He didn't say much. His assistant does most of the talking."

"But he's paying you a retainer to look into this."

"Sure. He may have a legitimate negligence suit if Hawai'i EcoTours didn't warn his son of dangerous water conditions, or if the equipment was defective."

"How will you find out?"

"We know Brock went out two weeks ago because we've got a charge on his credit card for March 26th. The morning was calm, but the surf had risen considerably by early afternoon."

"How old is he?"

"Twenty-six."

"Pretty young."

"Old enough to be an executive at Pacific Shipping and Transport. He also sits on the board. Missed a board meeting for the first time ten days ago."

Storm squinted at him. "He grew up in the islands, didn't he? He'd know how treacherous the ocean on those unprotected shores can be."

"I've still got to check it out." Hamlin looked away from her. "Brock is Liu's only son. Devon Liu is pushing eighty and looks like he's aged a decade in the last two weeks. Plus, he's not an easy man to ignore."

"I see." Storm didn't want to argue. They'd had disagreements before about personal injury suits and had different points of view on the topic. Hamlin was more ambitious in terms of his client list and their connections. Storm maintained that she didn't want her job, and her life, to revolve around social connections and the size of her paycheck. She also wanted her vocation to be about good will, and didn't hesitate to point out to Hamlin that it was working; she'd made enough money on her last case not only to pay her share of office expenses, but to put a generous hunk into an IRA.

Tanner Williams' phone call had been a surprise, a voice from the past. The last time she'd seen him, he'd saved her from a dismal science grade. That was the year she'd transferred to O'ahu from the Big Island, a lonely, displaced sixteen-year-old.

Though they'd never discussed it, she'd known that Tanner had his own struggles. He was a year older than the other seniors. According to rumor, he repeated his junior year because of health problems and was monitored by a doctor on his home island of Moloka'i. Students whispered that none of the Honolulu specialists had found anything wrong with him. He was just *mental.*

Tanner never discussed personal issues, and he rarely sought the company of other students. But he'd been honest, kind, and smarter than anyone else in the school, including a lot of the teachers. He'd given Storm support when she needed it, and now she would do the same for him.

Not that she needed much of an excuse to come to Moloka'i, especially when Uncle Keone and Aunt Maile were going to be there. They didn't often leave Parker Ranch, on the Big Island of Hawai'i, where Uncle Keone was one of the long-time *paniolo* and a ranch foreman.

Hamlin caught up to Storm and gently touched her arm. Storm could tell he knew he'd touched on a sensitive area and wanted to change the subject before it grew into a dispute. They needed this long weekend to linger over wine-soaked, unhurried dinners and breathe deeply of the peace that was Moloka'i. They needed long walks under the stars, cuddling before the cozy fireplace of the Lodge, and retiring to the sophisticated and cozy cabin-style rooms.

"Devon Liu's situation is sad, that's for sure," Storm said, to put the difference behind them. She was glad to be distracted by the sight of a bandy-legged, cowboy-hatted figure who stood by the low platform that passed for a baggage claim, just inside the chain link fence.

"Uncle Keone," she shouted, and dashed toward him.

The man, whose skin was darkened by the weather to a leathery mahogany, wrapped his arms around her. "Hey, honey girl. It's been way too long."

"That's cuz you won't leave the Big Island and come to Honolulu," Storm teased.

"Not. We just been plenny busy lately, clipping calves and training colts. I been meaning to come see Dusty Rodriguez for months. When Maile and I found out you'd be here, nothing would keep us away." The lines around Keone's eyes radiated like the warmth of the sun. "Plus, get chance to pick out some good cutting horses. Dusty got the best."

"He gets his cattle from Parker Ranch, doesn't he? We once helped him round them up and load them on the barge."

"Sure enough." Keone sighed. "That was quite a few years ago, back when your daddy was still alive."

Hamlin caught up to Storm and Keone. "Keone, it's great to see you. How's life on the Big Island?"

"It's good," Keone said and grabbed Hamlin in a hug. "But it'd be better if we saw more of you two."

Storm linked her arm with Keone's. "When can we see the horses?"

"Soon," Keone said, and gave Hamlin a wink. "Depends on what else you need to do."

"I need to make a run into Kaunakakai, but other than that, I'm going to relax," Storm said.

"From what I hear, you need a vacation."

"I'm fine," Storm said, but her smiled disappeared as she took in the glance that passed between Hamlin and Keone. "I wasn't hurt in that cave, just scared."

"You were damn lucky not to end up drowned like those surfers," Hamlin said.

Keone put his arm around Storm's shoulders. "Let's just thank our lucky stars that you and Aunt Maile's *'aumakua* got the job done."

Storm's hand went to the little gold pig she wore on a chain around her neck. Aunt Maile was not only a registered nurse, she was a *kahuna lā'au lapa'au*, or native healer, and believed deeply in the ancient Hawaiian traditions. She'd sent the necklace, their shared family totem, to Storm during her last case. The emerald-eyed charm had been a gift for Storm's thirtieth birthday, and Maile's timing with its arrival had been prescient. The case, though Storm would never admit it, had left a thread or two of silver in her dark hair.

"Where is she?" she asked.

"Out gathering *limu* before the tide comes up. She'll meet us at the ranch."

"What's the medicinal use for *limu*?" Hamlin asked.

"All kinds of things." Keone grinned. "But mostly it makes me happy, especially when the chef has fresh ahi tuna coming in. He and Maile are in cahoots. They going make one fresh *poke* to have with our beer, um, cocktails tonight."

"Yum," Storm said, conjuring pictures of her aunt in the kitchen with the chef, adding the fresh seaweed, ground kukui nut, and other seasonings to the raw fish dish.

A golf cart pulling a trailer piled with bags drew parallel to the baggage claim counter. No mechanized, hidden workers or conveyor belts here; bags got piled on and off by hand and in one sweep.

"Dusty's out front," Keone said, and pointed to a white van with the Moloka'i Ranch logo printed across the side. Like most things on the island, the vehicle was covered with a layer of red dirt.

Storm remembered Dusty from his visit to Parker Ranch because at fifteen, she'd thought he was hot. Especially for an old guy. Now she realized he'd been around thirty, or her present age. But he'd seemed so different than Uncle Keone, who'd essentially raised her, and the other men she knew. Keone may have been a father figure, but Dusty definitely wasn't. He'd been sort of an unattainable movie-idol type, like that Magnum P.I. actor Tom Selleck, though she would have swallowed her tongue before she told anyone.

One day, Storm rounded a corner of a barn and saw him leaning into a woman, one hand on the wall behind her and one inside her blouse. The woman, a pretty brunette named Darlene, was fast closing the gap between them. Storm had whirled on the heel of her boot and scooted back around the barn, her face burning with embarrassment.

A few days later, she'd overheard Aunt Maile whispering to Keone, who chuckled. "Guess he hasn't grown up yet."

Maile made a snorting noise, kind of like a horse when you tighten a girth too quickly. Storm knew that noise; the last time she'd heard it was when she got caught playing hooky with Howie DeSilva and had to spend an entire weekend weeding Aunt Maile's herb garden.

Storm regarded Dusty's approach with interest. He was still over six feet tall, and broad shouldered with thick black hair shot with gray, but his eyes had changed. His gaze was direct, not flirtatious, and conveyed a touch of sorrow.

His quick grin erased any sadness Storm thought she'd seen and he grabbed her in a jovial hug. "More beautiful than ever," he said, and Storm was glad her blushing cheeks faced away from Hamlin and Keone.

Dusty, oblivious, released her and grasped Hamlin's hand. "Great to meet you." He grabbed their bags. "You two travel light."

Storm and Hamlin were the only passengers in the van, so they sat on the bench behind the driver's seat. Keone rode shotgun to Dusty, who asked Hamlin if he'd ever been to Moloka'i.

"This is my first time. Storm's told me about it, though. She loves coming here."

"How long since you been here?" Dusty asked Storm. He regarded her in the rear-view mirror. "I haven't seen you since the Big Island."

"That was a long time ago. I was here with friends about ten years ago, right after the fire on Moloka'i Ranch."

"A brush fire?" Hamlin asked.

"If only," Dusty said. He turned left onto the highway, a winding picturesque two-lane road that led east, through grazing lands and fallow fields toward the town of Maunaloa and Moloka'i Ranch. There was a long pause before he continued.

"Someone burned down the ranch owner's home one night. Those were hard times." The corners of his mouth turned down at the memory.

"Are people more accepting of the ranch's presence these days?" Storm asked.

"I think so." Dusty shrugged. "But it might be that we're all getting older. Ten years ago, there was a lot of friction. Seemed like the ranch owners were just here to make money, wouldn't pay any heed to the people who call this place home." The sadness returned to his eyes. "People lost their favorite fishing spots, couldn't get to the old Maunaloa cemetery to visit their families' graves. They felt betrayed."

He pointed to a sign that greeted visitors leaving Moloka'i Airport.

ALOHA
SLOW DOWN
THIS IS
MOLOKA'I

"We want to keep the lifestyle here. The population's only about seventy-five hundred people and half of 'em are related.

Still no traffic lights, you know? But it's hard, and maybe not realistic all the time. We can't close ourselves off from the rest of the world. We talk more now, have meetings."

"How did the land owners and the local people get so far apart in their points of view?" Hamlin asked.

Dusty took a deep breath before he answered. "My opinion, for what it's worth, is that big land owners and locals, they have different perspectives. In the old days, land was the source of life for the Hawaiians. They didn't have a western concept of land ownership."

"Like Native Americans on the mainland?"

"Similar." Dusty's expression became thoughtful again. "We all know it's hard to get people to accept change, and who knows how much to accept. But if we're going to survive as a culture, we need jobs. Moloka'i's unemployment is the highest in the state." He looked briefly into the back seat at Hamlin and Storm. "What's the rate in Honolulu?"

"Things are good right now. It's under ten percent," said Hamlin.

"It's twenty, thirty percent here. We need work, but just when we think we can trust a big land owner to give us fair jobs and still honor our lifestyle, you get someone like that software guy, McAfee, who begged to buy a big wedge of land from an old family, then auctioned it to the highest bidder." Dusty shook his head with disgust.

Hamlin had been staring out the side window. "I can understand people's reluctance to give up their land, but violence just antagonizes people. That protest ten years ago—didn't someone die?"

Dusty didn't answer for a second or two, and Storm saw his shoulders rise and fall with a deep breath. "Yup. Those were bad times." He seemed to settle himself deeper in the driver's seat.

A few uncomfortable seconds passed before Keone spoke. "Storm, you been riding much since you moved to the city?"

"No, and I miss it. I guess I could go to Waimanalo, but I haven't had the time lately."

"Dusty's got a roundup tomorrow."

Dusty perked up. "She's good, you know," he said to Hamlin. "Won a coupla trophies for barrel racing back in her teens."

Hamlin's eyebrows shot up and he looked at her. "She never told me."

Storm shrugged in embarrassment and poked Uncle Keone in the shoulder. "Tell him the real story."

Keone chuckled. "How old were you? Thirteen? You'd been training Butterfly for weeks, getting ready."

Storm turned to Hamlin. "Butterfly was my mare. Best horse in the world. We'd been looking forward to the all-state rodeo for months. The best *paniolo* in the islands compete there. Butterfly could feel my nervousness, and she wanted to do a good job for me. When I let her go at the gun, she jumped out so fast, I lost my seat and bounced over the back of the saddle. All I could do was flop around and hold on to the saddle strings. The reins were flying behind and I didn't even have my feet in the stirrups."

Keone and Dusty were laughing out loud. "And she won."

"Butterfly won. I had nothing to do with it."

"People thought it was an act. You should have heard the applause," Keone added. "But when the announcer called Storm's name, a silence fell over the crowd cuz nobody believed the race was for real. And Storm walked right up to the microphone, grabbed it, and proclaimed that her horse had won the race. She stuck a carrot—you had those in your pocket the whole time, right?—in the big silver cup and let Butterfly work it out with her lips. The audience loved it."

Hamlin grinned at Storm and her discomfort. She rolled her eyes at him, then caught sight of a hand-lettered sign by the side of the road. *A'ole La'au* and right under it, *Momi's Organic Foods, 7 p.m. Tuesday.*

"Is that one of the meetings you were talking about?" Storm asked, trying to change the subject.

"What's *a'ole*? Hamlin asked.

"Means 'never,'" Dusty said. "As in 'never develop La'au Point.' And that's a meeting, all right. Activism isn't dead and gone, just more stable."

"Same people who were protesting ten years ago?" Hamlin asked.

"Some of 'em. A few, like Lambert Peole, dropped out. I hardly ever see him, though I heard a rumor he's been calling on a woman in Kaunakakai. Jenny Williams, a nice gal with a real smart kid." A note of regret seemed to linger in Dusty's voice.

Storm didn't dwell on that, because the name caught her attention. Jenny Williams was Tanner Williams' ex.

"Lambert Poele was the leader of the protest group back in the nineties. He got arrested for the fire, right?" she asked.

"They let him go. No evidence against him, just hearsay. He was the only suspect without a good alibi."

"Was anyone else arrested?" Hamlin asked.

"Nope. Tanner Williams and Skelly Richards were with women that night and Connor's mother said he was home with pinkeye."

Interesting detail for Dusty to remember, Storm thought, and almost missed Hamlin's next question.

"Skelly Richards. Isn't he the guy that owns Hawai'i EcoTours?" Hamlin asked.

"Yeah," Dusty said, and pulled into the drive leading to the Lodge, a rustic yet sophisticated structure with spectacular views in all directions. "He's had his troubles, too. Got into using meth for a while, but he's gone to NA for a decade and he's had his little business almost as long."

Storm stole a sidelong glance at Hamlin. This was the guy Devon Liu, owner and CEO of the mega-business Pacific Shipping and Transport, wanted to sue for millions. She wasn't sure, but Hamlin might have slouched a bit in his seat.

"You ever meet a guy named Brock Liu?" she asked.

Dusty hopped out of the driver's seat and opened the van's sliding door. "Sure, he stayed here a few weeks ago. Had a fancy room and ordered a lot of room service." He shrugged at Storm's inquisitive look. "He had a girlfriend, from what I hear."

"That the heavy-handed guy your appaloosa gelding dumped?" Keone asked. "I think I saw him the weekend I was here checking out your brood mare."

"The same," Dusty said.

"Thought so." Keone grinned and turned to Storm. "Why you asking?"

Hamlin answered. "He may have disappeared in a kayak accident."

"Here on Moloka'i?" Dusty asked.

"He rented a kayak from Hawai'i EcoTours and never came back."

Dusty screwed up his face. "I carried his bags to the car the morning he left and could have sworn he said he was heading for the airport."

"You know what day that was?" Hamlin asked.

"Not offhand, but we can find out from the hotel registration desk," Dusty said.

"Did you drive him?"

"No, he had his own SUV. Musta had it shipped over, cuz nobody rents them here. Dollar and Budget are the only car rental places, and they don't want people going off road. Too dangerous. Landslides, flash floods, private land and all."

"Maybe he borrowed it from a friend."

Dusty looked doubtful. "It had Honolulu plates."

Dusty took Storm's and Hamlin's duffel bags and put them on a waiting cart. "He got sort of friendly with one of our cow-hands. Let's get you checked in, and we'll head to the stables. We've got a mare about to deliver and Makani will be there. You can ask him."

"We'll meet you at the stables," Keone said. Hamlin nodded his agreement.

Storm kept her mouth closed. She'd meet them, but later. She couldn't help feeling Dusty knew more about Brock Liu than he let on. He knew Skelly Richards and his personal history, he knew about Lambert Poele's love life and the rumor that Brock had a girlfriend. The coconut wireless worked faster than electricity on this island, so why hadn't he heard where Brock had gone? And where was that conspicuous SUV?

Chapter Three

Storm stowed her clothes in a dresser drawer and put on jeans and a t-shirt. She turned to Hamlin, who was still unpacking. "I'll meet you later. I need to run into Kaunakakai and visit Tanner Williams' ex. I also want to pick up some things."

"Don't you want to see the mare give birth?"

"I'll probably be back before that happens. And you can talk to Makani about Brock Liu."

Storm didn't like seeing the disappointment in his eyes, but she wanted him to talk to the cowhand and think about Devon Liu's case. Liu was a powerful businessman in Hawai'i, with land holdings throughout the islands. He was the type who met senators for an afternoon drink and knew their kids' names. He'd be hard to say no to, even if there was no proof the tour company had been remiss. Plus, there was no evidence yet that the son had died. What if Brock Liu had a sweetheart here that his father, a highly opinionated individual, didn't approve of? Or if Brock had tired of working for his father?

But Storm had a bad feeling this wasn't the case, though she couldn't put her finger on why she felt this way. Probably it was because when people in Hawai'i disappeared, the outcome was often an unhappy one. Though the vast majority of island citizens were friendly and helpful, avarice, addiction, desperation, and malevolence existed here, like anywhere else. Plus the towering cliffs, miles of rocky coastline, impenetrable jungle, and the unpredictable geology of old and active volcanoes made it easy to get rid of someone. Storm wasn't even going to consider Aunt Maile's ghostly legends: she didn't want to believe Night Marchers, malevolent spirits, or angry warriors of old were among the reasons Brock Liu missed his board meeting. She worried, though, that the young man had suffered an accident, probably in the ocean.

Then there was the rub with Hamlin, who was less discriminating than she when approached by influential clients. Storm believed many people who filed negligence or wrongful death lawsuits found it easier to live with the idea that someone else was responsible for a death than the deceased or, God forbid, themselves. And she didn't care how much influence certain clients had.

She walked back through the Lodge, head down, lost in thought. In Hamlin's defense, it would be difficult to turn away a client with Devon Liu's clout, as any other lawyer would pounce on the case without a second's hesitation. And Liu, as president and CEO of the billion-dollar Pacific Shipping and Transport, could put a serious crimp in the practice of an attorney who pissed him off.

Then again, maybe Hawai'i EcoTours neglected to include Brock's lifejacket with the kayak, or a paddle had broken. Hamlin was right, he had to check it out.

Meanwhile, she needed to check on Luke Williams, as per Tanner's request. She needed to see for herself whether Tanner had a reason to be concerned about Jenny's mothering abilities, because that's what he'd asked her to do.

Storm figured she'd be less conspicuous asking questions in the small town of Kaunakakai if she was alone. Her half-Hawaiian, half-Japanese ancestry made her less of an outsider than Hamlin's green-eyed, sandy-haired fairness. On an island that didn't even have traffic lights, she'd be spotted as a stranger, but she looked more local, and unfortunately, that sometimes made a difference.

She had also told her best friend Leila, who ran a bakery in Honolulu, that she'd bring home a few loaves of the renowned Kanemitsu's Moloka'i Bread. It would be a good idea, too, to pick up some crack seed, dried cuttlefish, and fruit for between-meal snacks while she asked some low-key questions about Jenny, Luke, and Tanner Williams.

When Tanner called last week, he mentioned that he'd seen her name in the paper. The murder of Nahoa Pi'ilani, a renowned surfer, was big news, and she'd been caught up in the rash of deaths. In one of those odd connections that sometimes happens, she'd recently thought of Tanner, too, because she read an article about the East Coast pharmaceutical company where he'd once been a prominent researcher. Some years ago, a rumor circulated that he left the company and moved back to Moloka'i in some kind of disgrace. But there'd always been gossip about Tanner, and Storm ignored it just like she had in high school.

Outside, Storm squinted into the oblique rays of the sun. The white van that had brought them from the airport sat a few yards away. Someone's rear end, encased in tight jeans, bobbed in the opening of the driver's side door.

"Hi," Storm said, stepping aside to avoid being hit by a jettisoned paper cup that missed the trash bag sitting beside the vehicle. "You know if anyone is going into Kaunakakai?"

The jeans straightened and turned to face Storm's question. There'd been no question that the derriere was a woman's, but Storm was surprised to be staring up at a set of false eyelashes as dark and heavy as moth wings. The woman was in her mid-thirties and big, a good two inches taller than Storm's five-eight. She outweighed Storm by twenty pounds, and the bright mid-day heat had caused her blue eyeshadow to collect in the creases of her upper lids. Perspiration ran down her neck into a bosom that stretched the ribbing flat on her striped tube top. She could pack a sandwich and spare change in that cleavage.

"When did you want to go?" the woman asked.

"Whenever the bus is leaving."

"Give me a couple more minutes. I'm headed into town for supplies." The woman bent over, grabbed a whisk broom, then stood up again. "I'm Delia."

"Thanks, I'm Storm. Can I help?"

"Nah, I'm almost done. Let me just…" Storm lost the rest of the sentence because Delia dove between the front seats. She came out with a clipboard and an empty Doritos package, which she tossed into the rubbish bag.

She readjusted her tube top. "Okay, you ready?"

"Yeah, thanks." Storm got in the passenger side and noticed that Delia had taken out one of the back seats and loaded a couple of ice chests. "You going to the grocery?"

"The docks," Delia said, and pulled out onto the road. "Fresh catch is mahi and ahi. Dinner's going to be great. You eating at the Lodge?"

"I think so. I'm here with my aunt and uncle. He's here from the Big Island, buying horses."

"You're Keone Mapuna's niece." Delia's face cracked into a smile. "I'm from Hilo."

"The big city," Storm said, and they both laughed. It was, compared to Pa'auilo, where Storm had grown up. Still, with a sedate population of about forty thousand, there wasn't much for a young person to do in Hilo except smoke pot and dream about leaving. Moloka'i made Hilo look like a teeming metropolis.

"You been here long?" Storm asked. The van was at a high point, where the women could see ocean on both sides of the island. Storm felt as though she were on a precious gem at the center of a vast, sparkling dome of Pacific blue. They could have been in orbit. It was simultaneously breathtaking and remote.

"About twelve years. I moved here when I got married, but that didn't work out so well." Delia shrugged. "The marriage, I mean. Working for the ranch is fun, and the pay's decent."

"Seems like you'd meet some interesting visitors."

"Sure, from all over the world." One corner of Delia's mouth turned down. "Haven't really connected with anyone, though. If you know what I mean." Delia tugged at her tube top again.

"Um, yeah," Storm said. "You ever meet a guy named Brock Liu?"

Delia was looking straight ahead when Storm asked, so Storm couldn't tell if the woman's face froze from sadness, distaste, or some other emotion.

"Yeah, his family owns land here." Delia's full lips thinned with her answer, and she didn't say anything else for several miles. She broke the silence with, "You want me to let you out in town?"

"Is there a general store? Maybe a place to get snacks?"

"Try Amos' Crack Seed. And Ishiro's Market is right down the street." Delia pulled into a parking slot, but left the van's engine running.

Storm climbed out, then leaned in the open door. "You going back soon?"

"Yeah, I can meet you on the main road in about an hour." Delia avoided Storm's eyes.

"That would be great," Storm said.

The women exchanged mobile phone numbers and Delia drove off. Storm hopped out, wishing she knew why Delia had shut down at Brock Liu's name. She liked Delia and wouldn't mind having someone to chat with about Moloka'i life. Squinting into the angled rays of the setting sun, she decided she'd share Delia's odd reaction to Brock Liu with Hamlin, and let him decide what to do with it.

Chapter Four

Amos' Crack Seed reminded Storm of favorite stores from her childhood. Like the Hilo and Hamakua shops she remembered, it probably hadn't changed much since the day it was built, not long after World War II.

The three long fluorescent tubes in the center of the ceiling were no competition for the bright outdoors. One of them flickered and buzzed like a trapped fly. Shelves of big glass jars filled with dried, preserved fruits lined the walls of the single room. A rack right inside the door, with which Storm had almost collided in the gloom, hung with home-sealed packages of Betty's Chocolate-Dipped All-Butter Shortbreads, chocolate chip macadamia nut cookies, and something called Melting Moments.

A spicy sweetness saturated the air, and Storm's salivary glands ached with longing. She grabbed a bag of Melting Moments—anything with that name was worth a try—and headed for a wall of jars. There she paused, scooper in one hand and empty cellophane bag in the other, paralyzed with delicious indecision.

Prune mui, black cherry seed, or pickled mango? Maybe the shop owner would let her sample. Just a little taste from a jar or two.

She looked in the direction of the cash register, where he sat in the shadows, hunched like a stone Buddha. Only the glint from his eyeglasses revealed that he drew breath. Nearby, a flock of noisy adolescents clustered around a big refrigerator-freezer. The light from the appliance tinged their skin blue.

"Hey, Roly-Poly, what you eat today? One case Haagen-Dazs, thirty-five Snickers bars, a kālua pig or two—"

Someone in the group snickered.

"Shut up, Hogan," came a boy's voice, authoritative in its nonchalance.

Another voice, a girl's raspy alto, chimed in. "Yeah, Hogie, like you're skinny or something."

The girl who'd spoken moved shoulder to shoulder with the kid who'd stopped Hogan's teasing. He was the smallest of the boys, and he casually tossed an apple from hand to hand. Storm guessed his age at ten or eleven. Hogan, a husky kid who now stood alone, had the shadowy beginnings of a moustache on his upper lip.

Hogan sneered at the girl and teased in a sing-song voice. "Haley's in luh-uv, Haley's in luh-uv."

The other girl began to giggle, but Haley's glare stopped her stopped mid-titter.

"Puh-leeze," Disdain dripped from Haley's voice.

The smaller boy stepped to the counter with his apple and a can of Dr. Pepper. "Rolly, you got any li-hing mango?"

"Sure, Luke." A chair creaked and the huge man rose, then stooped behind the counter. He brought up a stack of plastic containers from under the counter. "Your mother'll want some, yeah?" He spoke softly and wheezed from exertion.

"Sure." Luke dug in his pocket for his wallet.

"No need." Rolly waved off Luke's money. "Tell your mom I got some of those other supplies, too."

"Thanks, Rolly."

Haley handed over money for a soda and followed Luke out of the store. Neither Haley nor Luke looked back at the other kids.

When the others finished buying their items, Storm stepped to the counter and laid three bags of cracked seed and her Melting Moments before the big man. Despite the ceiling fan whirling above them, his dark skin, pulled tight across a face as wide as one of the glass jars, glistened with sweat. The size of his head dwarfed his smudged eyeglasses, and he peered through them, unmoving except for the rise and fall of his shoulders.

"You have any more of that fresh mango?" Storm asked

The man's breath wheezed out, then in, before he answered. "You want with li-hing or plain?"

"One each, if you have."

The man heaved himself to his feet and reached under the counter again, where he apparently had a small refrigerator. He was breathing hard when he put the plastic containers on the counter.

"How hot are the firecrackers?" Storm asked.

"This batch plenty spicy. You like chili pepper?" He pronounced it *cheelee peppah.*

"Not if it's so hot I can't taste the fruit."

"This crackseed a good batch." He pointed with a finger the size of a bratwurst at the jar next to the one where Storm had found the firecrackers.

"Same dried plum, no chili pepper," he explained.

"I'll take some of both. I'm going to share with friends."

"Where you from?" he asked.

"O'ahu." Storm extended her hand. "Storm Kayama."

Rolly's hand was the size of a dinner plate. "Roland Pauoa. Friends call me Rolly."

"You grow up here?"

Rolly nodded and jotted some numbers on a pad. "Five-fifty," he said.

Storm got out her wallet. "I went to high school with Tanner Williams. You know him?"

"Yeah." He jutted his chin at the door. "That's his son."

"The boy named Luke?"

Rolly nodded.

"Seemed like a good kid. His father tutored me."

"Luke's smart like his dad."

"Tanner still around? I'd like to say hello."

Rolly's gaze shifted away, toward the big refrigerator. "Hard to find since his divorce."

"He always liked peace and quiet. Didn't hang out with most of the other students."

"Hasn't changed." Rolly slowly placed Storm's purchases in several small brown paper bags and seemed to reach a decision. "Tanner visits Luke when Jenny goes to work."

"When does she work?"

Rolly shrugged. "Her shift changes."

"They live around here?" Storm looked toward the door, where the boy had gone.

"Two blocks away." Rolly's face split in a smile. "Even I walk that far." He handed her change for her ten. "He might be there now. Kukui Place. Second house on the right."

Storm was halfway up the walk when she heard the man and woman shouting. It sounded as if they'd paused for breath, and then started again. Or maybe Luke had interrupted them. He was only five or ten minutes ahead of her and if he'd dropped Haley at her house or paused to finish his soda, he'd just be getting in.

Storm slowed, hating to witness the pain and fury in the couple's voices. What should she do? Just as she was about to make an about-face, the noise dropped as if someone had put a lid on a jar of angry bees. Damn, they'd seen her.

A thin blonde appeared several seconds after Storm's knock. She had on a scrub top, the kind hospital personnel wear, with tiny yellow teddy bears on a blue background, and reading glasses perched in her hair. Tired eyes scrutinized Storm's face.

"Yes?" Her voice was husky and low.

The woman looked worn out. Maybe it was a day's hard work followed by a fight with the ex, but Storm got the feeling Jenny's struggle had gone on longer than this afternoon.

"I'm sorry to bother you."

Jenny had opened the screen door and Storm could see that the house was neat, but far from plush. Both the carpet and the sofa were worn and a card table with two brightly colored woven place mats and folding chairs were positioned where one would expect a dining table.

Storm wondered how Jenny's life had been when Tanner had lived with them. He'd never told her why they split up. He hadn't told her much at all, come to think of it.

"You from the Catholic Charities?" Jenny asked. "I can't give anything right now. Sorry."

"No, my name's Storm Kayama. I went to high school with Tanner. I'm just here for the weekend and thought I'd say hello." Storm shuffled her feet. "He got me through Biology."

A shape moved behind the woman and caught Storm's attention.

Jenny's eyelids flickered, but she didn't turn around. "He's not here."

"Do you know how I could get in touch with him?"

The woman blew out a breath of air in what seemed like exasperation, and Storm smelled alcohol on her breath. She could also see a long-neck bottle on the heavy glass and stone coffee table in the living room. It was the one piece of furniture that had substance, a sense of permanence, and Storm remembered hearing that Tanner had married a sculptor. The woman before her, in hospital scrubs, didn't look like Storm's idea of an artist.

"Try calling one of his friends," she said, then whirled and shouted over her shoulder. "Get back in your room."

The motion startled Storm. She wanted to cover her surprise and establish some kind of rapport with this woman. "You have children?"

"One." Jenny attempted a smile. "A son."

"About getting in touch with Tanner, would you know a name I could contact?"

Jenny turned away. Storm thought for a moment she had been dismissed, but the rustle of paper kept her waiting for a moment longer. Jenny returned with a lit cigarette between her lips and a note in her hand. When she opened the door to hand it to Storm, she released a cloud of smoke and fresh beer.

Storm glanced down and squelched the jolt of surprise that passed through her. There was one name on the paper, and it was one Storm had seen before.

"Thanks." Storm jammed the note in her jeans pocket.

She waited until she got halfway down the street before she reached in her pocket to take another look.

Chapter Five

Storm's cell phone rang and she paused to dig it out of her pocket.

Delia's voice crackled. "Ready to go?"

"Yes, where are you?"

"Kaunakakai Ball Park."

"I'm at Kukui and Ilio." The white van rounded the corner a couple of blocks down the street.

"I see you."

When Storm climbed in with her packages, Delia said, "You got what you needed?"

Storm held out the bag of firecracker dried plum. "You like 'em hot?"

Delia grinned and took two.

"You know Tanner Williams?" Storm popped a spicy plum in her own mouth, bit down, then sucked air through her teeth. "Whew, he told me these were spicy."

Delia was already rattling ice in a cooler behind her seat. She handed Storm a can of diet soda, then popped the top on another and swilled half of it before Storm had her own open. It smelled faintly of fish.

"You always full of surprises? Burn my mouth and ask me about a crazy guy at the same time?" Delia burped loudly.

"Crazy?" Storm took another cooling swallow. "I went to high school with him."

Delia glanced over at her. "You look younger."

"Two years. He was a senior when I was a sophomore."

"Coulda fooled me. I'd have thought you were five or ten years younger." Delia shook her head and steered a corner one handed. "Maybe it's because he spends a lot of time outdoors. He's really tan, kind of weathered-looking, you know? Must be sun damage," she said and stuck her own face up to the rear-view mirror. "I gotta remember to wear sunscreen."

"You know if he lives near his ex?" Storm asked.

"I get it. You had a crush on him." Delia grinned. "You can tell me."

"No, I haven't seen him for years. I just admired him. He was really smart."

"Yeah, sure." Delia spit a pit out the window. "I admire some guys, too. You got any more of those hot ones?"

"He got me through Biology." Storm felt sixteen again, and the spark of defensiveness she felt was surprising. "Last I knew, he was married and had a good job on the mainland." She held out the bag of firecrackers.

Delia popped a few into her mouth. "He's not married any-more, but he has a kid, and they say he adores his boy."

Was Delia still being coy? Storm didn't want to play high school games anymore. Let Delia think she had a spark of unrequited love. Storm had bigger concerns. "Who's 'they,' and who says he's crazy?"

She thought back to Tanner's phone call. He had been low-key and articulate, and he'd voiced his concerns about Luke's mother without sounding like a jealous lover. But Storm hadn't seen him for years, and she knew from personal and profes-sional experience that some guys hid their inner furies well. If Tanner had periods of paranoia or was obsessed with his lost love, Storm wanted to know. And not for the reasons Delia suspected, either.

"People around here. Everybody talks, you know? They say he has a chemical imbalance." Delia had her face back in the mirror, this time gouging a piece of fruit peel from her front teeth.

The young woman managed to keep the van between the curving lane lines, but it had to be by some non-visual sense. Storm put a hand on the dashboard. "Chemical imbalance? Depending who you talk to, that could be anything from a cold to schizophrenia."

"I guess." Delia took a half-minute to mull over the question. "I've seen him, you know. He talks to himself, or talks like someone's with him. When there isn't." She rolled her eyes in Storm's direction. "I've also seen him when he said good morning just like anyone else in town."

"Do people say he takes drugs?"

Delia reached for the bag of spicy seed. "You think he might have a crystal meth lab or something? He used to work for a drug company, you know."

"No, I just wondered what the rumors are." The last thing Storm wanted was to start any more.

"No one's said anything about Tanner using coke or ice, nothing like that. Not like some other people I've heard about." Delia chewed, rolled the seed around in her mouth. "One of my friends says he's manic. He's supposed to take medication for it."

Storm's stomach dropped. She hadn't heard the term "manic" for a while, in part because people who knew her well avoided it. Storm's mother had suffered from bipolar disease, and committed suicide when Storm was twelve. Storm's adolescence had been a rough road. It was part of the reason she'd ended up on O'ahu as a teenager.

"Manic?" Storm repeated.

Delia heard the uneasiness in Storm's voice and shot her a glance. "Yeah, there's a term for it. Bi-something. You know, manic-depressive. Brilliant people often have it."

Storm swallowed. Delia made a sharp right turn into the Lodge's parking lot and Storm was glad for the excuse to hold on to her seat. "Bipolar," she murmured.

"That's it." Delia pulled to a stop in front of the Lodge. "You all right?"

"Sure." Storm opened the door and climbed out of the van. "Hey, thanks for the ride."

Storm waved to Delia and headed directly for the winding walk to her room, glad she didn't have to go through the lobby. She wanted to be alone, think about the news she'd heard. It rang true, and it had resonated on a level she hadn't expected.

Chapter Six

Tanner stuck to residential streets and open lots on his way to Maunaloa Highway. It was only a half mile or so, and it would be easy to hitch a ride once he reached the highway, but he wasn't ready to see anyone yet. He needed to think, and walking helped, even if he sometimes had to go a long way. He'd been dealing with this problem a long time, and he figured he knew best how to take care of himself.

His thoughts and emotions sometimes tangled like long, snarled fishing lines. Clumps and masses of thoughts and beliefs, which he had to sort through. Something else went on, too—elation and adrenaline in an electrifying blend. It felt good, but was a sensation he'd come to realize didn't work if he was around other people.

He needed to be alone to pick among the electrical impulses ricocheting inside his skull. Time and energy was required to release and separate the strands, get rid of the scrambled knots of sensation: the pounding pulse, burgeoning ideas, rampant desire mixed with paranoia, jealousy—and anger. It was his burden in life; easier than some people's, harder than others'.

He looked down at his feet in his comfortable, but muddy sneakers. They were his outside shoes, the ones he used to hike the path back to his cabin. He'd have to clean them. No, maybe leather shoes would be better when he went to visit people. Too late now, but next trip. A new shirt, too. One for himself and one for Luke. And the haircut, he'd drop by Skelly's for that.

Connor might be there, though. That's okay. He'd deal with him. Plus, Connor was growing up.

Jenny would at least know that he tried. Tried to be a good father. He was still trying, and wanted to do it better—and more often. Christ.

Take a deep breath, swing his arms into the walk. Look around, the setting sun turning the ocean to a plate of molten steel. If he went down to the pier, he'd see the boats unloading their fresh catch. Muscular tuna, glittering *mahi mahi*. But not now. He had other things to do.

Tanner checked his pulse. He didn't have to put his fingers on his wrist or neck to do this; he could monitor it by thought. His brain working again. His breathing was deeper and easier now. He'd covered at least a mile and was calmer. He could stand still. It was one of the little tests he gave himself. Next test was to stand on one leg. If this worked, he would do one of the yoga moves he'd been learning from the new teacher in Kaunakakai, the Tree Pose, Vrksasana. If he could do that one, he was ready to interact with people without disturbing them. Tools to integrate mind and body, like the yoga instructor said. It wasn't magic, but it helped.

He stuck out his thumb, but the car, which looked like a rental, flew by. That was okay. Someone who recognized him would come by and pick him up.

It was a little over ten miles to Kamalo, where the Richards brothers had their EcoTours business. The shop was in a great location for the service they provided. On the ocean, near Kamahuehue fish pond. Skelly didn't live in the little apartment adjacent to the office any more, but he left a hidden key and let Tanner know he was welcome to use it. Tanner could shower and shave, and if Skelly was there, he'd not only help with a haircut, but give advice about Luke. Connor occasionally used the apartment when he wasn't shacking up with his latest girlfriend, but Tanner looked for signs he was there and tried to avoid any conflict.

Skelly had had his wild days, along with his brother, but he'd been married for three years now to Helene, a good woman, and he was father to eight-year-old Amy, Helene's daughter from her first marriage. Luke called Skelly Uncle, and Skelly not only filled the role, but furthered it by acting like the brother Tanner never had. It was Skelly who got Luke interested in baseball, which was a source of pride and self-respect for the undersized eleven-year-old.

Tanner made a mental note to talk to Storm about Skelly and Luke. If anything happened to him, he wanted some kind of legal document so that someone could take Luke in. Either Skelly or David Niwa. Niwa had also been a childhood friend, and his daughter was a friend of Luke's.

That was the way friends worked, wasn't it? Skelly knew he could count on Tanner, too. Every week or so, when the weather was calm, Tanner would take a group out for Hawai'i EcoTours. He never took money for it. Instead, he convinced Skelly that he enjoyed taking out the mainland groups. Funny thing was, he did—he took real pleasure in it. Consequently, he'd turned into the brothers' most popular guide.

Tanner watched another tourist car go by. C'mon, it was getting time for the locals to head home for dinner.

His own stomach growled, but he ignored it and thought about tourists and smiled. Even his psychiatrist worried at first that herding a half-dozen affluent visitors from Michigan or New York through the wilds for several days would make him crazy, though Dr. Campbell used the words "distract" or "unnerve." Tanner liked to say crazy, or lolo. It's what it was.

The first group he'd taken out was when Skelly was desperate—he had two groups scheduled, Connor had taken off suddenly for O'ahu, and Skelly's other employee had the stomach flu. Tanner did it because Skelly had no one else to turn to, and neither of them had been sure if the trip would work out.

The excursions brought Tanner satisfaction not only from the experience of camping under stars thick as frost on a mountaintop, but also from interacting with the clients. The groups visited isolated beaches and tide pools, where if they saw anyone, it was a shore fisherman who waved a greeting to Tanner and continued with his own activities. Tanner gave lectures on unique examples of flora and fauna, plus he got the chance to look for rare seaweeds and other plant life.

He'd already found several edible seaweeds in varying water depths and was especially searching for *Bryopsis plumosa*, a source of kahalalide F, a possible treatment for a handful of serious diseases, including AIDS. Visitors were invariably fascinated with his work and some had intelligent and useful suggestions. He'd even made a serendipitous acquaintance, a Ph.D. at UCLA named Alex, who had taken his two sons kayaking for the weekend to celebrate the younger one's birthday. Alex was very interested in Tanner's work.

Tanner wished Jenny would let him take Luke along on some of the expeditions, especially if children his age were along. But Jenny clung to her bitter righteousness like *'opihi* to their wave-battered rocks.

He and Jenny had once shared so much. Tanner made a noise that sounded like someone had jumped on his chest. Herein lay one of his quandaries: if he took his pills, they insulated him from the cutting pangs of loneliness, the knowledge of how much he missed living with Luke and Jenny. But the pills had the same effect on his brain that dropping milk into water had; they blurred the clarity of his thoughts along with his emotions.

He and Jenny once shared synergy; they had been greater than the sum of their parts, especially when Luke came into the picture. Tanner knew his family was far bigger than he was alone. He felt as if it was an entity that protected, sustained, and even imparted life force. With a start, he realized why Jenny looked stringy and pale. She had to come up with the energy to keep going on her own, and it was sucking the juice out of her. But so were her habits and negativity, he reminded himself.

The sight of a big blue and white sedan cruising down the road pulled Tanner from his ruminations. He waved at the familiar vehicle. Enough of Jenny-thoughts, it's not healthy to keep playing the same loop over and over. What he needed to deal with now was the fact that her fear and anger were keeping Luke from him.

The police car pulled to a stop without bothering to pull to the side of the empty road. "Hey, Tanner," Sergeant David Niwa said, "where you going?"

"Skelly's place. You headed that way?"

"Sure, I'm on the way home. Hop in."

Tanner got in the front seat, next to Niwa, whom he'd known since they were in grammar school. Niwa lived about a mile from Skelly's and Helene's house, and the EcoTour office was on the way to both their homes.

"Howzit?" Niwa asked.

"Okay." Tanner knew right away the answer betrayed his frustration.

Niwa drove one-handed and glanced over at him. "You been up at your old place?"

"Yeah."

"You get to see Luke?"

"A little."

"Jenny okay?"

"I guess."

Niwa shook his head sympathetically. "Divorce with kids sucks."

"No kiddin'."

"Luke's got a big game tomorrow, doesn't he?"

Goddamn, if he'd known, he'd forgotten, and Jenny hadn't reminded him. But he could have asked Luke, too, instead of jumping right into an argument with her.

Niwa was watching him, and he was very good at watching people.

"What time's the game?" Tanner asked.

"Five-thirty," Niwa said. "Haley's pitching."

"That's great." Haley had been competing with one of the other kids for the position. "She deserves it."

"We'll see," Niwa said. He twisted his mouth. "Next year, she has to play softball."

"Doesn't seem fair."

"Yeah, I'd have to agree. How's Luke doing?"

"Okay." Tanner paused, then decided to voice a concern. "He told me Jenny stayed out all night a week or ten days ago."

One of Niwa's eyebrows rose. "Was he frightened?"

"Worried about his mom. He worries about me, too. Doesn't seem fair."

"She wasn't working a shift at the hospital, I gather."

"No." Tanner clasped and unclasped his hands. "Seems like she's been drinking a bit, too."

Niwa turned into the drive for Hawai'i EcoTours. "I'll keep my ears and eyes open for you. Luke's more mature than most eleven-year-olds. He'll be okay."

"Yeah, thanks."

Niwa peered at the office through the darkening foliage. "Don't see any lights on in there. You want a ride someplace else?"

"I've got a key."

"Okay then. See you tomorrow at the game?"

"Wouldn't miss it."

Tanner made his way along the round stepping-stones that paralleled the tangled and drooping *hala* trees to the paved walk, which was lined with herb pots. One of Helene's hobbies, and one that everyone who knew her appreciated. She was an excellent cook and generous with whatever she had on hand. She declared the plants grew better at the office than on their too-shady home lot, which was a couple of miles inland. Tanner looked around to make sure he wasn't observed, then made his way to a rosemary bush and tipped the pot just enough to pull a key from underneath.

He clattered around opening the door, went back to replace the key under the pot, then stepped inside. The office was dark, shaded by the thick hala grove outside the window and the low angle of the setting sun. A bank of light switches was right next to the door, he knew, and he ran his hand along the wall and hummed a song that had been buzzing through his head.

But before he found the light switch, a hurtling weight flattened him against the wall. Stunned, his breath rushed from his lungs in a grunt and the strength left his legs. It was all he could do to gasp like a speared *ono* before he collapsed to the rough carpeting.

Chapter Seven

Storm opened the door to the hotel room and closed it carefully behind her. "Hamlin?"

No answer. He must still be at the barn. She walked into the room, flicked on the lights, and sat down on the bed to pull on her boots. Instead, she flopped backward and stared up at the ceiling.

Luke was eleven, very close to the age she'd been when her mother died of the same affliction Tanner apparently suffered. One day, she'd come home from the seventh grade and found her home full of people. Concerned people, who didn't know how to tell an emotional and confused twelve-year-old girl what was wrong.

It had been Aunt Maile who'd grabbed the flustered adolescent and taken her outside to the peace of the garden. Under the shade of a mango tree in the front yard—Storm still associated the over-ripe smell of fallen mangoes with loss—Maile told Storm that her mother had taken an overdose of sleeping pills. Yes, that meant she had died. Her spirit had joined the ancestors. Yes, she was now with *pueo*, the owl, her totem, her *'aumakua*. Apparently she'd taken the pills not long after Storm left for school in the morning. No, there was nothing Storm could have done to stop her. She was sick, my dear one, you couldn't have known. You couldn't have known.

Storm had spent months looking for owls, her mother's spirit animal. In trees, under the eaves of neighbors' homes, storage sheds, whatever shadowy lair tugged her eyes and hopes. Owls came to her in dreams, singing in her mother's rich mezzo-soprano. These days, Storm didn't see them often, but they still captured her attention and she always sent a mental greeting to the animal. Sometimes she asked the winged creatures why.

Storm felt a bond with Luke. One of the difficult aspects of having a parent with bipolar disorder or mental imbalance was that not everyone viewed mental illness as a disease. To some, it was a weakness. And some scrutinized the sufferer's children. These things could be inherited, couldn't they?

Through much of her youth, Storm alternated between the concern that she might have inherited the disease and angst over her own self-absorption. She was alive, wasn't she? She also had Aunt Maile and Uncle Keone, who had stuck with her through the ordeal of losing her mother and then through the more ordinary adolescent ordeals.

Storm remembered drawing comfort from Aunt Maile's story of how Storm's mother had chosen the owl *'aumakua* from their mother's side of the family, whereas Maile and Storm had chosen *pua'a*, the pig, from their father's side. It gave Storm some distance from her mother's choices, yet still connected her to the strong framework of the family.

She knew she had always been lucky to have loving family and friends. When her father died of kidney disease, she'd been sixteen and a rebel. Not a particularly likeable person, yet they'd all stood by her.

Who did Luke have? Jenny looked haggard and worn, and Storm had seen her with a beer at four in the afternoon. An early cocktail after a fight with the ex might be an exception, but Storm had a hunch it wasn't. The woman didn't exude an aura of happiness.

She needed to keep Tanner's request in mind, though it had become more complicated. The gossip from Moloka'i's coconut wireless needed to be verified. Luke's best interests were tied not only to Jenny's parenting skills, but to Tanner's.

Storm sat up and pulled on her boots. She had a nice long weekend to sort through Luke's situation. A scrap of paper peeked from her jeans pocket and she pulled it out. And then there was Jenny's note, another surprise. *Skelly Richards, 567-3208.*

Hamlin was going to find this coincidence and Delia's reaction to Brock Liu very interesting. Storm rose to her feet with a surge of anticipation. For a few hours, she could put aside her empathetic yet gloomy thoughts on Luke's welfare and enjoy herself. Her loved ones, horses, and a new baby foal were only minutes away.

Chapter Eight

"Get off." Tanner's plea was muffled by the rough indoor/outdoor carpet. Imbedded sand made it more abrasive and his assailant knew it.

"The fuck you doin' here?" The words were borne on breath like burning rubber. The attacker made a phlegmy chuckling noise and rolled up from Tanner's head and neck, but sat with his full weight in the small of Tanner's back. Now Tanner could hardly breathe.

"Connor, s'that you?" His words were almost unintelligible.

"Tanner, you dumb fuck. I should call the police."

"The police just dropped me off." Tanner hoped that the forced whisper of his response covered the rising—and irrational—amusement he felt. Like Connor would call the police; he avoided contact with uniforms of any kind. But Connor weighed about a hundred pounds more than he did and Tanner knew he didn't want to antagonize the oaf.

"What do you think you're doin'?" A rancid cloud of halitosis followed Connor's gleefully menacing words, but at least he slid off Tanner's back.

Tanner took a deep breath of relief, then sat up slowly and wiped his nose, which was bleeding, but didn't seem to be broken. It wasn't painful, anyway. "Skelly around?"

"Maybe. Whaddya want?"

"Thought he might give me a haircut." Tanner sneaked a peek at Connor, but he couldn't gauge the size of his pupils in the dark room. He'd better act as if Connor had been using either crystal meth or anabolic steroids, both favorites of Skelly's younger—and bigger—brother. That meant avoiding any kind of a challenge until he knew Connor had calmed down. And people thought *he* was crazy. Christ.

"You're a stupid lunatic, you know it? Breaking in here in the dark." Connor grunted to his feet. "You want me to call him?"

Tanner knew he referred to Skelly, not the police. "Sure. He home?"

"Yeah." Connor walked to the desk, still in the dark. The numbers on the squat, solid phone glowed softly. Tanner heard seven tones as Connor punched the keys, then the sound of a woman's irritated voice over the line coincided with the crunch of feet on the gravel outside. "Connor, is that you again? I told you—"

Connor slammed the phone down as the door opened.

Skelly took in Tanner's form, hunched and still seated on the floor, and his shoulders slumped. "Shit, Connor."

"Hey, I'm protectin' the business."

"We don't need protection from Tanner."

"I'm not so sure." Connor gave Tanner an evil look and loudly cracked the vertebrae in a neck the size of Tanner's waist by jerking his head from side to side. He clomped off.

Tanner watched his departure. Connor reminded Tanner of a semi-tranquilized rhino. No intellect, and powder-keg impulses. Rhinos might be more predictable.

"You okay?" Skelly reached down and pulled Tanner to his feet. "You've got a raspberry on your cheekbone. That hurt?"

"I guess I startled him."

"Yeah." Skelly snorted. "You and everyone else. He took a swing at Bob Crowder last week." Crowder was the easy-going handyman who kept the kayaks in good repair. He lived out by Halawa Bay and had three kids of his own, plus he'd taken on his sister's three because of her deteriorating health. Usually two or three of the adolescents were around the shop, helping him, so they'd probably seen the altercation, too.

Tanner winced at the image. "Thanks for coming down so fast."

"Good thing Luke called ahead." Skelly sighed. "Connor's supposed to take a group out this weekend. He's in no shape right now for a group of tourists, though. He'll get 'roid rage if some kid can't figure out how to fasten the lifejacket." His eyes met Tanner's and a plea crept into his voice. "You got plans for the weekend?"

"Luke's got a game tomorrow afternoon. When do they get in?" Tanner's mind raced over the logistics.

It was an hour drive to where the road ended at Halawa Bay and Hawai'i EcoTours had a supply hut filled with boats, camping equipment, and an assortment of gear right on the beach. At the hut, he'd need to load the boats with camping paraphernalia, tie them together, and paddle his way up the coast. He wanted to make sure everything would be perfect for the visitors when they arrived. Fresh water, the outdoor shower set-up with solar heating, canvas tents.

"I pick them up at the airport tomorrow afternoon, but they're not going out in the boats 'til Saturday." Skelly's voice was so hopeful that Tanner had to smile, which reminded him he had a fat lip. No, Connor couldn't take these people out.

"Is Crowder there?" Tanner asked. If he was, the effort would be easier not only because he'd have help loading the boats, but because he and Crowder—and maybe a couple of his kids—could each take a kayak. This would cut the set-up time in half.

"I can get him there," Skelly said eagerly.

"What're you going to tell Connor? He'll be way *huhu*."

"He'll be pissed, but I'll make it look like I need him somewhere else."

"If I go out early tomorrow, I can still get back for the game," Tanner said thoughtfully. "I'll need you to set up the second campsite, but you can do that Sunday while we're paddling to Saturday night's site." He watched the worry lines lift from Skelly's brow and felt the glow of being of use to someone.

"Brah, you are one true friend." Skelly grinned and threw him a towel. "I'll give you a ride to the end of the road. Just tell me when you want to leave." He picked up the desk chair and moved it into the bathroom. "Sit down. I can sweep up better in here."

Tanner sat down and wrapped the towel around his neck. "What's roid rage?"

Skelly's smile disappeared. "You just saw it. Irrational anger, one of the side effects of anabolic steroids. 'Roid. Get it?"

"He got any other symptoms?"

Skelly nodded and looked sad. He didn't elaborate and Tanner didn't ask. Instead, he sat quietly and listened to the gentle snipping of the scissors. Connor once idolized his older brother. It was painful for Tanner to observe the change. He could imagine what Skelly felt.

Skelly was the first to break the silence. "How's the research going?"

Tanner's eyes lit up. "I've got two nibbles on the new substance I've isolated—Whole Health Medicines, which is a good-size American company, and an Australian one I want to check out."

"For the seaweed extract?" Skelly made a little grimace. "It had better be real healthy, cuz it looks like shit." He laughed.

Tanner grinned. "It does, but we'll figure out some way to package it. It's great for you, you know."

It wasn't worth going into a detailed explanation of how certain antioxidants tied up harmful free radicals, or how he had simplified an extraction technique for kahalalide F. Tanner knew Skelly accepted his word that it was good for him, and was glad his friend was finally having some commercial success.

Skelly ran a comb through Tanner's hair and snipped at a few wayward ends. "Did that guy you met last year on our tour with one of the companies help you?"

"The physiology prof? He gave me some tips on getting grant money from the NIH. Federal money. Can't knock that."

"Way to go, dude. Hey, I oughta make you pay for haircuts."

Tanner smiled. "I'm not getting rich, but it helped me buy equipment and it got the companies' attention. Gave me legitimacy."

"You did all this in your cabin out past Keawenui Bay?"

"Yeah, once we got my generator set up. I sure appreciate your help with that." Tanner's smile faded. "You still have those pills I asked you to keep for me?"

An expression of approval spread across Skelly's face. "You're going to take them when you talk to the pharmaceutical people, right? That's a good idea, you know. Hey, can you get your head farther into the sink?" Skelly tested the water temperature and began to wash Tanner's hair. "You're gonna make this happen. Hah! My *lolo* friend, the rich Moloka'i chemist. What's Jenny going to say to that, eh?"

Tanner shrugged and the towel fell to the floor. His next words held a tinge of urgency, even though they were spoken into the sink. "How about Luke's meds? You keeping extra in the fridge for me?"

"No worries, brah."

"That's more important than my pills."

Chapter Nine

Storm was halfway up the hill leading to the rodeo arena and stables when she ran into an ebullient group that included Hamlin and Aunt Maile.

"Auntie Maile," she cried out, and the women threw their arms around each other.

The men stood grinning, and Hamlin couldn't contain himself. "We saw the baby horse just getting to its feet. A half-hour old. It's a girl."

"Yup, it's a filly," a young man chimed in. "A cross between one of our quarter horse stallions and an Arabian mare."

Dusty spoke up. "Storm, this is Makani Kekapu. He's our rodeo foreman."

Makani stuck out his hand. "I heard you hold your own on a horse."

"These days, I'm lucky to stay on," Storm said.

"Not the rumor going around. We should have a paniolo competition. A little round-up and barrel racing."

From the corner of her eye, Storm saw the skin tighten around Hamlin's eyes. A round-up would be way out of his comfort zone.

"Maybe just a picnic ride," she said.

Storm took Hamlin's hand on the walk back to their room, but he took it loosely and walked faster. "I've got about five minutes to shower and get ready for dinner," he said.

"They'll only get a cocktail or two ahead of us."

"Right." Hamlin opened the door to their room and immediately peeled off his dusty, straw-speckled jeans. He threw them onto a growing pile of dirty clothes on the closet floor and headed for the bathroom.

"You can use those to ride in tomorrow," Storm told him.

He turned on the shower and stepped in. "I'm from Detroit, remember? I play basketball and hockey. The horse stuff I'll leave to you and your pals."

"Okay, okay." Storm backed off the riding idea, and told him about her trip to the crack seed store while she washed up at the sink. She related what she'd found out about Hamlin's case, which included Tanner's friendship with Skelly Richards and Delia's reaction to Brock Liu. She decided to save her description of Jenny Williams for later, when Hamlin seemed in a better mood.

"Didn't you tell me everyone knows everyone else on this island? Is this surprising?" He got out of the shower, wrapped in a towel.

"Hamlin, are you mad at me or something?"

"A little. I mean, you're the one who complains when I don't stay by your side at business functions, and we're both in the same profession. This is your element, not mine, and you ditched me this afternoon." He jerked up the zipper on a pair of pressed chinos.

"Those business functions are *your* clients' cocktail parties, political rallies, stuff like that." Storm heard the petulance in her voice. "I guess I thought you'd want to talk to Makani alone. Did you get the chance?"

"Are you kidding? He was up to his shoulder in a horse's ass. I thought he was going to crawl in."

"The foal was breech?"

"I didn't ask. I was trying not to barf on his boot heels."

"Wow. Wish I'd been there."

"How'd I know you'd say that?" Hamlin turned toward the door. "Are you ready for dinner? I need a drink to get my appetite back."

Hamlin had a few more than usual, but Storm didn't say anything. Instead, she enjoyed her wine and tried to converse with all their dinner companions. It was a fun group. When they got back to their room, Storm took a shower. By the time she crawled into bed, Hamlin was already asleep.

Storm tossed and turned during the night and was relieved when she saw the silver halo of morning bleed around the closed drapes. For a split second, she contemplated the mournful bird cry she'd heard before she'd opened her eyes, but she didn't think about it long. Over dinner the night before, she and Aunt Maile had decided if Storm woke up in time, she'd join Maile for some plant-gathering. Storm peeked at her watch. It was 6:30; she had fifteen minutes. Maile would forgive her if she didn't show up, but Storm wanted the time with her aunt.

Hamlin was still snoring with deep, rhythmic breaths. If she was lucky, he'd just be rolling out of bed about the time she got back. Storm propped a note in front of the bathroom mirror. "Meet me for breakfast at eight. Free coffee in the foyer, next to the concierge. Love, me."

That's where she found both Aunt Maile and Uncle Keone, mugs in hand. "Are you coming with us?" she asked Uncle Keone.

"No, I'm going to check on that new baby up at the barn. Where's Hamlin?"

"Still sleeping." Storm filled one of the mugs the hotel staff had set out for guests and turned to Keone. "Say, if you see him, will you try and talk him into a nice, easy ride later this morning? If he hears from you what a breathtaking view the trail follows, he'll be more inclined to go along."

"I'll do my best."

Aunt Maile had an eyebrow raised, though, and Keone got busy adding more sugar to his coffee. "Come on, honey. We need to drive toward Kaunakakai."

"We're not hiking around here?" Storm hustled to keep up with her aunt, who'd given Keone a quick kiss and headed out the front door.

"Not today. I want to see if we can find *'awa*, and it's too dry in the gulches around the ranch."

"*'Awa*? May I keep some?"

"You having trouble sleeping?"

Storm ignored the question and climbed into a small van with the ranch logo on the side. "The ranch loaned you this?"

"Yup. We're also going to get some *'awapuhi* for the manager's wife. She fell the other day and sprained her wrist. Some *koali* might help, too." Maile put on her seatbelt. "What's going on with you and Hamlin?"

Storm slumped. "I don't know where to start."

"Start with your seatbelt."

Storm fastened it. "Part of it has to do with work."

Aunt Maile's face softened. "I wish I had some magic answer for you."

Storm couldn't remember when the first little glitches had popped up. She hadn't wanted to admit they were there, and now they were spreading like eczema. "It seems like we're disagreeing more and more, like we don't have as much in common as we used to."

"He's a good person, a kind man."

"I know." Storm barely whispered.

"That's not a criticism of you, either. He's lucky to have you, and he knows it." Aunt Maile reached out and squeezed Storm's hand. "Meanwhile, try to listen to your heart and what it's telling you."

"I am."

"It takes practice."

Storm opened her mouth, then closed it again.

A gentle smile creased Aunt Maile's face. "I know you'll do the right thing."

The tightness in Storm's throat eased a bit. "I'm glad I got up in time to go with you."

Several comfortable miles passed quietly before Storm broke the silence. "Say, what kind of bird cries early in the morning? It woke me up."

Maile shot Storm a quick look. "It could be any number of birds."

"Really?" Storm wasn't fooled. "You were thinking of a specific one, though."

"I thought of the ʻalae. But it couldn't be."

"A mud hen? Why not?"

"They're endangered. There are some on Oʻahu, but no one's seen them on Molokaʻi for decades."

"Why'd you think of the mud hen?"

"Hmmm." Aunt Maile tapped the steering wheel in time with the melody they'd picked up on the radio, a station from nearby Maui. Storm had a hunch her aunt was deciding whether to relate some Hawaiian legend that had been passed around since her great-great-grandmother's days. They sometimes disagreed about the importance of these old tales in modern life. Most of the time, Storm tolerated her aunt's stories; her aunt was an intelligent, well-educated woman. A registered nurse, and also a teacher of the old ways, a respected *kahuna*. But this time, Aunt Maile just continued to hum.

An hour later, Storm and Maile had climbed up and down several ravines and gathered two full baskets of plant cuttings. Aunt Maile looked satisfied and Storm had sweated through many of the concerns buzzing around her head. Not that she knew all the answers, but she'd made some decisions about her own behavior. For a start, she'd decided not to railroad Hamlin into a ride. She'd ask how he wanted to spend the day and go happily along with his wishes.

When she and Aunt Maile got back to the Lodge, they found Hamlin and Uncle Keone, who looked like he hadn't moved, next to the coffee urn. Storm wrapped her arms around Hamlin's waist and he returned her hug.

"I went with Keone to see the baby horse," he said, grinning. "It looks completely different this morning. I mean, it has a fuzzy coat. And it's starting to scamper on those long legs."

Keone beamed. "The mare came over for an apple I'd been saving, so the little filly followed." He put his hand on Hamlin's shoulder. "We're going to turn this man into a horse lover yet."

The four of them went into the dining room and ordered breakfast. After Hamlin had downed about a liter of fresh orange juice, he said to Storm, "You'll love her. She's already prancing around, and the mother horse watches her with the same expression humans have for their toddlers. Makani and I put a little harness on her."

Keone saw the question on Storm's face. "Makani puts an adult horse's halter over her head and fastens it around her chest, so she's easier to catch and handle. Says it socializes the foals easier. He's a real ranch man, that Makani. I'm going to take a few new tricks home to the Big Island."

"He wants to take us on a ride this morning," Hamlin said. A touch of uneasiness had crept into his voice.

"We don't have to," Storm said. "You want to go canoeing? Or out in a Zodiac? We could see if there are still a few humpbacks that haven't gone back to Alaska."

Hamlin looked thoughtful. "Maybe tomorrow. I'd like to try this ride. It's going to be a great view, and Makani and Keone are going to teach me some things. Plus, the Lodge is packing a picnic lunch for us."

Storm fumbled a huge bite of syrup-soaked taro pancakes into her mouth. "That sounds great." Later, she'd tell Uncle Keone what a genius he was. She didn't dare look at Aunt Maile, who was grinning down at her own scrambled eggs.

A half hour later, the four of them ambled up the hill to the stables, where they found five horses tied to a rail, spaced evenly so that Makani could move easily among them. At the moment, he was bent over the rear hoof of a big buckskin gelding. The horse blinked sleepily in the sun. His ears perked up at the approaching foursome, but he didn't put his hoof down.

Makani looked up. "Hi. You're early." He picked up the buckskin's other hind leg and cleaned the hoof. "Or I'm late. Thought I'd have these guys saddled up before you got here."

"We'll help," Keone said. "Hamlin, you can curry, especially on their backs where we'll put the saddle blankets. Storm, why don't you get the blankets and match saddles to the horses? Maile and I'll get the bridles."

A half hour later, Makani had them mounted and in single file, with Hamlin behind Makani's bay mare. Aunt Maile was next, then

Storm, with Uncle Keone bringing up the rear. For a half hour or so, the trail, often wide enough for two horses to walk abreast, crossed red-dirt pasturelands. Makani dropped back to ride next to Hamlin. Storm couldn't hear all their words, but she could see Makani gesture to Hamlin's hands and demonstrate how to hold the reins against the horse's neck, or use the calves of his legs and his body weight to urge the animal before resorting to his heels.

Storm smiled up at the sun warming her face. When they got higher into more forested land, she relaxed and let the leaves' shadows dapple her eyelids. This was bliss. Hamlin was learning an activity she loved, from a man who was a lot less threatening than if Storm had tried to teach him herself.

This was something to think about. What was it that had come up between them? Was she just feeling insecure? Or was it Hamlin? It seemed she rarely could take a teaching role in their relationship. Did she need more recognition than he was willing or able to give her? He was three years older, and like many men, he was a doer, a guy who felt most effective when he was active: fixing a convoluted legal problem, teaching law students, charming potential clients. His instincts were to lead, especially where she was concerned. And though she trusted that his intentions were good, their opinions often differed.

Sometimes she worried he felt underappreciated, even threatened, by her independence. She didn't know what to do about that in the long run, but right now was not the time to get bogged down with questions that had no answers. She could just be happy Makani was teaching him to ride.

Makani pointed to Hamlin's feet, then exaggerated his own heel position. He slid one hand up the reins, shortening them. Storm perked up. Sure enough, both Makani's and Hamlin's horses picked up their pace. Because horses are herd animals, the rest of the mounts followed and trotted up a long, gentle rise. When they slowed, Makani took his position in front and the troupe began to pick its way up steep, rocky cutbacks.

The ascent went on for nearly an hour, through low, foggy cloudbanks that dampened them, though the horses lathered into a sweat from the effort of the climb. The riders perspired, too, as they leaned forward in their saddles to help the horses' efforts. When Makani's and Hamlin's horses broke out of the forest, Storm saw Hamlin's head snap up. She caught his profile momentarily as he pushed his hat back and grinned.

In a moment, all five horses broke through the fog to the top of the hill, where the riders took in a vastness of sapphire deepening to indigo, where the earth curved into a haze that obscured the boundary between sea and sky. It was as if the heavens had come down to enfold them, and for long minutes, no one spoke.

Finally, one of the horses stamped a hoof. Makani hopped off his mare. "Whaddya think of this for a picnic spot?"

"Couldn't do any better," Keone said.

The others slid off their mounts. Hamlin flexed his legs a bit, and Storm reminded herself to check and make sure they had some ibuprofen on hand for tomorrow. She would use it, too; it had been a while since she'd exercised these muscles.

Makani had tied saddle bags onto his and Uncle Keone's horses and the two men unloaded the bags onto a level area. Makani hobbled the horses and set them to graze, then spread out a large, checked tablecloth. Keone unwrapped a couple of insulated packages that made clinking noises. One had five bottles of pale ale, the other an assortment of bottled waters and sodas. There was a box of cut and whole fruits, a loaf of sourdough bread, sliced avocados, condiments, and a variety of meats and cheeses. Memories of the big breakfast five hours before had faded with the foggy mists of the morning.

It was bright and sunny on their outlook, and though the breeze was cooling, heat rose from the earth. Along with the satisfying meal, the balmy air made the riders and their mounts sleepy. After lunch, the men covered their faces with their hats and rolled jackets under their heads. Soon, soft snores carried over the soughing of the wind.

Aunt Maile and Storm cleaned up the remnants of the picnic and Storm took apple cores to the horses, while Aunt Maile wandered to the edge of the forest to look for *popolo*, whose berries had antibiotic properties. Her horse, she claimed, had a cut on its shoulder, but Storm thought she might be wandering off to find a private bush. And that was fine with Storm, who thought she might look for one in the other direction.

When Storm got back from her walk, Makani and Keone had put the bridles back on the horses and retightened their girths. The haze that blurred the horizon a little over an hour ago was much closer. In fact, cloud banks shot with oblique streaks of sun and rain loomed so close they could smell the water in the air.

"We might get a little wet. Does everyone have a jacket?" Makani got on his horse. "Let's head back through the forest. There's a bit more shelter."

The horses knew they were heading back to the ranch, too, and with the wind at their backs, lengthened their strides along the path. Though the leaves rustled around them, the ride was cool and the horses moved in a comfortable rhythm. Storm could see Hamlin sat as relaxed as everyone one else on the ride, and she grinned. She didn't get away with it unnoticed, though, as Keone chuckled behind her.

"You're as transparent as a window pane, you know?"

"Shoots, Uncle Keone, I can't ever fool you."

But both of them were fooled. Stunned, in fact. The horses were in single file, Makani and Hamlin were carrying on a conversation, and Makani was turned in his saddle to talk to Hamlin. No one in the line knew if it was Makani's bay or Hamlin's buckskin who first snorted its warning. But Makani's horse reared and pivoted first, which led Hamlin's to do the same. The stench of death reached them a split second later.

Chapter Ten

Skelly Richards pulled into the driveway at Hawai'i EcoTours around eight a.m. He'd stopped for breakfast at an old friend's house on the drive back from Halawa Bay, and despite the coffee he'd taken for the road, was feeling the lack of sleep. The friend had called a few days ago to tell Skelly that he'd heard Connor at the gym, talking about some people from O'ahu who were looking for the younger Liu brother. He thought Skelly would be interested. That alone made Skelly uncomfortable, plus any discussion about the Lius was bad news. It was a long-known fact.

After last night's haircut, he and Tanner had reminisced about old friends and had a few beers. Actually, Tanner only had one. If he even finished it. Skelly didn't want to count the bottles he'd emptied—the throb behind his eyes told him too many.

The evening had been a pleasant buzz of friendship, except when Skelly mentioned the old gang. He'd also referred to the Liu kid, now he thought about it. But Tanner had just looked at him with a blank stare. After an uncomfortable moment, Tanner asked why he was thinking about them. The whole thing had been a bit weird, as if Tanner had forgotten he was part of the gang.

Granted, the beer had made Skelly talkative, but he thought it was okay to put out feelers with someone he trusted. He just wanted to know if Tanner had heard the same gossip the other guy phoned about. He guessed not, but he wasn't sure. That look had been odd. Could be that medicine Tanner was taking, though. It certainly made him sleep like the dead. He'd been tough to wake up.

They'd spent the remainder of the night in the office on a pull-out couch and chair cushions arranged on the floor. Skelly figured it was better than driving home, waking Helene and Amy on their entry, and again when they got up two hours before dawn.

It had been pitch dark, chilly, and raining when they loaded Skelly's faded red pickup with supplies and pulled onto the highway to Halawa Bay. At least they'd had time to brew a pot of coffee from the grounds Tanner had found. No milk or sugar, though.

"Probably from your last visit," Skelly said, sniffing at the bag of coffee, which was one of two things in the freezer. The other was a carton of freezer-burned ice cream. Chocolate chip cookie dough. He tossed that one into the rubbish can without sniffing.

"Means they're about six weeks old."

"At least."

They hadn't said much on the hour drive to the drop-off point where the road ended. They were both trying to wake up.

That was three hours ago, and the big stack of pancakes Skelly had eaten was making him so drowsy he could hardly keep his eyes open. Seeing Dave Niwa's police car in the drive roused him, though.

He braked to a halt and climbed stiffly from the truck. "What's up?" Two hours on the road and less than four hours of sleep hadn't left him in the mood to beat around the bush.

"Where've you been?" No joking around. In fact Skelly wasn't sure he'd ever seen Dave so serious. And he'd known him for ages.

"Uh, what's wrong?"

"Skelly, I mean it. Where've you been?"

"I took Tanner to Halawa to set up camp. We've got a group coming in tomorrow. What's going on?"

"You were with Tanner?"

"Yeah, since about six last night."

"That's when I dropped him." Niwa's sternness ebbed a bit. "He spent the night with you and Helene?"

"No, we stayed here. Had to get up too early." Skelly shut the truck's door. "What's up?"

Niwa scuffed a size thirteen in the gravel walkway. "Jenny Williams died last night."

"Oh shit." Skelly fell back against the truck as if someone had pushed him. "Shit," he repeated, much softer.

"Yeah."

"Where's Luke?"

"He found her."

"Oh no, man."

"Yeah. He called 911 for an ambulance this morning. They called me." Niwa's voice had a hitch in it. "I took him to my house."

"He's friends with your daughter, isn't he?"

"Yeah. You got any way to get hold of Tanner?"

Skelly pulled out a two-way radio. "Doubt if he'll have his on yet. Doesn't have a cell phone, either." He turned it on and keyed the transmission switch. "Tanner? Tanner, you there? Over."

The radio crackled, but no one responded.

"We get decent reception in the storage cabin, but once you start around the point, it's iffy. On the water, it's hit and miss."

"Any idea when he'll come back?"

"Dunno for sure. I'd say mid-afternoon." Skelly frowned into the climbing sun. "He'll need a few hours to set up. Say, until ten or eleven. Then it'll depend if he goes to his cabin, or turns around and comes back to town."

"Where's his cabin?"

"Somewhere near the north shore, back in Halawa Valley. He has a little research lab there."

"A lab?" It was Niwa's turn to frown.

"Yeah, he's working on seaweed extracts. Scientific stuff." Skelly sounded proud.

"Really?" This was news to Niwa. He didn't know Tanner had been doing anything but helping Skelly out.

"Yeah, he might have a job again. I mean, other than a tour guide."

"So he goes there when he's not working for you?"

"Mostly." Skelly shrugged. "I don't keep track of him."

"Did he say anything about Luke's game?"

"Yeah, he plans on being there."

"Was he going to contact you to pick him up in Halawa?"

Skelly shook his head. "Can't. I've gotta meet the tour group at the airport this afternoon, take them to the Lodge for the night, then stop in Kaunakakai for supplies."

"How's he planning to get back?"

Skelly mimed thumbing a ride. "You gonna look for him, tell him about Jenny?" Skelly sounded glad he didn't have to.

"I guess so." Niwa turned to go, but Skelly had another question.

"What happened to her?" Skelly's arms hung limply at his sides, the radio dangling from one wrist.

"Don't know yet."

"I mean, she have an accident or something? She's about our age, isn't she? Jesus." He whispered the last word.

"She hit her head. That's all we know right now." Niwa walked slowly to his car and got in. "She's younger than we are. Thirty-one."

"Wait." Skelly moved toward the car. "You gotta get Luke to that game, okay? The kid's gonna need it. So is Tanner."

Niwa nodded and waved as he pulled slowly away. Skelly keyed the transmit button again. "Tanner, you there? Come in, over." Static was the only reply.

He opened the office door and made his way to the phone on the desk. As he stabbed the numbers, he was glad Dave Niwa wasn't around to see the tremor in his fingers. He hit the eight button twice by accident and had to try again.

"Hey Connor, I need you at the office." His voice shook a bit, though he cut off his brother mid-sentence. "Don't give me that shit. Ten minutes ago, that's when."

Skelly was staring out the window over his desk when Connor tramped through the open door.

"What the fuck?" Connor's words sounded slurred.

Skelly stood up and braced the back of his legs against the desk. "Where've you been?"

"Delia's."

"You mean she hasn't kicked you out yet?"

"Fuck you. Like you don't have any problems."

"Okay, okay." Skelly took a deep breath. "Was she there?"

"Delia? Yeah, sure."

"The whole time?"

"Well, she had to work 'til eleven last night."

"So you were alone until then?"

Connor paused. "I went to Joey's Gym until about nine. Did some stuff there."

"Anyone else around?"

"Mike Ka'ana and Jeff Gibson were there for a while."

"You go calling on any old girlfriends?"

"No. What's—" Connor's tone was indignant.

Skelly dropped into the chair. "Jenny Williams is dead."

Connor's mouth dropped, though he did that to breathe. He made a snorting noise. "Hey, maybe there is a God."

"Give me a fucking break."

"She's a bitch and you know it. It's not like she doesn't yank your chain, too."

"Connor, I want you to shut the fuck up. Now."

Connor's jaw flapped like a Moray eel's before he caught the glint in his brother's eyes and his teeth clicked closed.

Chapter Eleven

It was all Storm could do to hold onto her own mount. Makani's and Hamlin's horses bolted straight for them, while Aunt Maile's horse, reined in firmly, rolled its eyes and hopped backward to avoid the oncoming animals. The last she saw, Aunt Maile and her mount had leaped off the trail into the woods and Storm didn't have time to wonder if Maile had allowed it or not. She was too busy keeping her horse from hurtling itself into the nearby rocks and brambles.

And the odor. The wind, which had been behind them, had twisted through the trees and returned bearing an awful message. As if Makani and Hamlin had broken through a bubble of putrefaction and let it escape like Pandora's horrors into the unwary world.

None of the horses could be stilled until they'd put some distance between the stench and their restless hooves. It wasn't until they'd all retreated about a hundred yards that Storm saw the riderless mount. It was Hamlin's buckskin, white-eyed and side-kicking.

"Oh, God. Where's Hamlin?" Storm jumped from her horse. Makani was right behind her.

He reached out and grabbed her by the arm. "Wait, I'll go. Stay here." With the other hand, he grabbed at the buckskin's trailing reins.

Aunt Maile and Uncle Keone were off their horses by then, and Makani handed the buckskin's reins to Keone.

"I'm going with you," Storm said to him. "Hamlin's back there, maybe hurt, by that dead thing."

"No, stay here." His eyes flicked back and forth on the path, not meeting the other riders' anxious stares. "It's probably a steer. Winter rains wash out the ranch fences."

Makani tied a handkerchief over his face and walked toward the smell. "I'll call if I need help."

Storm followed him anyway and held her sleeved arm against her nose. They hadn't gone ten feet when Hamlin appeared, pale and grimacing with pain. One arm hung at his side and he held it steady with his other hand, as if each step he took hurt.

Storm dashed past Makani, but Hamlin stopped before she reached him. "My shoulder's dislocated." His voice was a whisper. "It's happened before."

"Let me help you," Storm said, and reached for his good side.

Hamlin turned toward Makani. "Let's get away from the smell."

Makani let Hamlin lean against him and they walked toward the now-tethered horses and Aunt Maile and Uncle Keone. "Did you see whatever scared the horses?"

Hamlin spoke through gritted teeth. "Didn't try to. I knew what I'd done," he gestured to his shoulder, "and I wanted to get away."

He directed his words to Makani. Storm followed behind.

When they got close, Uncle Keone approached. "We can get that back in the socket, if you want. It'll hurt when we do it, but it'll feel a whole lot better after."

Hamlin nodded. "We better do it."

"I've got a poultice that'll help," Aunt Maile said. "And ice from the cooler."

Uncle Keone took Hamlin's good arm and led him to level ground, where they could sit. But he smiled at Storm. "Your aunt's got a bag of tricks. He'll be fine in no time."

Aunt Maile rolled her eyes and handed Keone a package. "Storm and I'll find some *kī* leaves. Once you get the shoulder reduced, we'll wrap the joint with kī, and apply this *koali* paste. Then we'll use the ice packs the drinks are packed in."

She and Storm headed into the underbrush that bordered the path. Storm felt as if her boots were filled with lead. Hamlin hadn't let her touch him, let alone give any comfort.

When they were out of sight of the men, Maile turned to Storm. "He's going to need some space."

"I didn't know what to do," Storm said. "He wouldn't let me near him."

"I know." She squeezed Storm's hands. "I think he's a little embarrassed."

"He should be," Storm said angrily, then shot her aunt a black look when Maile chuckled.

"I only mean he's ashamed that he fell off."

"That's not what I meant."

"I know." Aunt Maile grinned at her. "Just let him be for right now."

"I might have fallen off, too, if I'd been as close to that stinking thing as he was," Storm said. "But I wouldn't be so touchy."

"That's probably true, but people react differently."

"I'll tell him he hurt my feelings."

Aunt Maile raised an eyebrow. "You'd be better off lying low for a few hours. That shoulder hurts like the devil."

Storm snorted. "That's not the way he and I relate. We talk to each other."

"Yes, after a little break. Let him heal a bit, and not just the shoulder." Maile gave Storm a hug, then led her toward a tall plant. "There's our kī. Let's take some back to the men. Then we'll go check something else out."

The men still sat on the ground, Hamlin hunched forward, though it appeared his shoulder had been reduced. His face glistened with sweat.

"You feeling any better?" Storm asked.

He nodded. "I just need to sit a bit longer."

"No problem." Storm handed the kī to Uncle Keone, who gave her a secret wink, then walked back to Aunt Maile.

"What did you want to check out?" Her voice didn't carry much enthusiasm.

"The body."

"Not!" Now she looked up, her eyes round as Hamlin's horse's had been.

"I've got mint leaves to chew and two big handkerchiefs." She paused to evaluate the wind direction. "We'll go 'round the other way, make sure the breeze is in our faces."

"Let Makani check it out. He's the ranch man."

"Hah." Maile made a snorting noise. "I don't know who was supporting whom coming out of those trees."

"What? He's seen dead steers before."

"Yeah, and so have I. Smelled 'em, too." Aunt Maile handed Storm a handkerchief. "That was no steer, and Makani knows it."

Chapter Twelve

Luke's 911 came in at 5:11 a.m., and the responding officer, rookie Nettie Ching, called the station with a report of a suspicious death eight minutes later. The dispatcher immediately phoned Niwa as supervising officer. He got to Jenny's and Luke's residence at 5:25, heavy-hearted and showered but unshaven.

He helped secure the site as a possible crime scene, and couldn't help noticing that except for wear and tear, the place looked pretty much as it had eight or nine years ago when he and his wife spent evenings with Tanner, Jenny, and little Luke. Niwa took a deep breath and sought his reservoir of professional detachment.

It looked like Jenny had died of a severe head injury. That was bad, but for Niwa it was even worse that her son had to be the one to find her. Niwa wanted to ask the boy some questions, but the kid was too shaken up. He couldn't even remember whether he'd moved her, maybe in an attempt to revive her. It often happened.

The eleven-year-old was beside himself, and Niwa was devastated on Luke's behalf. A couple minutes after he arrived, Niwa made a flurry of phone calls. The first one was to his partner, Sgt. Steve Nishijima, then the morgue, the ID tech, his commanding officer, and his wife, Caroline. Officer Nettie Ching worked to comfort the boy, but Luke continued to tremble with what Niwa assumed to be shock. Between phone calls, Niwa popped into the bedroom to give Luke hugs and reassurance, but the lad looked pale and pitiful. He needed to be with people he knew and loved.

His dad was Niwa's first choice, but no one knew where he was. Haley and the Niwa family would do in a pinch.

Caroline said she'd roust Haley from bed and be there inside a half hour. Meanwhile, Luke's shaking grew worse despite the blanket Niwa and Officer Ching wrapped around his shoulders. His skin was taking on a waxy look and he felt clammy to the touch. Niwa speed-dialed his house, but no one answered the phone. This was good. Caroline was on her way.

Normally, he'd have waited for the ID tech's assessment to call the morgue, but Niwa wanted a jump on having Jenny's body examined. He knew all too well the logistical problems unique to his home island. Moloka'i was part of Maui County, and Dave Niwa and his Moloka'i colleagues were part of the Maui Police Department. The central office for the Maui police department was in Wailuku, Maui. So was Maui Memorial Hospital, where the very busy coroner did the bulk of his work. Therefore, suspicious deaths were flown over to Maui for forensic examination.

Niwa knew this could take a week, sometimes longer, and he had a bad feeling about Jenny's death. Her head injury looked worse than what he'd expect in an accidental fall, and whatever she'd hit it on wasn't immediately apparent. Nor could he see an obvious weapon. They'd find the answers to these questions, but he wanted a time of death, or as close as a couple of pros could come to it.

Meanwhile, Nishijima would scrutinize the house for what left the fatal dent in Jenny's skull as soon as Luke and the body left the premises. He was already unpacking the Luminal kit and putting up black-out drapes.

Niwa's mind kept returning to the boy in the bedroom, wondering how much Luke had seen of his mother's bashed head, and whether the carpet had wet the boy's feet as much as it oozed around his own. No kid should see his mom like that.

Niwa had gently questioned the boy about when he'd last seen his mother alive, and would do so again once the boy had settled down a bit. Right then, all Luke could say was that she'd been fine when he'd gone to bed at ten. He thought he'd heard voices later, but she often had friends over when they got off the late shift at the hospital.

The ID tech arrived at the Williams' house not long after Niwa, Nishijima, and Officer Ching. He underscored his examination of the body with lots of muttering, took pictures, and then backed up the detectives' request to send the body to Maui. The ambulance arrived around 6:00, soon after Caroline pulled in the drive to pack Luke into her car. Niwa was glad he wasn't around to see the EMTs load Jenny into the back of the quietly waiting vehicle. Her body on the gurney looked tiny, diminished by the absence of energy that is life. A testimony to loss, Niwa thought sadly.

After the ambulance left, he told his partner he was headed over to Hawai'i EcoTours to talk to Skelly. Steve Nishijima gave him a wave as he went out the front door. "I'm gonna go through the house, see what there is to see."

"I'll talk to her friends before the news hits the coconut wireless," Niwa said.

"Good idea. You better work fast." Nishijima nodded at a shadowy form that lingered in the next-door neighbor's side window.

On his way out, Niwa caught the ID tech alone, loading his car. "When do you think she died?"

The ID tech shrugged.

Niwa knew the tech didn't want any off-the-cuff speculations to come back later and bite him in the ass. "Unofficially. Come on, I need it."

Niwa looked around at the houses in the neighborhood. He was going to have to talk to all of them, too. They already seemed too quiet, with the expectant hush that accompanies someone else's misfortune. The few people that left for work scurried to their cars without looking toward the Williams home.

The ID tech gave him a dirty look. "Between two and four. Not too long ago." He got in his car and slammed the door. "But don't quote me."

Niwa cheerfully thanked the departing dust cloud. He then visited the houses on both sides of the Williams home. The shadow Nishijima had seen belonged to a woman about Jenny's age, who was bursting to know what had happened, but hadn't seen or heard anything unusual during the night. She told Niwa Jenny wasn't all that friendly, didn't go to neighborhood potlucks or visit with anyone. The woman figured Jenny worked a lot. Niwa visited the home on the other side of the Williams house, but no one answered his knock. Maybe they weren't up yet.

After that, he decided he'd return later to talk to other neighbors, and lowered himself on aching knees into his patrol car. When Niwa got to Hawai'i EcoTours, he took in the dark windows and realized Skelly probably didn't come to the office this early, especially if he didn't have any morning tours.

Niwa heaved himself out of the car and stretched in the cool morning air while he thought about Jenny's death. Telling people about it wasn't going to be easy, and he took a deep breath and looked out at the calm bay to gather his thoughts. Only a few minutes passed before the crunching of wheels on gravel distracted him from his ponderings.

Skelly looked hung over. He tried to give a friendly nod of greeting, but the effort fell flat, especially when without preamble, Niwa told him about Jenny's death and asked him where he'd been. Shock crossed Skelly's tired features, followed by a ripple of indignation. Niwa was glad to see it, and he was even happier when Skelly resisted calling him on it, recognizing that Niwa had an unpleasant job to do. Skelly was cooperative, though he couldn't raise Tanner on his two-way radio.

Niwa pointed to the radio. "Keep trying to raise him, okay? If you get him, tell him I'm on the way and call me."

Back in his car, Niwa called into the station and told the dispatcher he'd be cruising along East Kamehameha Highway. With any luck, he'd find Tanner on the side of the road with his thumb out. He hoped it would be that easy.

Niwa reflected that if he hadn't driven Tanner to Skelly's office late yesterday afternoon, he'd have been hunting a lot harder for the man. Even as he knew and liked Tanner, he never underestimated the ire of a jilted spouse. Especially one with documented mental illness, though Tanner didn't have a history of violence. Niwa had checked, just to make sure.

He did, however, have episodes of hallucinations and agitated behavior. The last time, a little less than a year ago, he'd stood on Ala Malama Street, in downtown Kaunakakai, shouting and shaking his fist at an invisible adversary. When Niwa arrived in response to a 911 call, Luke was dragging on one of Tanner's arms, trying to pull him away from gathering citizens. Niwa's heart had ached for the boy.

Negotiating a turn in the road, Niwa wondered if Skelly's tale of Tanner's research lab was true. Everyone knew Tanner had been brilliant at one time, but it was Niwa's impression that Tanner's illness had disorganized his thoughts to the point that he had trouble living within society's framework, let alone dealing with the burden of employment, meetings, and other hi-tech demands. This was a guy who refused to own a cell phone.

Skelly might believe Tanner's ravings, though. He probably wasn't very sophisticated when it came to Tanner's condition or the science behind his work. Skelly hadn't finished high school, and he had always idolized Tanner and his abilities. Niwa had the impression Tanner was expected to bring his friends glory by association. Particularly in Jenny's eyes.

Niwa dialed his home phone, but no one answered. That was normal; Haley would be in school and Caroline at the office. Had Luke been in shape to go to school, though? He doubted it, and wanted to get hold of Caroline at the pharmacy where she worked, but he was losing range on his cell phone and there was another call he wanted to make. He pulled to the side of the road, got out of the car, and faced toward Maui, then Kaunakakai, watching the reception bars on his phone. The Maui direction gave him two bars—intermittently. But he got through to a crackly Maui forensic pathologist's lab. The pathologist wasn't in, but the tech listened carefully to Niwa's description of the arriving body and his request for a time of death as soon as possible.

Niwa got back in his car and pondered a couple of rumors about Jenny that had been floating around. He would never have confronted Tanner with them before, but now he might have to. When he'd picked Tanner up yesterday, Tanner had alluded to Jenny seeing someone, and that tied in with recent gossip about an affair Jenny allegedly had. Still, Jenny and Tanner were separated, and no one in this insular and judgmental community should throw the first stone. Not that someone wouldn't.

The buzz he worried most about happened over a year ago. It involved Skelly, and Niwa dreaded implicating the one guy that Tanner seemed to confide in. Tanner was isolated enough. Especially since the story was pretty vague, and the outcome depended on who told it. It involved some water cooler gossip that Skelly and Helene had a big fight one night, and Skelly stormed out of the house and went to Jenny's. They were long-time friends and confidants, after all. Helene, the story went, gave him about an hour and a half head start, then threw open Jenny's front door and found the two of them groping each other on the couch. Or maybe they were talking—or Jenny was sobbing in his arms. This was where the story got fuzzy. One person asserted that Helene went over to apologize to Skelly for being bitchy and ended up staying for an impromptu beer party. A different raconteur said that Helene threw her handbag at the two and split Skelly's lip. Niwa navigated a curve in the road and sighed. Whatever happened, he hoped Luke had slept through it.

He drove all the way to where the road ended at Halawa Valley. It took him nearly two hours, partly because he stopped when Pete Oshiro and his son waved him down from the side of the road where they were changing a tire on a pickup truck that belonged in a Ford museum. The new tire's tread was almost as smooth as the old one's, but the beater couldn't go more than twenty miles an hour, and Niwa had bigger problems on his mind.

At the park near the end of the road, Niwa got out and went inside the restroom to use the facilities. It was a good hitchhiking spot, too, but Tanner was nowhere in sight.

On the way back to Kaunakakai, Niwa dropped by the Hawai'i EcoTours office once again. Skelly wasn't there; he'd gone home to get a few hours of sleep. Connor was as belligerent as usual and he had no idea where Tanner was. He wasn't that freak's keeper. He also had a list of places he'd been last night, and a phone call to his girlfriend supported his story for the later part of the evening. Niwa was inclined to believe her because she didn't sound happy about the visit.

By this time it was two and Niwa was ravenous. He was so hungry his legs felt shaky as he dropped into a chair at Kanemitsu's. He felt like he'd been working for nine days instead of nine hours.

He had a tuna salad sandwich for protein, and then he treated himself to a slab of the restaurant's special Moloka'i bread—warm, soft, and gooey with strawberry cream cheese filling. With a small sense of virtue, he refrained from eating a second helping. Last week, he'd shifted his belt buckle to a bigger size and his doctor, whose office was three doors down from the police station, was going to give him hell about his cholesterol levels. This guy would actually stop his patients (practically every adult in town) in the street. Niwa reckoned he'd better park his car at the other end of the block until this Jenny Williams crisis passed.

After eating, Niwa lowered himself back into his car with a groan, and dialed Hawai'i EcoTours again. To his relief, Skelly answered the phone.

"Did you reach Tanner?"

"He never did answer the radio call. But he left a message on the answering machine."

"What did he say?"

"He's in town, I think. Wondered if I would meet him at Luke's game."

"Did he leave a number?"

"No, and it sounded like he borrowed someone's cell phone. The number was blocked."

"You know what time that was?"

"Uh, I forgot to check. But I got in the office around one."

"You still have the message?"

"No, I erased it."

"I may drop by later." Niwa hung up.

Damn, Tanner probably went by about the time Niwa's head was parallel with the Oshiros' ancient wheel hub.

Niwa rang his own home next. "Hey, honey girl, you ready for the game tonight?"

"Hi Dad. I am, but Luke's sick."

"He is?"

"Yeah, he wanted to go to bed, but Mom wouldn't let him. She took him to the hospital."

"Where is he now?"

"You don't get it, Dad." Lord, she sounded like a teenager. "She had to take him to the Emergency Room. The doctors have to do some tests."

Chapter Thirteen

Storm heard the buzzing of insects before she smelled the body. Aunt Maile, who led on the narrow path, popped a sprig of mint leaves into her mouth, and Storm did the same, then tied the handkerchief bandit-style over her nose. Just in time, as the cloying stink of decay wafted toward them despite the breeze at their backs.

Aunt Maile turned to her. "It's pretty ugly. Bloated and black. You ready?"

"Tell me again, why are we doing this?" Storm's words were muffled.

"So we can tell the police if it's human. They're going to ask." Aunt Maile tied the bandana over her own face. "Maybe we can get a look at any clothing for identification, too."

Storm swallowed hard. "You're not going to touch it, are you?"

"No way. We're not going to get that close."

Thank God. Storm was beginning to feel queasy. "Can't you see enough from here? We don't want to mess up a crime scene."

"Animals have been here." Aunt Maile tiptoed closer, then stopped. Storm followed, watching her feet and the foliage along the path, anyplace except toward the dead thing. She almost walked into her aunt's back.

"It's definitely human, and I think it's a man. The hiking boots are pretty big." Maile's voice sounded thick in the stomach-turning atmosphere.

Storm tried not to inhale, but it didn't matter. The odor got to her even when she breathed out. And if Aunt Maile was close enough to see hiking boots and still couldn't tell if it was a man or woman, Storm *knew* she didn't want to see it. She kept her gaze on the grass along the path, which was thick and lush as if in defiance of death's putrefying presence.

Something glittered ahead in the green, about three feet away. Storm pointed over Maile's shoulder. "What's that?"

Maile went closer, made a choking noise, and wheeled around. She darted, fumbling with her bandana, toward a tree stump. Storm cringed at the sound of vomiting. That was a first; Maile was known for treating cancer patients, necrotizing infections, and crippling diseases with unruffled professionalism. Of course, those people were still alive.

The noise of her aunt's sickness made Storm's own bile rise, and she turned quickly to the sparkle in the grass. Keeping her eyes away from the corpse, she crept toward the shiny article.

It was a watch, and its crystal face shone in the sun. She could see it now, a Tag Heuer, one of those nice diving watches with a navy blue or black face. Hamlin had given Storm a Fossil for her birthday last year, a step up from the reliable old Casio she'd worn for years. She was pretty sure Tag Heuer watches were in a higher price class than what she was used to. She also had a hunch there weren't many Moloka'i people who wore them.

With her back carefully to the corpse, Storm looked around to see if any other articles lay in the grass, and noticed a scrap of reddish plaid fabric. She leaned over for a closer look, and recoiled in horror. The fabric was a flannel shirt cuff, and to her roiling disgust, a blackened hand emerged from it. Gagging, she reeled and dashed toward Aunt Maile, who leaned against a tree a good twenty yards away. Maile faced the direction of the breeze, away from the sickening stench.

"Oh God, a hand. It was a hand,"

Her aunt's voice held respect. "You got close enough to see it. The empty eye sockets were too much for me. And the maggots."

"That's disgusting." Storm suppressed another gag. "The hand was in the grass, away from the rest of him."

"Probably dragged off by scavengers."

"Dogs?" Storm bent at the waist, her hands on her knees. She sucked in air and tried to convince her stomach to get out of her throat.

"Or wild pigs, even cats."

Storm shuddered and shook the image of that hand out of her head. "Can we go back now?"

Maile nodded vigorously and started off with long strides. The women were a hundred yards away before they removed the handkerchiefs and gulped fresh air. "I can still smell it—must be in my hair, on my clothes. I want a long soak in the ocean," Storm said.

"I'll go for the chlorine in that nice, calm pool." Aunt Maile still didn't have her usual ruddy glow.

"That'll do, too."

They walked for several minutes, happy to be in the cleansing sunlight and sweet air, before Maile asked, "What was it that caught your attention?"

Storm described the watch.

"You're right, those are expensive. That should help the police."

"I have a bad feeling about this."

"You think it's Hamlin's client's son?"

"He's a missing rich kid, isn't he?"

"Yes." Maile sounded thoughtful. They were within sight of the men. Hamlin was on his feet and waving at them with his uninjured arm. His other was in a bandana sling. He looked much better than he had when they left, and Storm waved back.

The women told Hamlin, Makani, and Uncle Keone they'd confirmed a human body lay in the woods, and it had been there for a while. Weeks, maybe. The information subdued everyone, and Hamlin met Storm's eyes with a question in his.

She gave a little shrug, combined with a quick tip of her hand. Could be, but don't know for sure.

Before they climbed on the horses, Uncle Keone used a length of plastic food wrap to tie an ice bag around Hamlin's shoulder. He also led the buckskin to a stump so Hamlin could mount without having to pull himself up. Though Hamlin assured everyone that his shoulder was much better since it had been repositioned, Storm could see that his posture in the saddle was less relaxed than it had been before the horses shied. His entire arm probably still hurt, and she gave him a lot of credit for getting back on the horse.

To everyone's relief, the ride back to the ranch was uneventful, though there was a lot less conversation than there had been on the ride out. Only the horses were livelier, as they knew they were headed for the barn and full buckets of oats.

"Just tie your horses to the fence," Makani said on arrival. "I'll put away the tack and take care of the rest."

"We'll carry our saddles in," Uncle Keone said. He had Hamlin's horse tied and pulled the saddle as soon as the younger man's feet touched the ground.

Storm and Maile followed his lead, and within a few minutes the group of four thanked Makani and headed back to the Lodge. It was a little after three, a beautiful time of the afternoon, when the sun's rays cut a fiery swath across Kaiwi Channel between Moloka'i and O'ahu. They strolled along the gravel road back to the Lodge, each lost in his or her own thoughts. Even with the vista in front of her, Storm couldn't forget the body in the woods. She could still smell the cloying reek of death, and though she was pretty sure it was a memory, she felt like the odor clung to her.

"We may see the green flash tonight," Aunt Maile said, and Storm felt certain her aunt was looking for beauty as a means of escape from the gruesome images.

"I'd like nothing better than to sit on the lanai by the bar, watch the sun set, and have a cocktail," Hamlin said. "Or two."

"We can arrange that," Keone said.

"Not until we've talked to the police." Maile's voice was sad.

Storm nodded. "And then we'll deserve that drink."

"I've got another thing to do first," Hamlin said, and fatigue showed in his eyes.

"See the doctor?" Storm asked.

"No, I can do that later. The arm's not urgent." He moved it to show them he was doing better. "After my fall, when we were waiting for you two to come back, I had a chance to ask Makani about Brock Liu."

"Does he think that was Brock's body?" Keone asked.

"He didn't say, but I'm sure it's crossed his mind."

"What did he say?" Storm asked.

"There are some things he's not telling me, but he did talk about an old group of friends, the same guys who were involved in that protest Dusty Rodriguez told us about."

"Was Makani part of the group?" Storm asked.

"Didn't seem like it the way he talked, but he knew them. Remember the guy who died? Makani told me that was Alika, Brock Liu's older brother."

Several moments passed and the only sounds were the crunch of their feet on the gravel road. Finally Keone said, "I don't envy that father, no matter how much money he's got."

"Yeah." Hamlin's voice was low.

"If that's Brock, it doesn't look like he drowned in a kayaking accident," Storm said.

"True, but Devon will still press to see who and what is responsible for his son's death." Hamlin squinted down the roadway. "At my last meeting with Liu and his legal assistant, I got the feeling Mr. Liu knew the Richards brothers. It was just a hunch, then. Now it seems certain he knew them."

"How old is Makani?" Storm asked, and everyone looked at her. "I was wondering if he was part of that protest, but he seems younger than Skelly, Tanner, and those guys."

"I'd say he's in his mid-twenties, wouldn't you?" Keone said. "Plus, someone told me he was from Maui."

Maile had been following the conversation. "Makani may be just passing on hearsay."

"More questions for me to ask," Hamlin said.

"What was it you wanted to do before cocktails?" Storm asked.

"Go see Lambert Poele."

Storm frowned. "Wasn't he the ringleader of that protest group?"

"Yes, and Makani told me he had a big argument with Brock Liu right before Liu was to leave the island."

"Did he say what they argued about?" Storm kicked a pebble before her.

"Makani told me Brock had been buying parcels of land around where Poele lives," Hamlin said. "Apparently Brock Liu is pretty abrasive. And Poele doesn't like the Lius in general."

"What's Poele's livelihood?" Keone asked.

"Sounds like he's kind of a recluse. A hippy drop-out type, with a flock of goats. Sells his organic goat cheese to restaurants throughout the islands. He's not rich, but he does okay."

"Brock was probably representing Liu family interests," Storm said.

"Check how Lambert's land is zoned. And if he's on Hawaiian Homestead land." Aunt Maile took off her handkerchief and wiped her face. "Lordy, I'm looking forward to that drink."

"What's the significance of Hawaiian Homestead land?" Hamlin asked.

"If he's fifty percent Hawaiian and has leased the land under the Hawaiian Homes Commission Act, he has water rights. And he can only sell to another Hawaiian. Is Liu part Hawaiian?"

"No," Hamlin said. "But I bet Devon Liu could find some Hawaiian willing to stand in for him."

"You're kind of cynical about your client, aren't you?" asked Keone.

"Actually, he's realistic," Storm said.

"If that's Liu's body, it sounds like Poele might have a motive," Keone added.

"We can't tell until we talk to him." Hamlin wiped his forehead with his shirtsleeve. He looked tired. "There's another little problem."

"What's that?" Storm asked. The four had reached the Lodge's front door and paused before splitting off to their rooms. Uncle Keone and Aunt Maile's room was on the inside of the main building, like a hotel. Storm's and Hamlin's room had an outdoor, garden entrance.

"Makani says he'll probably only talk to a local—I'm too Mainland."

"He doesn't like *haole*?" Keone asked.

"Guess not."

"I'll go with you, if you'd like," Storm said.

"Thanks, that'll help."

"I'll ask Dusty if you can borrow his truck," Keone said. "His personal one, without the Ranch logo."

"And I'll call the police about the body," Maile said. "We'd better meet them before we do anything else."

Chapter Fourteen

Niwa hung up from talking to Haley and dialed his wife at the pharmacy where she worked.

"Caroline, Haley told me you had to take Luke to the hospital."

"Yes, did you know he's diabetic?"

"No." Niwa sat back in the driver's seat with surprise. "Like he needs insulin?"

"Yup. Recently diagnosed. The way I understand it, his insulin doses aren't quite regulated yet. The ER doc said he's brittle."

"One of the dispatchers is like that. If he misses a meal, or doesn't eat enough, he can pass out."

"Yeah, well it's worse for kids. Some kids, anyhow. Emotional traumas, unusual stresses can throw them way off kilter."

"Jesus, poor Luke. No wonder he looked so bad this morning."

"They're keeping him overnight for observation."

"Sounds like a good idea." Niwa looked at his watch. It was a bit before four. "I couldn't find Tanner, but he's supposed to come to the baseball game tonight. We can take him right to the hospital from there."

"Oh, honey." He could hear Caroline's sigh. "This poor family. On top of everything else."

"You mean Tanner's illness?"

"Yes, that and Jenny's problems. Just when I'd heard she was doing better—"

"Jenny's problems? What—" Niwa's phone beeped at him. "Shoots, the dispatcher's calling me. Caroline, I want to hear more about this, but I gotta run. See you at the game?"

"Sure. I better go, too."

Niwa got back out of his car and wiped his face with his sleeve. It was too damn hot to sit in that steel sauna and talk on the phone. He made his way back to Kanemitsu's and ordered that second slab of sweet bread. Hey, it was air-conditioned in there, and that alone had to be better for his blood pressure. He was making his way to a chair and getting the phone out when the office called again.

"You're gonna hate this." It was Jerry Sanchez, Niwa's favorite dispatcher.

"It can't get any worse." Niwa took a big bite of strawberry-cream cheese filling.

"Oh, it can always get worse." Jerry sounded way too cheerful. "We got a call about another body."

"You're shitting me." Niwa swallowed hard.

"Nope."

"You don't have to sound so happy about it." Niwa took another bite. "And Jerry, I gotta ask you about insulin and stuff. Seems Luke Williams is diabetic."

"Bummers. Sure, we can talk later. Kid that young, he's probably a Type I like me. Sarge, the people you need to talk to are up at the Lodge."

"Some tourist croaked? Am I a total prick if I hope it's something simple like a heart attack?"

"I have a hunch it's not so easy. The people who *found* it are up there."

Niwa made a noise between a moan and a grunt, ate the rest of his bread in a huge bite and lumbered to his feet. "Shoots. Later, Jerry."

Betty, the grey-haired counter clerk, shook her head at him. "Eating fass bad fo' da heart." She pronounced it *haaht*.

Niwa rolled his eyes at her and walked out the door to his car. Eating fast wasn't as bad for his heart as this day had been.

Fifteen minutes later, Niwa found three Hawaiians and a haole guy sitting around the bar at the Lodge, drinking cokes. They probably wanted a beer as bad as he did, but figured they'd better wait. Their expressions looked tired and serious.

After introductions, the two women alternated telling him what they'd found and how they'd come upon it.

"You sure the remains, they're human?" Niwa asked.

"Yes," both women said together.

"Can you tell me how to get there? I've been up in that area, but not for a while."

Keone, the rancher from the Big Island, spoke up. "I can. I've ridden that trail before with Dusty."

"Dusty Rodriguez?" Niwa knew the people heard the sharpness in his voice when four sets of eyes focused on his face.

"Yes," said Keone. "He's an old friend of mine."

"But he wasn't with you on this trip?"

"No, one of his staff guided us. Why?" the man named Ian Hamlin asked.

Niwa sighed and made a calculation. "Dusty's daughter disappeared about ten years ago. This was more than a skeleton, right?"

All four heads nodded. The younger woman spoke. "It looked like a man and it's probably been out there a week or two, not years."

Niwa felt a wave of relief, but the rancher looked pensive. "I remember that. The daughter and her baby, right?"

"Yes, everyone said she ran off to Honolulu, but we would have found her," Niwa said. "But I guess we'll never know for sure."

"Dusty never thought she ran off, either. He had a terrible time when it happened, it changed his life." The older Hawaiian woman nodded along with her husband's words. The younger pair looked back and forth between the older couple. They'd obviously never heard the story.

Niwa sighed. "I feel bad for the family of this person, but I'm glad to hear it's not Tia." He turned to Keone. "I think there's an old road back in there, so we can drive at least part way. You mind going along to help with directions? It'll save us some time and I'll have someone bring you right back."

"Sure," Keone said. Niwa pushed himself up from the table with an unintentional grunt. Keone stood, too. It went through Niwa's mind that the rancher was about twenty-five years older than he was and had been on a horse all day, yet he'd risen without any groans. Niwa vowed to himself that after this case, he was going to start exercising, lose some weight. He walked off a few steps while Keone kissed his wife and the younger woman on the cheek. He also handed a set of car keys to the haole guy. "Be careful."

Keone turned to Niwa. "Let's get this over with."

Storm, Maile, and Hamlin watched the two of them go. "Poor Uncle Keone," Storm said. "He's tired."

"That policeman looks exhausted," Aunt Maile said. "Bodies in the woods have to be unusual here. Moloka'i is a quiet, friendly place."

"Let's hope so." Hamlin didn't sound like he believed it, and he stood up as if his whole body hurt. "You ready to go?"

"You mind if I make a quick pit-stop on the way out?" Storm asked, anticipating the drive.

"No, but I'm with Keone," Hamlin said. "Let's get this over with."

Chapter Fifteen

Ten minutes later, Storm and Hamlin found Dusty's faded red pickup in the parking lot at the side of the Lodge. It would fit right into the Moloka'i countryside; the hood had rusted through in a couple of spots and a few bales of straw were piled in the bed. Hamlin opened the driver's door, took one look at the manual transmission on the column, and rolled his sore shoulder with a grimace.

"You mind driving?"

Storm took the keys. "No problem. You want to drop by the doctor's on the way?"

"No, there's nothing a doctor can do right now. I'll go see someone when we get home." He climbed in the passenger's seat, and got a folded paper out of his jeans pocket and opened it to scrawled directions. "Head toward Kaunakakai, but we'll turn before we get to town."

Storm followed his directions. "Where's he live?"

Hamlin looked at his notes. "Ho'olehua. You know that area?"

"A general idea. I think it's Hawaiian Homestead land."

Storm bumped down the driveway and out onto the road as gently as she could. Hamlin winced. "I appreciate your coming along."

Storm knew it would be hopeless to suggest the doctor again, so she just smiled at him. "So happens I like the company, plus I'm curious about this guy."

"Me too, but I wish he didn't sound like a racist."

"He's probably okay. Wasn't he the one arrested for that fire ten years ago? Sounds like he had some bad experiences with the law and local land owners."

"That's an excuse?"

"Course not. But it might be a reason he's wary." She remembered when she was picked up for growing marijuana in a sugar cane field on the Big Island. Aunt Maile, Uncle Keone, and Miles Hamasaki, her father's best friend and her own legal mentor, conspired to send her to O'ahu for the rest of her high school years. Only much later did she realize how lucky she'd been, and how narrowly she'd escaped a downward spiral of trouble.

"He was probably very frustrated," Storm said.

Hamlin made a snorting noise and Storm glanced at him, worried. Maybe his shoulder was more painful than he was letting on.

"Remember, back then, the ranch owners didn't listen—they weren't local." The minute the words were out of her mouth, Storm knew they were the wrong ones.

"You mean they were haole, don't you?"

"No, I didn't mean race," she said quickly. "I meant they didn't understand the needs of the people who live here."

"That makes it okay to break the law? Damage property? Kill someone?" Hamlin's voice rose with each question.

"We don't know he did that." Storm kept her voice calm and even.

"It couldn't be legally proven, you mean. People knew what happened."

"People talked because he was one of the protestors, but they didn't know who started the fire."

"In a community this size, people know. They stick together and don't discuss it with outsiders, then they ostracize whoever breaks the local code of behavior." Hamlin flexed his shoulder and winced. "Lambert Poele is probably a very bad dude."

He turned his head to look out the side window, and Storm could no longer see his face. What was eating at him? How had the conversation gone downhill so quickly?

"Let's wait until we meet him. If he seems hostile, we'll leave." She paused. "Maybe your client can tell you why his son went to see him."

"I called him when you went to wash up. He said he didn't know Poele, and asked me to look into why Brock visited him."

Storm sighed. That must have been a grim phone call, which might explain part of his black mood.

"Poele's not going to shoot us. The guy's not a maniac." She tried to sound reassuring.

"You're right, he's smart enough to realize people will know where we are."

"Right." Storm nodded and turned onto a dirt road that was pitted with a series of dusty potholes. They bumped along for several minutes.

"It's dry up here, that's for sure."

"This can't be an easy place to live," Hamlin said.

"Especially if you're being hounded to sell your homestead."

"I don't mean right here." He finally looked over at her. "I mean the whole island."

"Some people wouldn't leave for all the money in the world. It's loaded with history, legend, and folklore."

"Still, a community this small, without enough jobs. Idle people can be brutal. Imagine the discontent, the judgments, the gossip."

"Kind of like where I grew up. The Big Island was—still is—economically depressed. But people there stick together. They got me through my mom's death."

The truck crested a long rise and the two of them looked out over the Kaiwi Channel. The rounded green hills of O'ahu glimmered across the sapphire expanse.

"See?" Storm pointed. "Where else could you walk out of your house and see this?"

"It comes at a price. It's probably why Dusty's daughter left. What do you want to bet she had her baby out of wedlock?"

"She wouldn't be condemned for that. It's fairly common here."

"She'd leave out of hopelessness."

"Hopelessness?" Storm gripped the steering wheel. She was running out of patience. "That's a point of view, Ian. We don't know what these families feel. There's a lot to be said for the support and love of a small community." He knew her history; he should know better than to make negative comments about people he didn't know and a place he didn't understand.

Hamlin didn't reply, but the set of his mouth was hard.

Storm stopped about fifty yards from a small frame cabin that sat on posts about three feet off the ground. Five goats trotted toward the truck, while others lingered at the home's front steps to watch their approach. She took a deep breath to calm herself, and then opened her door. "Ian, let's not argue. Please? Let's see what Lambert Poele is like before we draw our conclusions."

They climbed from the truck, and Storm led the way to the simple little house. Hamlin walked stiffly a step or two behind. The goats moved next to them, observing with their cat-like pupils. They jostled to get closer, but didn't get near enough to be touched.

Storm and Hamlin were still twenty or thirty feet from the door when a muscular man in his late forties or early fifties stepped from the house. A few inches taller than Storm's five-eight, he had a red bandana tied around his head, Indian-style. He stopped on the over-grazed tufts of what might have been a front lawn and stood, wide-stanced, with his arms tightly folded across his chest.

"Hey, whassup?"

Storm introduced herself and Ian Hamlin, who nodded without speaking. They stopped at a polite distance, not close enough to offer a handshake.

"Not too many people come up here."

"Maybe we should have called first," Storm said.

"S'okay." He leaned to tousle the ears of a goat that nuzzled the pocket of his shorts, and Storm could see that his gray hair was tied in a ponytail that hung to the middle of his back. The black T-shirt he wore had been washed so many times its logo was an indecipherable smudge.

"I know why you're here. We need to talk story, figure some things out." Poele gestured to the front stairs and a tattered folding chair that looked as if it hadn't been moved from the hard-packed dirt for decades. "Excuse me, I don't get too many visitors. Only one chair, but please sit. The view's good, anyway."

Hamlin hesitated, then sat on the stoop and cradled his injured arm in his lap. Storm sat next to him. Poele reached behind them into the shade under the house, and pulled out a faded plastic cooler. The goats ventured nearer. There were at least a dozen of them in varying sizes.

Poele grinned at his visitors. "Cocktail hour." One of the goats butted his rear end gently when he bent over. He pulled four bottles of beer and a bag of pretzels from the cooler, popped one of the beers, and poured most of it into a battered Frisbee that lay on the ground nearby. He then threw out a handful of pretzels. A half-dozen goats clustered around the Frisbee and the rest went after the pretzels.

Storm laughed. "They drink beer?"

"Some of 'em. Funny, yeah?" He handed Hamlin and Storm their own bottles. "Sorry, no glasses. But I won't make you drink out of a Frisbee." He chuckled.

Storm wondered what tidbits of information had drifted along the coconut wireless to arrive at this remote spot. He seemed to have been expecting them. Local courtesy required the trio to go through a brief ritual of getting to know each other before jumping to business, and she hoped Hamlin would remember this.

Hamlin looked edgy, and so far he'd refrained from speaking, which was better than being too pushy. Poele either hadn't noticed his standoffishness or ignored it. The Hawaiian dropped into the old chair, which creaked with his weight, looked back and forth between the two of them, and downed half the bottle. When he lowered it, his smile had disappeared.

"I heard already," he said, and his eyes drifted, unfocused, toward the ocean.

"You heard?" That was fast, even for the coconut wireless. Storm wondered if Uncle Keone and Detective Niwa had reached the body yet.

"E hānai ʻawa a ikaika ka makani," he whispered, before his gaze met Storm's and she saw the shine of tears. "A prayer for the dead. That's why you're here, isn't it?"

Storm opened her mouth, thrown off balance by his emotion. No one else seemed to like Brock Liu.

Hamlin finally spoke. "How'd you—"

Poele ignored him and spoke to Storm. "You local?"

"Yes. Born on the Big Island."

"Hawaiian?"

"Half," Storm said softly. "My mother was Hawaiian. My aunt—"

"Is a healer." Poele picked at the label on his sweating beer bottle. "She'll know that prayer."

Hamlin tried again. "So when did you see him last?"

"What?" Poele frowned at Hamlin, his sad expression replaced with one of confusion. "Who?"

"Wait a sec." Storm laid a hand on Hamlin's arm. "Who's the prayer for?"

"Jenny. Isn't that why you drove up here? You knew her, right?"

Storm felt like she'd been punched in the chest. "Jenny Williams?"

"Yeah." Poele got to his feet. "Why are you here? What's going on?"

"I just saw her." Storm could hardly get the words out. God, poor Luke. About the same age she'd been when her own mother had died.

"Jesus, what time?" Poele stood in the shadow of his house, but his eyes burned as if lit from behind. "Was anyone else there?"

"Who the hell is Jenny?" Hamlin's tone cut through their shock.

Storm stood up and held her hands, palms out, toward both men. "Hamlin, remember I told you about my high school friend? We're talking about his wife. I stopped to see her yesterday afternoon, around four-thirty."

"She's dead, too?" Hamlin looked back and forth between Poele and Storm.

"She died sometime last night," Poele said. "But who are *you* talking about?"

"We found a body in the woods this afternoon," Storm said. He'd hear about it soon, anyway. "It's not identified, but it's been there a while."

"How long?" Poele asked quickly, and leaned toward Storm. He appeared to be holding his breath.

"We couldn't tell. A week or two, I'd guess."

Poele sat down in his chair with a soft sigh. "So why you asking me about it?"

Storm ignored the question and paced back and forth in front of the steps. "I can't believe Jenny is dead. How did it happen?"

Poele shook his head sadly. "Head wound, but so far, no one knows how she got it. Could have fallen, I guess."

"How did you find out?" Hamlin asked. He sat stiffly, with his arm draped across his lap. His good hand gripped a mostly full beer. Storm downed the rest of hers.

"I know a guy in the police department. He called me." Poele handed Storm another bottle and offered one to Hamlin, who shook his head. "Was anyone with Jenny when you saw her?"

"She called out to her son, but I didn't see anyone else." If she told him about the argument she'd overheard, the gossip would spread like a brush fire. "I talked to her from the front door."

"She didn't ask you in?"

Storm didn't want to make Jenny sound inhospitable. "She thought I was collecting for a charity."

"She was drinking, wasn't she?" He didn't say it as if he expected an answer.

"She didn't seem drunk."

Poele opened another beer and sank lower in his chair. "*Hā'awe i ke kua; hi'i i ke alo.* She was a woman with many burdens."

"Do you know Makani, the ranch hand?" Hamlin asked.

Poele nodded. "Sure, Makani Kekapu. He's been here since he was a teenager. Helps his uncle on the Ranch."

"His uncle?"

"You know. Dusty Rodriguez, the overseer."

Storm sat up straighter. She'd have to ask Uncle Keone about the daughter Dusty had lost. Makani would have been her first cousin.

"How about Brock Liu?" Hamlin asked.

"Brock Liu?" Poele kicked a small rock across the dirt yard. "That guy get one *chiisai chimpo*."

"What?" Hamlin's voice was sharp.

If Storm hadn't been so upset at the news about Jenny Williams, she would have laughed. Instead, she mustered up a smile for Hamlin.

"He's got a little dick," she said. "Metaphorically speaking."

"Right." Hamlin didn't smile. "When did you last see him?"

Poele took a long pull on his beer. "Two, three weeks ago. I forget the exact date. He left here in his big SUV after he made another offer on my land. I turned him down, of course, and he threatened me. Again. Nothing new." Poele squinted at Hamlin. "Why? You think that body is Brock?"

"He's missing. That's all we know right now."

"I'm broken hearted." Poele snorted. "Hope he stays that way. Missing, that is. And I'm not alone."

"He pissed off other people, too?" Storm asked.

"He's a shit. Ask Delia Tsue."

"They go out?" Storm remembered Delia's reticence when she'd asked about Liu.

"Used to. She kicked his ass out. Had to get a restraining order."

"Why?" Hamlin asked.

"He broke her nose." Poele popped open another beer. "At least, that's the part I know about."

"What did he threaten you with?" Hamlin asked.

"Told me I might have a fire. Out here, so far from everyone." Poele took a big swallow of beer and burped. He seemed about as disturbed as if Liu had threatened him with flat tires.

"As you may know, I have a rocky relationship with fire. His comment was in bad taste, to say the least." Poele's mouth twisted. "Then he told me he'd have my water diverted." With this statement, his face darkened. Storm had the impression he believed that threat.

"And then?" Hamlin asked.

"He left. Slammed the doors of his big truck and sent up a dust cloud that lasted hours." Poele waved his hand in the air.

"You haven't seen him since?"

"I don't know where he is. I mean that." Poele looked over at Storm. "You seen Tanner lately?"

"No, I was going to try to meet up with him tomorrow." Storm picked at the label on her beer bottle. "Did he know Brock Liu?"

"This is a small island and Brock Liu thought of himself as a big shot. Everyone knew him." Poele's answer was brusque. "How do you get hold of Tanner? He doesn't have a phone."

Storm pulled a note from her pocket and read what she had.

"That's the Hawai'i EcoTour number," Poele said. "Not a bad place to track him down. He works for Skelly sometimes."

"Do you see him often?" she asked.

"Hardly ever. Lotta wilderness out there. You can get lost on this island if you want to." He looked sad. "I wonder if he knows about Jenny yet."

"When did you last see her?" Storm asked.

"Last week, Thursday." He finished off his beer and popped another.

"Did she talk about any fears or problems?"

"Oh, no." A sly grin erased his previous expression of sorrow.

"I take it you two had a relationship?" Hamlin asked.

"I never kish and tell." Storm could see at least four beer bottles under Poele's chair. The conversation was going to deteriorate.

Storm got to her feet. "Lambert, thanks for the cocktail hour. You mind if I use your bathroom before we drive back?"

Poele threw a hand in the direction of the front door. "Down the hall to the right."

Storm went in and paused to let her eyes adjust to the small, unlit space. The setting sun had thrown the sitting room into deep shadow, but she could see the book-lined shelves that covered the walls. No TV, just books. A small, lumpy sofa and a comfortable recliner with a good reading lamp next to it. That's where he spent his evenings, she figured—after beers with the goats. No wonder he wanted them to know he had a relationship with another human.

Storm peered at the book draped over the recliner's broad arm. *Ka oihana kahuna mamua aku*, by John Webber. She picked it up to see if there was an English translation. Poele's facility with the Hawaiian language was impressive. No translation, but a flyer marked Poele's place in the book, and it was a lurid blue. "Paradise Quest, a development by Liu & Sons." Scrawled across the top was a phone number. She'd bet a six-pack it was Brock Liu's.

On the first trip down the short hall, Storm passed the bathroom and reached a small bedroom at the end. A twin bed and a desk took up the space, and both the bed and desk were covered with newspapers, manuscripts, and more books. Piles overflowed onto the floor. Storm took a step into the room, which looked like an office. She'd find a scrap of paper to record the phone number on the flyer. Just in case the two beers she'd gulped in quick succession on an empty stomach fogged her memory.

Right. If she was honest with herself, she wanted to find more information about the Lius' development corporation. A date of the visit would be nice, too. It would also be interesting to see what other books Lambert read in his spare time, considering his past activism.

She didn't dare turn on a light, but the titles that were in large, bold print were easy to read even in the fading light. They all seemed to be about Hawai'i. Treatises and newsletters from the Office of Hawaiian Affairs were anchored against the breeze stirred by the ceiling fan with George Cooper's and Gavin Dawes' excellent book *Land and Power in Hawaii,* Samuel King's and

Randall Roth's *Broken Trust*, and a few others. There were also stacks of well-worn sheaves of papers. They were manuscript-bound, like college term papers, only thicker. Storm didn't have much time to explore, nor did she want to leave Hamlin and Poele together alone for long. The rumble of male voices drifting through the room's open window seemed sociable enough right then, but leaving the combination of testosterone, beer, and Hamlin's bad mood to foment without her intervention seemed about as safe as barbequing in a fireworks factory.

Storm ruffled through a stack of typed manuscripts. Some were old enough to have been done on a typewriter. She looked around the room. No notes and no computer, but that could be in his bedroom—if he even used one. On her way down the hall, she'd counted only two rooms and the bath, so there weren't many places to search.

Storm pulled a document from the middle of the stack. *Pahulu* was typed on the title page, followed by *Li'i Kekapu*. They were names, and *Pahulu* sounded familiar, though the other meant nothing to her.

Nor did she have time to think about it. Hamlin's voice had risen in volume, and she heard Poele's deeper tones in response. Time to go.

Storm darted toward the door and knocked over a stack of unbound papers that had been sitting on the floor. Damn. Quickly, she bent to right the stack, and in the process noticed the first line of one of the pages. *Kāhuna 'anā 'anā, Kāhuna kuni*. She didn't speak Hawaiian like Poele, but she knew certain words. Kahuna was a broad term meaning teacher, priest, magician, wizard, or expert in just about any profession. The words *'anā 'anā* and *kuni* were modifiers, and they rang a warning bell in the recesses of her memory.

Storm righted the papers, making sure as well as she could that they were stacked as they'd been before she tripped. Now the name *Pahulu* came back to her, and Storm felt a wave of dread. *Pahulu* was a goddess of sorcery, though people rarely mentioned her name. Storm had only heard it because some children on the Big Island once threatened another playmate with her dark magic—until a set of parents put a swift end to the bullying. The kids had precipitated a bigger reaction by uttering her name than by spewing variations on the F-word, another popular playground activity.

Storm backed away from the manuscripts and covered the six or eight feet of space to the bathroom in two seconds. She didn't have time to use the facilities, so she flushed the toilet and hoped that the noise would reach—and distract—the men. Out in the hall again, she took two deep breaths, the first one shaky, the second deeper and more controlled, and sauntered through the sitting room and out the front door.

Chapter Sixteen

Tanner Williams asked old Mr. Yamaguchi, who'd picked him up not far from Halawa Bay, to drop him about a mile down the highway from Kaunakakai Wharf. He told Yamaguchi he was going to visit a friend who lived nearby, but in truth he needed time alone. Yamaguchi had heard about a local death on the radio, and blurted the story soon after Tanner got in the car. The old fellow had called his daughter-in-law, who lived in Kaunakakai, to get more information. It turned out that she lived two blocks from where the cluster of police cars and a silent ambulance had gathered. Tanner recognized the address Yamaguchi mentioned. The news caused him to hyperventilate, and he gasped for Yamaguchi to pull to the side of the road. Tanner stumbled from the car and threw up.

The gentle octogenarian felt so bad about Tanner's reaction he wanted to take him to a doctor, but Tanner mumbled that what he needed most was to get to Kaunakakai. After several miles of silence, Tanner borrowed Yamaguchi's cell phone and called the police station, but Niwa wasn't there and Tanner didn't want to talk to anyone else.

He knew his thoughts weren't hanging together. It was all he could do not to shout them aloud, which was his way of working out distress, kind of like discussing problems with himself. But that would really freak out old Mr. Yamaguchi, who was already glancing nervously at his passenger. After the call to the police, Tanner called Skelly, who wasn't there, either. He left a message, though. Nice and bland, so that Connor, if he intercepted it, wouldn't hear Tanner's angst. At least Tanner hoped he wouldn't—he wasn't sure how he sounded right then.

By the time Yamaguchi got his aging sedan to within a few miles of Kaunakakai, Tanner was beginning to twitch. Both men were relieved when Tanner climbed out of the car and mumbled his thanks.

He watched Yamaguchi drive off, then scurried through the long grass of a vacant field toward the ocean. He needed to sit and think, gaze out at the calm water and reflect on the news he'd received. He wanted to believe the radio had it wrong, that the report was a case of mistaken identity. Two doors down from the Williams house, the neighbors frequently had knock-down, drag out battles with shouts, crashing dishes, and slamming doors.

It could be that woman, Tanner thought. And Luke? Tanner's heart froze in his chest at the thought of Luke in a house of danger and death. When Yamaguchi related the news, Tanner had gasped out a question about a boy, but Yamaguchi said the radio mentioned only a woman, nothing about a child or even another person.

His medication was making his hands shake and his brain fuzzy. The pills had induced a deep sleep last night, though he'd risen at the pre-dawn hour he'd told himself to awaken. That system always worked for him, though four hours of sleep weren't enough. He'd drunk an extra cup of strong coffee that morning to mask the sensation that his brain was in slo-mo and his synaptic network had dead spots. As in memory blanks. Unfortunately, he didn't feel much better twelve hours later.

He remembered having part of a beer while Skelly had a few. Skelly was accustomed to it, though. His old friend asked questions about the past, too, but Tanner couldn't quite recall what they'd been, yet he knew they'd made him uncomfortable. Or was he confusing that disquiet with the distress brought on by the news of Jenny's death?

There had to be a mistake. Jenny was too young. And Luke needed her. Thoughts of Jenny stirred up strong, conflicting emotions in Tanner. Though he had tender memories of her from the time they met to a couple of years after Luke's birth, anger lay just below the surface. She'd changed from a gentle wife and mother to a complainer, one of those people who relish their victimhood and seek a target for their hostility. He was the target, and it pissed him off.

Tanner sank onto the beach a few feet from the ocean. The tide was coming in, lapping a little higher with each wave. He focused on the grains of sand, distinguishing the ridges of shell fragments, and the gentle hues of sea glass.

He was forgetting something, whatever had triggered this sense of foreboding. It seemed as if it came from an incident last night, when it had been so dark that his senses couldn't make out what had nudged him toward consciousness. A movement or a noise, perhaps. He wasn't sure. It could have been a nightmare, the rustle of a stray cat, Skelly's apneic snores. He was having trouble discerning imagination from reality, though he'd taken his medication. It was probably due to lack of sleep and the shocking news he'd received, but he thought the cloud hanging over him preceded Yamaguchi's bombshell. It might concern one of the Richards brothers. That or the questions Skelly brought up, the ones Tanner tried to keep buried in the past, and which crept into his dreams.

He dug in his pocket for the amber vial with his pills and swallowed one dry. It would gather his scattered thoughts, though it would also blunt his insight. Tanner sat for a minute more, then stood to make his way to Kaunakakai Ball Park. He wanted to see Luke so badly, he vibrated with yearning. Finding his son and talking with Dave Niwa about the circumstances of Jenny's death were now his top priorities.

Chapter Seventeen

"Hamlin, it's extremely unusual to have something written down about Hawaiian sorcery. It's bad luck. And he had manuscripts about it." Storm peered down the unpaved trail as far as the truck's misaligned headlights would allow.

"Most cultures are like that. Who wants to admit their lives are dictated by superstition?" Hamlin slid down in the truck's passenger seat and slumped back against the headrest.

"No, I mean some people wouldn't utter the words." She looked over at him. "Are you all right?"

"I'm okay. What words?"

"The sorcerer's name. It's a Hawaiian goddess."

"'In revenge and in love woman is more barbarous than man.'"

Storm hit a pothole. "I can't believe you said that."

"I didn't. Nietzsche did."

"What's wrong with you?"

"Sorry, I guess I'm hungry." He looked at his watch. "No wonder, it's 7:45. You think Maile and Keone will wait for us?"

As in answer, Storm's mobile phone rang. One hand on the steering wheel, she dug the phone out of her handbag.

"Why don't you stop to answer that?" Hamlin asked. "How many beers did you have?"

She gave him a poisonous look. "Uncle Keone? How'd it go?" She slowed down and stopped at the trail's intersection with the paved road. Not another car was in sight, and the night was as dense and opaque as black velvet. The moon hadn't come up yet and Moloka'i had little ambient light. Storm knew if she looked out the truck's windows, the sky would be filled with stars thick as falling snow.

"I stayed where we waited for you and Maile," Keone said. "The cops went into the woods, and they came out pretty fast to call for help. A couple of the younger ones looked downright green. Glad I didn't have to go in there."

"It was not a pretty sight."

"I can imagine. Where are you two? We're getting hungry."

Storm grinned into the phone. "Get a table and order drinks. We'll be there in twenty minutes."

When they got back to the Lodge, Storm dropped Hamlin, then parked the truck and stopped at the front desk, where she was told that Dusty had found a ride home and would pick up his keys in the morning. Her stomach growled loudly as she made her way to the table. Hamlin had already gone into the dining room, so that he could tell Aunt Maile and Uncle Keone to call for menus.

Maile had one of Hamlin's hands in hers. As Storm approached, she could hear Maile ask, "Can you feel this? How 'bout here?"

Hamlin mumbled his replies, and Maile wore a frown. "Where do you feel the most pain?"

Storm took the empty chair across from Hamlin and picked up a menu, though she listened for his answer.

"It's a general ache, kind of hard to pin down, but my shoulder and elbow feel weak and this hand is getting so numb I can hardly use it," he said.

Storm couldn't help but look over the menu at him. "Why didn't you tell me? We should have had your shoulder packed in ice."

"It's okay, Storm," Maile said. "He'd still have the symptoms, though his arm and shoulder are swelling, and that makes the ache worse. I think when you fell, you stretched your brachial plexus, the nerves that run down your neck into your arm. We need to get you back to Honolulu to see a specialist."

Hamlin looked alarmed, and Maile laid her hand gently on his. "It's reversible. The symptoms will go away over time, but you do need to have it looked at."

Keone closed the menu he'd been reading. "The last flight left at 6:30, but we'll get you on an early one tomorrow morning."

Hamlin sighed. "Not before seven, okay? I'm going to have a stiff drink and try to get a good night's sleep." He caught the eye of a waiter and waved him over. "A dry martini with onions, please."

Storm waited for the waiter to leave before she leaned inward. "Do you know anything about sorcery?" she whispered.

Uncle Keone sputtered on his beer. "I haven't heard anything about that since I was a kid." He looked at his wife. "How 'bout you?"

Maile looked about as happy as if Storm had announced she'd uncovered a stash of pornography. "Not lately. Though Moloka'i is known for its powerful sorcerers. Why do you ask?"

"Poele has manuscripts on the topic."

"Those tales are almost always passed on orally. It would be almost unheard of for someone to write that kind of thing down."

Hamlin lowered his drink. "He's probably just interested in Hawaiian history. People don't believe in sorcery any more, do they?"

"Some do." Maile raised one eyebrow in his direction. "There are things we grow up with that never leave us. Many of us believe our *'aumakua* protect us. Others believe priests turn wine into the blood of Christ."

She looked back and forth between Storm and Hamlin. Storm suppressed a smile. *'Aumakua* were a tradition that even mainland-born Hamlin bought into. He'd checked to make sure she was wearing her pig charm before they left for Moloka'i. He'd also been the one to present the gold necklace with its mischievous emerald-eyed pig to Storm on Uncle Keone's and Aunt Maile's behalf for her thirtieth birthday.

"Hawaiian leaders used sorcery," Keone added. "Kamehameha made sure all the strongest sorcery gods were aligned with him and his chiefs when he organized to unite the islands. He built god houses and keepers for their worship."

"I thought those were for his *'aumakua* and those of his warriors," Storm said. "To protect his rule."

"That's true, but it went beyond than that." Maile looked at Storm. "The ancient Hawaiians, before the language was written, established *'aumakua* by dedicating the bones of an influential family member to a powerful god, like that of the shark, owl, pig, or another animal. They believed the dead person was transformed into that animal, and if the animal was then worshiped by the family, it would protect that family." She took a sip from her wine glass. "Conversely, if the animal's worship was neglected or its sacredness forgotten or ignored, the *'aumakua* would seek vengeance on the family."

"But certain people abused this belief," Uncle Keone said.

"I'll bet, considering how brutal some of those chiefs were." Storm might argue with her aunt about the role these stories played in her present life, but she loved hearing the old folklore.

Hamlin flagged down the waiter for another martini, and Aunt Maile waited for the young man to get out of hearing range before she quietly resumed her tale.

"Kamehameha and other *ali'i* believed that gods could possess a living person. Those people were called keepers, and they were sent to harm people who were seen as a threat. Kamehameha allegedly used sorcerers' power to gain control of the islands."

"How were these spirits supposed to get to their victims?" Hamlin asked.

"People kept pieces of keepers' bodies, or relics. Even an image, object, or parts of an image could be charged with the spirit's power, or *mana*," Maile said. Storm's fingers crept unconsciously to her charm.

Maile continued. "They directed the spirits' mana through chants. Eventually, people in the general population began to use this power, and the chiefs became very concerned."

"So they made laws against it, which just pushed the practice into secrecy," Keone said. "By this time, everyone suspected everyone else. People began to hide their family *'aumakua*, because even those were feared. Others claimed to have the ability to use sorcery to combat sorcery. It got very complicated."

"To answer your question, Ian, there were *kāhuna a'o,* or teaching sorcerers. There was also someone known as a *kahuna ho'opi'opi'o,* who could inflict illness—and there were others."

The waiter showed up to take their orders and all four of them had to take another look at the menu. Storm's stomach had growled all through Maile's and Keone's tale, but she'd barely noticed. Now it let out a grumble that turned Hamlin's head, and he flashed his first grin in several hours.

As soon as the waiter left, though, Hamlin asked, "What others?"

Maile gave a little sigh. "Before we go on, I want to know a thing or two. What did you talk about with Lambert Poele? And where were these manuscripts?"

"We mostly talked about Jenny Williams' death and when he'd last seen Brock Liu." Hamlin looked over at Storm.

"Then I had to go to the bathroom," she said, and she related her detour into Poele's office.

Keone's eyes widened and Maile sat back as if she'd been pushed. "He'll know you snooped."

Storm shrugged. "I just peeked. And he wasn't trying to hide anything."

"He wasn't expecting visitors, dear."

"Ask them, Storm," Hamlin said.

"Ask us what?" Keone asked.

"What's a *kāhuna 'anā 'anā*, and a *kāhuna kuni*?"

Uncle Keone leaned back in his chair. "I'm losing my appetite."

"I haven't heard those terms in years, and I've never seen them in print." Aunt Maile was pale, but she spoke after carefully looking to make sure no one could overhear. "A *kāhuna*

ʻanā ʻanā is an expert in praying someone to death. A *kāhuna kuni* has the ability to burn someone to death."

"And who is Pahulu?"

"Oh, my," Aunt Maile said.

"She was the most powerful sorcerer of all," Uncle Keone whispered. "The chief of evil beings, the *akua*. She lived here, on Molokaʻi.

"And some people say her descendants are still here."

Chapter Eighteen

Haley's game was the only thing David Niwa had looked forward to all day and he was more than a half hour late. Christ, what a day. Two suspicious deaths in a twenty-four-hour period might be a first for the island. Hell, for the whole Maui Police Department, even if one victim had been dead for a week or two. Niwa felt like he still stank from that one, but he had a hunch he smelled worse from the fact he'd been on the run ever since his five a.m. shower. That was more than twelve long hours ago, and the temperature was still about eighty degrees. For April, that was hot—and they said global warming was a myth. And who were *they*, anyway?

Niwa turned into the baseball park's dirt lot, turned off the ignition to his patrol car, and sat for a moment to gather himself. He was off the clock and it was time to shake the stifling mantle of distress he'd worn since finding Jenny Williams. Haley wasn't going to be pitching baseballs much longer; self-appointed sports authorities were going to move her to softball. This is not the time to think about this, he told himself. Light thoughts—no cynicism or bitterness right now. Niwa hauled himself out of the car.

"Dave, I hear you had one busy day." The second-string shortstop's dad had pulled up next to him. Niwa couldn't remember the guy's name right then. Kind of new to the island, some guy who moved his family from O'ahu to do aquaculture. Nice enough fellow.

"Yup. You have one, too?"

"Yeah, I hate being late like this. Wonder how we're doing. Hey, I'm glad Haley's pitching."

Both men looked at the slender figure on the pitching mound. Only the ponytail that stuck out from the back of the cap revealed that the pitcher was a girl. That wasn't a sure tell, either. The catcher, a hundred-eighty-pound twelve-year-old with the beginnings of a moustache, also had a ponytail. Kid needed an exercise program, Niwa thought, then reminded himself that he could use one, too.

The men walked toward the crowd of parents gathered on the sidelines. Caroline waved from the low bleachers and gestured to the seat she'd saved. The other man split off to greet his wife.

"Bottom of the fifth, we're tied two-two," Caroline said, and kept her eyes on Haley. "She walked two batters."

Niwa winced. "She's distracted."

"Probably."

"You seen Tanner?"

"You're distracted, too."

"I've got to find him. You heard anything new about Luke?"

"Not since I talked to you."

Niwa stood. "I'll be right back."

She shot him a sharp look, but there was nothing he could do. If his child was hospitalized, he'd want to know immediately. Any parent worth his salt would, and Niwa thought Tanner, despite his weaknesses, was a caring parent. He also figured someone had told Tanner about Jenny by now, and he wondered how the guy was coping. The least he could do was reassure Tanner that Luke was being cared for, but he hoped from the bottoms of his aching feet to the top of his sweating scalp he wouldn't have to leave the game to take Tanner to the hospital.

Niwa stood to scan the crowd, but Tanner wasn't among them. Niwa hadn't really expected him to be in the bleachers. He shaded his eyes against the sun to view the other side of the field where a smaller group sat in the shade of a large monkeypod tree.

One of them looked like Connor Richards, and the other three looked like fellow gym rats. No women. Connor was probably the last person on the island Niwa wanted to talk to, but it was likely Tanner had approached Connor if he was looking for either Skelly or Niwa.

The younger Richards brother watched Niwa's every step across the far end of the field, and made sure Niwa knew it. When Niwa was within about twenty feet of the group, Connor stood up and did some kind of shrugging motion that made his trapezius muscles bulge like twin hillocks under his cutaway tank top.

Niwa stifled a derisive snort and addressed his greeting to Jeff Gibson and Mike Ka'ana, who were beginning to rise from their folding chairs. "Howzit."

"Hey." Jeff and Mike stood and offered their hands, which Niwa shook. All three men ignored Connor. The thought crossed Niwa's mind that Connor might start pawing the ground if this went on for long.

"You seen Tanner Williams?"

"You're late, as usual." Connor did the shrugging motion again, and added a head roll to the motion. Probably thought he looked like Rocky IV—or IX.

Jeff Gibson made sure Connor wasn't looking his way and rolled his eyes at Niwa. "He was here, but he left with Skelly. They went to the hospital."

"Good, that's what I wanted to know." Niwa nodded at Jeff and Mike. "Thanks."

He turned and left. Halfway around the field, he pulled out his cell phone to call his partner and got Steve Nishijima's voice mail. "I'm at the ball field for Haley's game. Gimme a call. Tanner Williams and Skelly Richards are on the way to see Luke at the hospital."

Niwa hung the phone back on his belt and climbed up in the bleachers next to Caroline, whose face showed relief. "I was afraid you'd have to leave."

"I think things are under control for the time being."

"It's about time." Caroline smiled up at him. "You brought her luck. She struck 'em all out this inning."

Niwa looked out on the field and was swept with melancholy. Probably it was brought on by the day, but right then he wondered about luck and what, exactly, he could do for his daughter—or anyone, for that matter.

Like Luke, his daughter was at the mercy of so much that was out of his control. Right now she was the starting pitcher, but Casey Onoue, the second-string pitcher, was going to eclipse her in size and strength as soon as surging testosterone hurtled him into puberty. In a few months she'd slide, not completely comprehending why her almighty father couldn't protect her, to the far less admired women's softball league.

Caroline, as if she could read his thoughts—and she probably could—leaned her head against his shoulder. He put an arm around her shoulders and drew her close. What else could they do?

Chapter Nineteen

In the eighth inning, one of Haley's teammates batted in three runners on a rogue grounder fumbled by the opposing team. Niwa and Caroline rose to their feet with the rest of the parents to roar their delight. Haley took the mound and struck out the next three batters to win the game 5-4. Niwa watched Haley's ponytail, nearly lost in the jubilant huddle of her fellow players, bounce with congratulatory nudges, and his melancholy began to lift. Okay, maybe things weren't so bad after all. His daughter was a winner, and always would be. Even if it was softball. Or the swim team, in which she'd recently expressed interest. His family was fortunate, and he'd better get over his funk and remember.

Niwa looked down at his wife with pride and affection in his dark eyes. "Great way to end a hard day."

"I'll bet." Caroline's eyes searched his face. "You look tired."

"I am. Say, earlier today you mentioned problems Jenny was having. Anything I should know about?"

Caroline gave him a wry smile. "You're always the last one to know."

"People gossip too much," Niwa growled softly and looked around at who might overhear their conversation.

"True, but you could keep your ears open." Caroline gave him a soft punch on the arm.

He gave her a hug. "That's what I've got you for."

"And you're damned lucky."

"Not a day goes by, my dearest."

"Just as long as you know." She leaned against him as they made their way toward the cluster of players and parents. "Jenny hasn't had it easy."

Niwa knew better than to rush her. Caroline would reveal what she knew in her own organized way.

"Sue Murakami has known her for a long time." Sue was a friend of Caroline's from their exercise class. "Jenny used to be a talented sculptor and had a growing reputation on the East Coast."

"Wow, and I thought she worked at the hospital."

"That's probably what most people think. She got that job when Tanner took a turn for the worse. I don't know if she's ever been a happy person, but Sue says she's become more bitter over the years."

"Couldn't she do art on the side?"

Caroline shot him a look. "There are only so many hours in the day. She's a mom, too."

"So they moved back here and she got a job when he got fired from the pharmaceutical company?"

"Not exactly. He was having problems, true, but when they moved back here, he was still working. He was supposed to see his therapist here and follow up on the work he'd been doing on the mainland. But then he had some kind of breakdown and couldn't work at all. That's when she went to work at the hospital."

"When was this?" He'd get more from Caroline and her friends than going through traditional channels. He'd be lucky if the doctor admitted Tanner was a patient. He made a mental note to check Jenny's employment records with the hospital.

"A few years after they came back to Moloka'i. I got the feeling the company paid worker's comp for a while, but finally stopped."

"You know what year they moved back?"

"About ten years ago. According to Sue, a few months before the fire." She gave him a meaningful look.

Niwa's face creased with thought. With the discovery of the body in the woods, the same seed of thought had begun to grow in his mind. He was still waiting for confirmation that the body was Brock Liu's, but he already knew the watch and clothes corresponded to items Liu owned. "Does anyone talk about that?"

She cocked an eyebrow at him. "People usually give each other meaningful looks and change the subject." She stopped and looked up at him. "Brock Liu's older brother died in that fire, didn't he? What was his name again?"

Niwa nodded. "Alika. All the guys implicated in the protest were friends of Tanner's."

"Then Tia Rodriguez and little Tommy left, soon after the fire."

"Do you think she left?"

"Honey, I hope so." Caroline's voice was low and sad.

They were nearly within earshot of some of the parents.

"So what was Jenny up to lately?" Niwa asked quietly. "Did she fill Luke's insulin prescriptions at your pharmacy?"

"Sometimes. One morning, she came in to pick up some syringes and Ted said he could smell alcohol on her breath."

"No kidding." Ted Yawahara, the owner of the drug store, was known for his discretion.

"I think he was worried. He lives down the street from her, you know. There was gossip about her late night visitors, too."

"As in men?"

"I guess so. He didn't say any more. You know Ted."

Niwa just nodded. Parents were beginning to look their way and offer greetings, and Haley jogged over to them.

"Dad, you made it."

"It was the high point of my day," Niwa said honestly. "You were great, honey."

The Niwas hung around for the potluck, a traditional after-game occurrence. Four families had brought hibachis and people arranged an assortment of teriyaki chicken, freshly caught fish, hot dogs, steak, and kal-bi on racks over the coals, which had been lit between the eighth and ninth innings. Caroline reached into the tote she'd been carrying and pulled out a covered chocolate sheet cake. Mothers uncovered sushi platters, poke, macaroni salads, greens, fruit, fried rice, char siu bao, Chinese noodles, and various sweets.

As always, Niwa marveled at how efficiently the spread materialized. Folding tables, coolers, and eating utensils appeared. Parents had this system down cold. Normally, he looked forward to these post-game festivities, which went on win or lose, and would pile a paper plate until it sagged. But this night Dave Niwa followed his wife and daughter through the line and helped himself to less food than they did. He even got a Diet Coke, which got Caroline's attention.

When he whispered that he wanted to stop by the hospital to check in on Luke, she agreed. "We'll follow. Haley will want to see him, too."

A half hour later, they stopped at the front desk to get directions to Luke's room. They were still a half-corridor away when they knew something was wrong. Three nurses and a pediatrician, the same woman Haley saw, shot out of his room.

Niwa's casual stroll turned into what Haley called his cop-walk and Caroline and Haley struggled to keep up.

"Dr. Peterson, is Luke all right?" Niwa called out.

"He's not here, and he needs to be." The doctor's expression was grim. "His father was in a few minutes ago with Skelly Richardson."

"Did Luke leave with them?" Niwa was hopeful.

One of the nurses shook her head. "No, Tanner rushed out when he saw Luke was gone. Skelly was trying to keep up."

The sound of swift footsteps down the hall caught the group's attention. Skelly Richards rounded a corner, his worried eyes scanning the hall.

Skelly practically shouted. "Hey, where is he?"

"Tanner?" Niwa asked. "I thought he was with you."

"He's freaking out, man. He ran outside." Skelly's shoulders sagged. "I made Tanner stop for something to eat before we came. If I hadn't..."

"You were helping Tanner." Caroline put a hand on Skelly's forearm. "Luke was probably already gone."

Niwa turned to the hospital staff. "When did you last see Luke?"

One of the nurses answered. "I stopped in after his dinner was delivered. That was about six."

Everyone looked at their watches. It was 7:49.

"He was okay then?" Niwa asked.

"He looked asleep. I went back a half hour later to make sure he ate dinner, but his bed was empty. I figured he was in the bathroom."

"His food was there?"

She nodded. "He'd eaten some of it, and I thought he was coming back to finish."

"We think he ate the sliced turkey, fruit cocktail, and pudding," Dr. Peterson said. "And his roll and butter."

"He probably took some of it with him," Haley said.

Everyone looked at the little girl.

"Why's that?" Dr. Peterson asked gently.

"Because he's careful now. He always takes food with him." Haley reached into the pocket of her pants and pulled out a napkin-wrapped bundle. She opened it sheepishly. "I brought him a manapua."

The pork-stuffed bun was dented on one side, but Niwa thought it still looked tempting, especially after hearing what the hospital served.

Caroline hugged her daughter to her.

"Listen, man, we've got to find Tanner," Skelly said, his voice panicky. "He's flipping out."

Dr. Peterson cut him off. "We've got to find Luke. He'll die without insulin. Or enough sugar. He's very brittle." She turned to Niwa. "Can you get some cars out looking for him?"

Niwa was already punching numbers into his phone.

"I just pray we got him stabilized," Dr. Peterson muttered, more to herself than to anyone else.

"When's his next shot due?" Caroline asked.

"At bedtime," the doctor replied. "About nine-thirty."

Everyone looked at their watches again.

"How long can he go without it?" Caroline asked.

"That's not the whole problem." The area around the doctor's mouth was white with tension. "Hypoglycemia could be even worse. His metabolism is up and down. He needs insulin, but his doses are changing, especially with the stress he's under. He'll get disoriented and feel dizzy first. He could misinterpret his symptoms, give himself what would be his normal amount, and put himself in a coma." She swallowed. "We've got to find him soon."

Chapter Twenty

The mischievous god Māui labored to put Kalā, the sun, in its place above the volcano Haleakalā, trailing the pink mists of dawn over the down-turned bowl of the Pacific. The air was fresh and cool; it smelled of hay, keawe, and red earth.

Storm steered Dusty's pickup around a curve in the road. "I'll catch a later flight. I can be home this afternoon to help you."

"That would be silly." Hamlin kept his eyes on the brightening sky in the east. "No need to cut your vacation short. At least stay until Monday, when Aunt Maile and Uncle Keone go back." He gave her a wry smile. "You could go on another ride without having to baby me."

"No one babied you. In fact, most people wouldn't have gotten back on their horse."

"Hmmm."

"I doubt I would have." Storm signaled for the turn to the airport. "Your appointment is at eleven, right? Call me right after. I can catch a two or three o'clock flight."

Hamlin waited a couple of seconds. "There is something you could do."

"Yes?"

"You were planning to talk to Tanner?"

"I left a message for him this morning before we left. I figure Skelly Richards can find him, if anyone can."

"Could you ask him about Brock Liu? If he saw him, if he ever took out a kayak?" Hamlin shifted in his seat. "Be indirect.

You're good at getting people to talk. I'd like any information about where Liu was last seen."

"I'll be glad to. His dad told you he took a kayak, right?"

"Liu's assistant told me. I guess they have a charge receipt."

"It doesn't look like he even made it to the water."

"If that was Brock in the woods."

"True. We should find out soon. Word'll hit the coconut wireless sometime today, I'll bet."

"The police will tell Devon first. I'll call the assistant this afternoon for an update."

"If that's Brock in the woods, then there's no lawsuit against Hawai'i EcoTours, is there?"

"We'll see."

Storm slowed on the airport access road. There were two cars in front of her, a veritable traffic jam for the eight-thirty to Honolulu. She stopped at passenger check-in and got out of the car with Hamlin, who held his carry-on duffel bag.

"Call me after you leave the doctor's. Please?"

She slid her arms around his waist and he leaned in, though his good arm held his duffel and he winced when he reached out with the injured one. "I'll talk to you soon," he said and kissed her. "I'll feel better in a day or two."

"I know. Have a safe trip." Why did she feel like he was going farther than a twenty-five-minute flight and thirty miles?

Though airport security was a lot more easy-going than Honolulu, the guard was ambling her way. Just doing his job, and at least he wore a smile. Storm slowly climbed into Dusty's truck, which he'd cheerfully volunteered that morning before rushing off to the barn. She drove at a crawl past the small terminal, out onto the highway, and a mile or two to the nearest gas station, where she filled the tank.

On the ride back to the ranch, she contemplated how to tactfully question Dusty about his missing daughter. Her own concerns derailed her thoughts, though. Was it only Hamlin's injury that was making him seem distant?

What she really wanted was to talk to Aunt Maile and hear that she was fretting about nothing. But Aunt Maile and Uncle Keone had planned to leave early that morning, too, for a visit to Pala'au State Park and the area around Phallic Rock, a place of great power on the island. They would be gathering plants and absorbing Hawaiian culture until dinner time.

So Storm corralled her thoughts on the road back to the ranch, drove past the Lodge and up the hill to the barn. As the truck crunched its way over the crushed coral drive, she could see Dusty in the rodeo arena, working with a handful of young paniolo and their cutting horses. He looked up at the sound of the approaching vehicle and waved.

A few minutes later, he led his lathered horse, an appaloosa with bright, inquisitive eyes, out of the arena.

"What a gorgeous horse." Storm wished she'd brought a carrot or apple for the handsome gelding. She reached out to the animal, who snuffled the palm of her hand.

"Hope I'm not interrupting. Thought I'd bring the truck to you." She handed over the keys. "Thanks for loaning it to us."

"You're welcome." Dusty pocketed the keys.

"Moonlight's a new arrival to the stable, and he's going to work out just fine." Dusty gave the horse a pat and tied him to a rail. He removed the saddle and handed it to a young man who'd approached to help. "We're training for the Makawao Rodeo."

Some of Storm's worries lifted as she watched Moonlight's skin twitch with delight. Butterfly used to do the same thing. "You going to cool him down? I'll walk with you a bit."

"Sure, a walk would be good. The air up here is good for the soul." He attached a lead rope to Moonlight's halter. "How's Hamlin doing this morning?"

The kindness in his voice caught Storm off guard. She looked down at her feet and waited a moment for the tightness in her throat to subside. "He's okay. His arm's a bit sore, I guess."

"I heard he needs an X-ray or something."

"He might have some nerve damage."

"Is Maile taking care of him?"

Storm nodded.

"He'll be okay, then." He paused. "Time will help."

Storm had the feeling he wasn't just talking about Hamlin's shoulder. She changed the subject. "Have you always lived here?"

"I grew up on Maui, but I'm old enough to say I've lived most of my life here." The lines around his eyes appeared to deepen. "I raised my daughter here."

"I heard about her last night."

The clip-clop of Moonlight's hooves were the only sound for a second or two. "I didn't think I'd survive losing her."

"She's missing, right?"

Dusty gave her a sad smile. "That's what death is, isn't it? When you know you'll never see a person again?"

A wave of sorrow passed over his face and Storm knew what he'd look like when he was an old man. Regret that she'd brought the subject up rolled through her, but to her relief, he broke the heavy silence.

"I was supposed to watch Tommy that afternoon. He was crawling and really scooting around. You couldn't leave him alone for a second." Dusty smiled at the memory. "She was going to drop him off, then go to town to help some of her friends make pickled mangoes for a fundraiser." He patted the horse's neck.

"She didn't drop him off?"

"She was always late, so I waited about an hour before I called to see if she'd decided to take Tommy with her." He turned his head away and rubbed Moonlight's head. The horse snorted gently, and Dusty continued, his voice matter-of-fact. "We got a lot of people to look for her, for her car."

"What happened?"

"Her car was at the airport."

"The police thought she'd left the island?"

Dusty stopped to adjust the horse's halter. Storm couldn't see his face behind the horse's curved neck. "Some of them did. But cars get abandoned there."

She recalled Sergeant Niwa's comments last night. "They probably scoured the other islands."

He nodded. "Mainland, too. The local police sent pictures to other police departments. A photo of the two of them is still on the Internet."

Dusty's gaze was on the ground in front of his feet, but Storm could see the muscles in his jaw working. "What about Tommy's father?"

"He was a wreck, too. Worse than me."

"Is he still on Moloka'i?"

Dusty's dark eyes met hers. "Sure, you met him yesterday."

The first name that popped into Storm's mind was Makani, but first cousins would be a little too close, not that it didn't happen. The next name that came to her was Lambert Poele, and she murmured it aloud.

"Lambert worshiped her, and his son. It was Tia who wouldn't get married. She wanted to finish college. That's the reason some people think she left." Moonlight, Dusty, and Storm had reached the end of a path, and Dusty turned the horse. "She would have told us, though."

"How did Lambert feel about her taking classes?"

"He wanted her to be happy. And Tommy, we wanted the best for him, too." Dusty frowned into the distance.

"When did this happen?"

"Nine years, eleven months, and eighteen days ago."

A long time to be counting days. "I remember my mom 'disappearing,' too. I still look for her *'aumakua*."

"Tia's is *puhi*."

"The eel, a fierce warrior." Storm wondered about Tia, who with her desire for education, sounded like a woman who faced down small-town expectations. A fierce warrior. "Mine is *pua'a*."

"The mischief-maker. I could believe that." Dusty smiled at her. "Though pigs are revered, too."

"She disappeared March twelfth?"

"The eleventh."

The fire he'd mentioned when he picked her and Hamlin up from the airport had taken place around the same time. A death due to suspected arson would shake a community the size of Moloka'i to its core. Follow that with the disappearance and possible death of two others, and devastation would spread like poison in water.

Poele, Tanner, Skelly, Conner, the Liu brothers, Dusty, and Tia were all friends, relatives, or colleagues. Kids who'd grown up together and knew each other well. Makani, though his mother lived on Maui, had probably spent a lot of time with them, too. They were all tied to the fire.

"When was the fire on Moloka'i Ranch?" Storm asked. "The one you told us about?"

Dusty's face darkened and he quickened his step. "Why you want to know? Lambert has suffered enough without bringing that up."

Chapter Twenty-one

Niwa sent Caroline and Haley home and headed for his patrol car with Skelly Richards, who needed a ride back to his office. The urgency of finding Luke had given him a surge of energy, and he absently rubbed a spasm that had been passing through his stomach for the past couple of weeks. Luke's doctor couldn't give Niwa a specific time frame, as too many factors affected a diabetic's blood sugar levels. It turned out Luke had received a small dose of insulin before his nap, and the floor nurse planned to check his glucose levels after he ate and again before bed. But Dr. Peterson stressed how volatile his levels were, and how they were affected by many factors, particularly the trauma of his mother's death. The boy probably wouldn't last twenty-four hours without a monitored balance of insulin and nourishment.

The first stop Niwa made was at Luke's home, and Niwa scanned the entire route for both Tanner and Luke. He saw two people walking dogs, but no one else.

Once at the house, he had to pick the locks to get in. Steve Nishijima had carefully locked up when he and the ID techs finished that morning. Ironic, because Jenny probably didn't bother. Most of the neighbors didn't; Niwa rarely locked his own house, though he thought he'd probably begin.

His next stop would be to drop Skelly at his business, where he could phone the police station if father and son stopped by. Skelly thought there was a good chance Tanner and Luke would spend the night there. Tanner knew where he hid the key and Skelly kept coffee and other supplies on hand for his friend. Tanner did it all the time; he and Luke might even be there now.

Niwa's mind was churning with questions and he found Skelly's frequent inquiries and opinions an annoying distraction. Why had the kid left the hospital? If he was desperate to find his dad, where might he go? Why was he running? That thought chilled Niwa, and made his apprehension worse.

"Where's Tanner's cabin?" Niwa asked. "The one where he does his research?"

Skelly looked startled. "That's supposed to be a secret."

"This is an emergency."

Skelly gnawed on the inside of his cheek. "It's been a long time since I was there, and Tanner led me into the valley. I don't know how to get there alone."

His evasiveness in the light of Luke's danger made Niwa want to bite his head off. He controlled the urge. "So where do you think it is?"

"Someplace back in the valley, before you get to Keawenui Bay. He hikes in or takes a boat."

"Which does he usually do?"

"Kayak or canoe is probably faster. Depends on the ocean, though."

"Does Luke know where it is?"

Skelly nodded. "But it's too far to go tonight. That's why they'll probably spend the night at the office." He continued to chew on his cheek. "Or maybe my house."

"You got a cell phone?"

"We don't get reception at the house. Sometimes works at the office. I think it's 'cause it's on the water."

"Right." Niwa didn't have time for Skelly's ramblings on why cell phone signals worked in some places and not in others on the island. If he listened to that, he'd be there all night. Some people thought spirits interfered with the signals.

He handed his phone to the man. "Try to call both places. And wait here. I'll be back in a few minutes."

Niwa was in the kitchen, looking for insulin in the refrigerator when Skelly banged through the front door. He stopped dead at the blackening stain on the worn carpet.

"Ah, shit, man." Skelly's voice broke.

"I told you to wait in the car." Niwa had had trouble skirting the stain, too. It looked bigger than it had when Jenny was lying on it.

"I wanted to tell you…shit, man." Skelly turned and let the door slam behind him.

A few minutes later, Niwa was out at the car. There had been a small carton of insulin vials in the refrigerator, with one vial missing. Niwa found it, empty, in the trash. He also checked the boy's bedroom, which was even messier than Haley's. Niwa counted four sets of Hanes tighty whities, five T-shirts, dirty, and two pairs of cargo shorts on the floor. The bed was unmade and cold; the small dresser's few drawers were filled with what looked like clean socks and underwear, a few sets of faded shorts and shirts. It was hard to tell, but Niwa didn't think Luke had stopped by the house. If he was careful enough to carry extra food, he would have taken the other insulin vials, wouldn't he?

Niwa was concerned that Luke might be outside at that moment, but wouldn't come in if he suspected someone was waiting for him. Niwa didn't want to scare the kid off, because Niwa's top priority was for the boy to get his insulin. Second on the list would be to convince him to come back to the hospital. According to Dr. Peterson, Luke knew how to give himself the shots, but he was too recently diagnosed and his doses too variable for him to know if he was getting the right amount. If he got dizzy or disoriented, his judgment regarding his doses would fail, too.

Niwa left a note under a magnet on the refrigerator door. "Call me. You're safe with us." He signed it Uncle Dave, Aunty Caroline, and Haley, and then plodded back out to the car with a prayer for the boy in his heart.

Skelly was leaning against the side of the car, head cradled in folded arms. He looked up when he heard Niwa's footsteps on the drive.

"Did he come home?" Skelly asked.

"Doesn't look like it. You see anyone hanging around?"

"No, and I watched." Skelly opened the door and got in the car. He handed Niwa's phone back. "No one answers at the office. I got enough of a signal to get Helene, and no one's gone to our house. So far, anyway."

Twenty minutes later, they pulled up to Skelly's office. "Who closed this afternoon?"

"Connor didn't come in today." Skelly's tone was flat. "I closed around three to pick up some folks at the airport and take them to the Ranch. I went straight to the game from there."

"Tanner was already at the ball park?"

"I told you he left a message, right?" Skelly sounded as if the day had finally gotten to him. "That's where I met him."

The men got out of the car and made their way along the uneven paving stones to the door. The moon was nearly full and cast deep shadows that made the path hard to navigate. The only sound was the mournful lowing of two buffos competing for a mate in a nearby marsh.

Niwa thought the big toads were repulsive, but refrained from saying so. He illuminated his Casio and checked the time, which was a couple minutes to ten. "Pretty quiet around here."

"Yeah, maybe they're asleep already." Skelly banged on the door. "If he's here, I don't want to startle him." He looked at Niwa. "He was in a state when he left the hospital."

"What do you mean?" Niwa figured it was time he found out more about Tanner's illness and temperament. Caroline had mentioned a breakdown; Niwa wondered how frequently those occurred, and exactly what happened. When he'd given Tanner the ride to Skelly's office, which seemed like longer ago than just Thursday, Tanner had seemed preoccupied with his son, but his overall behavior had seemed calm and rational.

Skelly shrugged. "Mostly, he talks to himself." He looked at Niwa as he dug in his pocket for his key. "I do that too, but I hope I don't sound like I'm having a conversation with someone in my head. He can get pretty excited about stuff."

"I'd get excited, too, if my sick son was missing from the hospital."

Skelly got the door unlocked. "Yeah, but you probably wouldn't hop around, break into a dripping sweat, and then run away."

He stopped inside the door. "Tanner, Luke, you guys here? It's me, Skelly." No one answered. "He can't help it, though. It's a chemical thing. Tanner, you here?"

Niwa reached behind and found the light switch. The overhead brightness made them both blink. The room looked like an empty office, waiting for the next day to begin, nothing else.

"Crap," muttered Skelly. "Doesn't look like anyone's been here."

Niwa felt like crap, or worse. Skelly clomped around the corner, into what Niwa presumed was the kitchen area of the small, office-adapted apartment. Niwa made his way to the desk, where he hoped against hope to see a note, even the blinking light on the answering machine, telling them that a message waited. Skelly ran a fairly neat office, though, and the desk was clear of papers. The answering machine sat quiet and uncommunicative.

"Hey, Dave. C'mere."

Niwa hurried toward the sound of Skelly's voice. "What's up?"

"Someone broke the window over the sink. I know I latched it when I closed up for the night. And he cut himself." He pointed out a couple pinkish droplets in the sink to Niwa, then turned to open the refrigerator door. "Luke's insulin is gone."

Thank God, it looked like the kid might have been there. "Does he know where you hide the key?" Niwa felt upbeat for the second time that day, considering Haley's game was the first time.

Skelly scrunched his face in thought. "I don't think so." He walked out of the kitchen, passed through the office and out the front door, where Niwa could hear the clunk of stone. He got there in time to see Skelly let go of one of the herb pots that lined the paving stones and move to another one.

"It's supposed to be under the rosemary," Skelly said. "Tanner always put it back in the same place."

"So what are you thinking?" Skelly's search was giving Niwa bad vibes. His mood was starting to plummet again.

"A couple of days ago Connor got mad at Tanner for using the apartment."

"Are you telling me Connor took the key?"

"Maybe."

"But it looks like Luke broke in," Niwa said. "Right?"

"I've got to check something." Skelly hurried back inside, with Niwa lumbering behind. He went straight to a cupboard that held five or six coffee mugs and a few mismatched plates and bowls.

"Fuck."

A wave of fatigue swept over Niwa that threatened to collapse his legs. "Now what?"

"Tanner's pills are gone, too."

"So maybe Tanner took 'em."

"Yeah, maybe." Skelly didn't sound like he believed it.

"You think Connor took their meds?"

"I've got to talk to him."

"Yes, you do. Right now." Niwa rubbed at the pain that shot through his belly.

"That wouldn't be a good idea," Skelly said softly. "If I want to get the truth, I need to wait for him to have his, uh, medication and some coffee."

"Christ, Skelly, we need to know who's got the meds, whether it's the people that need 'em or your self-absorbed idiot of a brother." Niwa knew the minute the words were out of his mouth, he'd put his foot in it. "I'm sorry, man. It's been a long day and I'm worried sick."

"Me, too. You think I like suspecting my brother?" Skelly's voice rose in indignation.

"I was out of line." Niwa shuffled toward the front door and turned back to look at Skelly, who was gazing at the broken window. "I need some sleep. We both do. Can I call you tomorrow?"

"Yeah." Skelly didn't look at him.

"Hey, Skelly. I'm really sorry. Call me tonight if you hear anything. From anyone."

The fluorescent overhead light made Skelly's face look grey. He just nodded his response.

When Niwa crawled into bed next to Caroline around two, she woke enough to ask him if they'd found Luke.

"No," Niwa groaned, and despite his exhaustion, slept with his hand outstretched toward the phone on the bedside table. Other patrol cars were searching for the boy, too, with directions to call if anyone spotted him. Niwa woke gritty-eyed and hungover around seven the next morning with the sick knowledge that Luke was still out there.

Chapter Twenty-two

Storm walked the gravel road back to the Lodge and her stomach growled angrily. She wished she'd had time for breakfast with Aunt Maile and Uncle Keone—or at least someone cheerful and uncomplicated. The two men she'd talked with so far that morning had been enough to make her want to crawl back into bed. The fact that she'd had a youthful romantic obsession for one and was involved with the other wasn't helping.

The aroma of coffee lured her into the dining room. It was only nine o'clock; the room was filled with families and delicious aromas. A hostess appeared right away and Storm let herself be led to an outdoor seat with a panoramic view.

"Coffee?" the hostess asked, and Storm nodded gratefully. The hostess filled a mug and left Storm a menu.

Storm opened the menu, but her mind drifted to Dusty's abruptness when the subject of the fire came up. He had discussed Tia's and Tommy's disappearance and the subsequent search for them without much hesitation, but he'd shut down fast when she brought up the fire. It made Storm wonder if Tia's disappearance and the fire were related. Otherwise, why not tell her about it? Especially since he'd brought it up on the drive from the airport Thursday afternoon. Or had she or Hamlin brought up the fire? She wasn't sure any more. Dusty had talked about it, though.

Storm took a grateful swallow of coffee and noticed that her waitress was back. "Scrambled eggs and fruit salad, please.

Toasted taro bread sounds good, too." Storm eyed the pot of *poha* jam on the table. A relative of the gooseberry, *poha* jam was an island delicacy she didn't get very often.

Breakfast was just what she needed. Stoking a hundred percent improvement in her mood, Storm devoured everything on her plate and signed off on the check. On her way out the front door of the Lodge, she was contemplating filling another mug from the coffee urns by the foyer when Makani ambled through the front door with his own extra-large mug in hand.

"Hey, Storm," he said. "How's Hamlin this morning?"

"Still kinda sore. He went back to O'ahu to see the doc."

"Bummers."

"Yeah." A thought struck her. "Makani, could I buy you breakfast and ask a couple questions?"

"You don't have to buy. You want to know about Brock?"

"That and how he ties in to Lambert, Tanner, and that whole group of guys."

Makani gestured to a soft leather sofa in front of a big fireplace in a comfy log chamber that served as gathering space and lobby for the Lodge. "Let's sit down."

"Dusty told me Tommy was Lambert's child," Storm said.

Makani ducked his head and slurped at his coffee. It took him just a beat too long.

"What?" Storm asked quietly.

"You get right to the big stuff, don't you?"

She hadn't meant to, but there it was.

He looked down at his mug. "Alika Liu was probably Tommy's biological father." He swirled his coffee around. "But Tia left him for Lambert."

Storm sat back on the sofa. "I didn't know that. When did she leave Alika?"

"When she was pregnant. He was an ass." He grimaced. "Kind of runs in the family."

"Was Alika angry about that?"

"Nah, he didn't want the responsibility. In fact, he might have been the one to break it off."

"How did Dusty take this?"

"He was glad it was over. No one in our family liked Alika."

Storm nodded. "Dusty and Tia must have been close, right?"

Makani sipped his coffee. "Dusty took care of her real good, and he absolutely adored Tommy."

"I never hear anyone talk about Tia's mom. Where is she?"

Makani sighed. "She died in a car crash near Lahaina. That's when Tia moved here to live with Dusty. She was sixteen."

So Dusty had exaggerated a bit about how he'd raised his daughter on Moloka'i. She'd only lived here for three years.

"You grew up together, then?" Storm asked.

"She was like my big sister. If a girl could be a best friend, she was mine. She could ride like the wind, throw a baseball, shoot hoops—and all the older guys wanted to be my friend cuz they wanted a date with her."

"How much older was she than you?"

"Two and a half years. Seemed like a lot when I was ten or twelve."

"Is she the reason you moved here?"

He winced. "Not exactly. As you probably guessed, my mom was plenty *huhu* with her brother. Dusty cheated on Liza, and she and Mom weren't only sisters-in-law, they were best friends. He took a long time to grow up, and by then it was kinda late." He stirred his coffee again.

Storm stayed quiet, and he finally mumbled down at his mug, "A couple years after Tia moved, I got into some trouble at school."

"Sounds like me at that age." Storm grinned at him.

"Really?"

"Big time. I got busted for pot." A waitress wandered by and Storm ordered more toasted taro bread. She waited for the young woman to leave. "I was kind of a rebel, too."

This confession seemed to delight Makani, and he continued. "Mom was worried about Tia. She knew Tia was involved with these activists. One of them was Tommy's father, and she knew that wasn't going well. Meanwhile, Tia was starting to see another one."

"So she got you to watch over each other?"

"That was the plan. Plus, Mom wanted me away from some bad influences on Maui." The waitress came in to put the toast, a tub of butter, and a couple of pots of jam on the coffee table before them. Makani looked at it hungrily. "That does look good."

"It's for you, I already had some."

Makani spread butter and jam on a piece, took a bite, and chewed a while before he spoke again. When he did, his voice was sad. "I let 'em down."

"What do you mean?"

"Both of them, my Mom and Tia." He slumped in his seat, and crumbs of toast fell on his shirt front.

Storm touched his shoulder lightly. "What do you think you could have done?"

Makani brushed at the crumbs. "Watched her better? Kept track of who she was seeing?"

"Did she act worried or scared?"

Makani finally slid his gaze to meet Storm's. "I've thought about this a lot, you know. A lot probably went over my head." He shook his head sadly. "I was in school, then I'd rush up here to help Uncle Dusty here at the ranch. Trying to be good."

"And she was busy, too. She had a baby. Did Dusty act like anything was wrong?"

"Yeah." Makani chuckled, but it held no humor. "He was pissed."

Storm sat up straighter. "About what?"

"A lot of things, I think. The fire was one of them. Remember, he worked for the Ranch, and people were split over the Ranch's development."

"Did he seem angry with anyone in particular?"

"The guys who started it, I guess. But no one knew who that was," he said quickly. "And anyway, they were his friends. Even if he didn't agree with them, they'd grown up together."

"It was like that where I grew up, too." She took a sip of coffee. "Do you remember the date?"

Makani frowned into the distance. "Not exactly, but we saw Tia, Tommy, and Uncle Dusty at Christmas and everyone was talking about it."

"And she disappeared in March?"

Makani just nodded.

"Do you think she left the island?"

"I've wondered a thousand times." His dark eyes clouded with melancholy and remorse. "She wanted to go to O'ahu to finish school, you know. But she was in the middle of a journalism class here on the branch campus and she loved it. I'm sure she wouldn't have left without finishing."

He sighed deeply and stood up. "I'd better get going. Dusty probably wonders where I've gone."

"Thanks for explaining some things," Storm said. "One last thing—do you know if Brock Liu went kayaking during his visit here?"

Makani looked down at his dusty boots. "He mentioned wanting to go, but I didn't see him after that. He came and went without explanation, so I figured his dad had called him home, you know?"

He trudged off, and Storm sat for a moment and nibbled on the last piece of toast while she mulled over the conversation with Makani. She hadn't found out any information for Hamlin, but Tia sounded like a young woman she would have liked to know.

Makani had been sixteen or seventeen at the time of the fire. The discussion had obviously dejected him, and how could it not? Like tangled and hungry flames, tendrils of violence reached from the past and tormented individuals today. She wondered again if and how Jenny's and Brock's recent deaths fit into the puzzle of the past. And yes, she thought the body in the woods belonged to Brock. But how did he die? And Jenny—where did she fit in?

Storm rose to her feet. It was time to track down Tanner and Skelly, which was probably going to take some effort. With that thought, Storm acknowledged she wasn't going to head back to O'ahu that afternoon. She looked at her watch. Eleven-thirty. Hamlin should have seen the doctor by now, but he hadn't called.

She dialed him and got his voice mail. Okay, maybe he was delayed at the doctor's. But she was itching to know if the police had contacted Devon Liu. She also wanted to hear how Hamlin felt, and get a read on his mood. She was bothered that he'd been so aloof that morning. What was bugging him now? Storm left a message to call her back and wandered out of the Lodge, squinting in the bright sunlight.

Chapter Twenty-three

Luke felt shaky and weak, but before he left the hospital, he'd used a glucose monitoring kit, which he hated because his fingers ended up poked full of holes. His numbers were in the right range. He knew he needed rest, and he'd been dozing fitfully ever since Aunty Caroline had brought him to the ER this morning. But he couldn't let himself fall soundly asleep, not where everyone and anyone could come into his room. No, not after he'd glimpsed the hulking, shadowy figure in the living room last night. Worse, the figure had looked directly at him.

It hadn't been difficult to sneak out of the hospital; it was dinner time, the patients' call-buttons kept the nurses scurrying, and it was visiting hour. Luke fell into step behind a father and two kids who'd come to see their new little brother and walked out the front door. It was only a half-mile to his house, where he sat down to rest in the dark shelter of the banana trees in the back yard. He'd come back for the insulin vials in the refrigerator, but now he couldn't make himself go inside. His legs quivered at the thought.

Luke rubbed a hand across his eyes as if he could wipe the memories away. Like a video loop, they'd been running through his mind since early that morning. It seemed longer ago than that, though.

A thin, high cry had jarred him from a deep sleep, a noise that would haunt him forever, because he knew now it had been his mother's last appeal. And he'd been as effective as a slug. It was over before he knew what was happening. Oh, God, if he could only have another chance, turn back the clock, try again.

In the moment that had changed his life, he'd stumbled from his bed, stupefied with sleep, and felt his way down the hallway and into the dark living room, where he must have made a noise because a large, dark figure raised its head from Jenny's prone form. It looked right at Luke, who stood as if struck senseless. By the time he scrubbed the sleep from his eyes, the shadow had slipped away.

But a residual image was burned into the boy's brain. Thick fingers of moonlight crept through the blinds on the front window and striped his mother's body like the moray eels down by the pier. The figure hovering above her was noticeable for two reasons: it was a featureless silhouette, backlit by the strips of light, and a wink of light had flickered from the area of the hulk's head, as if it wore glasses.

Before Luke understood what it all meant, the figure merged with the shadows by the front door, the screen door squeaked and then fastened with a click. That's when Luke finally moved. On jellied legs, he tiptoed to his mother and grabbed her arm to give it a shake. It flopped bonelessly and he didn't like the way a slice of moonlight reflected a dull gleam in her half-closed eyes. He ran to the kitchen phone and dialed 911. He'd still believed everything would be okay and his mother would later tousle his hair and give him a hug for helping her out.

But he knew better now, and he felt gutted and hollow. Thoughts skittered through his mind like cockroaches fleeing light. They lacked logic or order, and drifted away before he could hold onto them. Dull fear prodded, reminding him he desperately needed to think.

The house squatted darkly, its windows mirroring the street lights with the same dullness his mother's eyes had reflected, like they needed to be cleaned. It transmitted its desolation to the boy, who knew he wouldn't enter, not even for his medicine. He could get insulin from other places; in fact, he'd travel around the island before he went into that place of living nightmares.

A man who knew his mom from the hospital picked Luke up and gave him a ride to Uncle Skelly's office. That building was locked up, too, but the kitchen windows had louvers he could remove. It wasn't as simple as he thought, though. The screen came off without too much trouble, and he got the first pane out, but the second pane was jammed tightly into its corroding aluminum frame. The glass broke in his hands, slicing the base of his thumb and nicking a couple of fingers. Luke dropped it in the gravel under the window and sucked at his new wounds.

The opening was big enough to crawl through. Being small occasionally had its advantages. He went in headfirst and slithered across the sink onto the countertop. The first thing he did was wash the cuts on his hands. He even found Band-Aids in the cupboard with the coffee mugs. They were next to a giant bottle of aspirin, which he left alone.

But when he opened the refrigerator, it was empty. No insulin, though Uncle Skelly had put the vials in a couple of weeks ago. He looked through some other cupboards and even checked the main office for possible storage sites, but the insulin was gone.

This was not good. He'd come all the way down here for nothing. It made him want to cry, or throw something, but that wouldn't do any good.

He had one more person he could turn to before he found his dad. He'd have to go back to Kaunakakai and wake him up, which would take a bit of effort. It was a last resort, but that's where he was.

What he wanted right then was to lie down on the couch here for the night, but he was afraid he wouldn't wake up. Nor did Luke want to risk running into Uncle Skelly's brother, who had bad breath, a nasty temper, and little piggy eyes. The fellow in town had the medication Luke needed, and a safe place to rest. The shadow who'd been in his house wouldn't think to look for him there.

◇◇◇

Tanner jogged from the hospital to his former house, his breathing ragged with anguish. Sometimes he shouted out loud, calling for Luke, and discussing with himself where the boy might have gone. Whenever a car went by, he ducked into hedges or behind trees, though he knew hiding wasn't rational. Most of his former neighbors would willingly join the search for Luke, and Tanner wanted to see Dave Niwa. Niwa could call his colleagues into the search, plus Tanner knew that Niwa and his family genuinely cared for his son.

But Tanner knew he looked distraught and out of control. He knew the symptoms, had studied them, in fact. His right eyelid had developed a muscle spasm and he could barely swing his arms, let alone unclench his trembling fists. If someone stopped him, he might not be able to stand still, and if the person showed a kindness, Tanner wasn't sure if his reactions would be socially acceptable. His emotions were too close to the surface. Tears, laughter, or a combination could boil over in a noisy outburst. If he encountered someone who showed irritation or indifference, Tanner wasn't sure he'd be able to walk away. Nor did he want anyone to challenge his progress through the neighborhood, as some of the newer members might if he was seen scurrying along the sidewalk.

So he headed through back yards, avoided houses with dogs and fences, and circumvented street lights. When he got to within sight of his house—or Jenny's and Luke's, he reminded himself—he stopped several yards away and looked at the dark, blank windows. His hopes plummeted. What did you expect, he asked himself. Luke is running, and would be careful not to leave any sign of his presence.

Tanner crept through his neighbors' yards to the back of the house. He sneaked up the two steps to the back door, jiggled the doorknob, and was surprised when it was locked. Jenny almost never locked the house.

Oh, shit. Jenny hadn't closed up, had she? Reality hit him with a blow that nearly knocked him down. She was gone. Forever.

Tanner stumbled back, missed the step, and fell to his knees on the ground. He muttered a few words, and heard his own voice wobble with physical and psychological pain. Moisture seeped through his slacks and left blotchy mud spots. After a few moments of self-pity, he stood, knocked softly on the door, and certain that Luke either hadn't been there at all or had already left, headed back to the main road. This time, he walked down the sidewalks as if he belonged.

It took him three rides and over an hour to reach the Hawai'i EcoTours office. It too, was dark and closed up, but Tanner was prepared for that. What he wasn't prepared for was when he tipped the rosemary plant and the key wasn't there. Two thoughts went through his mind. With the first, his hopes soared: Luke had been there. But he wasn't sure if Luke knew about the hidden key, as he'd never had a need for it. When he'd been to the office, he'd been with Tanner or Skelly.

The second thought precipitated a kick to the large concrete pot, and the shock that traveled up Tanner's leg gratified him somehow. It's what he'd like to do to Connor's face. That would take some fast footwork, though. If the oaf had turned up right then, Tanner would have taken him on, inflated brawn and all.

Tanner tried the front door, but as expected, it was locked. Luke knew there was insulin in the refrigerator. What would he do if he were Luke? Tanner remembered the time Luke climbed through a window one night so that he and Jenny wouldn't know he'd sneaked out to play with friends.

A couple minutes later, Tanner discovered the broken kitchen window and smiled with relief. He couldn't get through the opening, so he shouted into the kitchen. No answer. Tanner walked around to the office, where a big picture window looked out to the ocean. He cupped his hands around his face and peered in. He couldn't see into the corners of the room, but he could see the desk, couch, and two chairs, and no one was in them. He knocked loudly on the glass. "Luke, are you there?"

By the time Tanner made his way around the building, he was fairly certain Luke had been there to retrieve his insulin and had left. Tanner knew that Luke needed medical supervision, and he needed it even more since he'd suffered the shock of Jenny's death. But he also had confidence in Luke's knowledge of his illness, and felt a sense of relief that Luke had picked up his medication.

A couple of years ago, when Tanner moved out, he and Luke devised a system to leave messages. There was a loose brick at the ball park pavilion in Kaunakakai, where people had their potlucks. Tanner and Luke had used it a number of times; it was how Tanner took Luke places Jenny didn't approve of, like the cabin, or on short kayak trips.

He'd check there and see if Luke had left a note. He hoped so, because he was sure Luke wouldn't head for the cabin on the north shore until daylight. So the next question was, where would the boy choose to spend the night?

Tanner didn't know where to spend the night himself at this point. His first plan, the office, wasn't an option. The next best thing would be to get back to Kaunakakai, check the pavilion for a message, and crash on one of the benches there. He needed to rest and get on the road early, so that he could leave a message for Luke at the ball park and the cabin before he met his group of tourists at Halawa around noon.

Tanner walked back along the uneven, narrow shoulder of the highway, carefully veering off the road into the lush foliage if a car came by too quickly. He knew Friday night traffic—people partied, then drove too fast. The bright lights of a speeding car caused him to hop into a thicket of tall grass and oleander. It wasn't until it passed that Tanner identified it as a police vehicle with two people in the front seat. The driver was about the size and shape of Dave Niwa. Tanner clambered back onto the pavement, jumped up and down, waved and called out, but they were too far down the road to notice.

Chapter Twenty-four

Niwa and Skelly rode in silence from the office to Skelly's home. The lights were still on and Helene stepped out the front door wearing a cotton robe and slippers.

"Any news?" she asked. Out of politeness, she asked Niwa in for coffee.

"No thanks, Helene. We've got squad cars looking for Luke and Tanner. I've got to get some sleep."

Helene and Skelly watched until Niwa's car was on the main highway. "I always told you they were no good," Helene said.

"Don't start." Skelly's voice was low and cold. Without another word, he went into the house, grabbed a jacket from a rack inside the door and his car keys from the table. He pushed by Helene, back out the door.

"Where you going?" She clutched her robe around her.

"I've gotta talk to Connor."

Helene bit her lip and went into the house. She turned out the lights one by one as she made her way upstairs.

Fifteen minutes later, Skelly banged on the door to Connor's apartment. He hoped Connor was there, and not at the girlfriend-of-the-week's. He banged again, waited what was probably only fifteen seconds, and considered calling some women he knew Connor liked, when he heard a thump from inside, followed by a string of swear words.

One eye appeared at a crack in the door. "This had better be a big emergency."

"It's me." Skelly's voice was a low growl.

"Yeah?" Connor opened the door the width of his head.

Skelly pushed it the rest of the way and walked in. "Anyone else here?"

Connor smirked. "She left about an hour ago." He pulled at his worn, discolored Fruit-of-the-Looms.

"I doubt it."

"You jealous?"

"No," Skelly snorted. "I'm pissed."

Confusion crinkled Connor's brow. "Why? What did I do?"

"The key."

"The key? You mean the one under the pot?"

Skelly moved fast as a snapping dog and shoved his brother with a smack to his bare chest. Connor fell back onto the coffee table behind him, collapsing two legs as if they were cardboard.

"Hey, stop." Connor held up a hand, no longer so tough. "I'm just being safe. We could get robbed." A whine crept into his voice. "It's my business, too."

"You took the insulin and Tanner's pills."

"I've got it in my fridge. I was going to give it to you."

Connor struggled to his feet, and Skelly pushed him again. Connor sat back down on the coffee table and the other two legs buckled.

"Luke's sick and needs that stuff. As in last night. He looked for it and it wasn't there." Skelly took a deep breath, sucking it through his teeth. He gave his head a shake, as if to resume control. "We let a kid down, a little kid who's sick."

"I'm sorry, man." Connor almost sounded contrite.

"You need to stop the 'roids. I'm putting the word out."

"I can't. You can't make me." Connor's face turned purple. "I mean, I can't stop them all at once."

It took a moment for Skelly to answer and Connor retreated a few inches. When Skelly answered, his voice was low and dangerous.

"You want to keep your part of the business? You can't control yourself when you're hyped on this shit. I need you to get it together."

"I am. I—"

"No." Skelly leaned over him. "You'll be in the office at eight this morning. And you'll be clean."

"But—"

Skelly's breath hissed through his nose. "And one more thing."

"I can do that." Connor scrabbled to stand up. "What?"

Skelly clenched and unclenched his fists. "You've been blabbing."

The color drained from Connor's face. "Skelly, no. I never—"

"I keep my mouth shut all these years. Ten years. Protect you, and what? You shoot off your big fat mouth."

"When? When did I ever?" Connor got to his feet again, and did his trapezius-flexing move in an attempt to stand up to Skelly. He gave Skelly a push. "Whaddya mean, you protected me?"

"Mom and me both did. I told her, you know. Told her you ran outa the house first, screaming. That you were the first one to know it was on fire." Skelly was red-faced and shouting, but Connor tried to hold his ground.

"You think I—" Incredulity raised the level of Connor's voice to a near-squeal.

"You were where it started. Fire inspectors can tell where it starts, you know." Skelly put his face right up to Connor's. "Mom and I both lied for you, you miserable runt."

"Never. And stop shoving me around." Connor gave Skelly a hard shove, but Skelly was ready. He hit him with a closed fist, and Connor hit the floor with a crash, then a whimper.

Skelly pivoted, hunched his shoulders as if he expected a blow to his back, and slouched out the front door. He didn't see Connor sit up and wipe the blood out of his eye, nor did he hear him repeat, "Never."

Chapter Twenty-five

Storm surveyed the Lodge's parking lot. She needed wheels and had no intention of asking Dusty to borrow his truck again. When she saw Delia working on one of the Ranch's big vans, she had an idea.

Delia saw her coming and waved in her direction. The bat wings fringing her eyes may have been factory-made, but the bosom swelling from her cropped fluorescent pink and silver sequined tank top was definitely the real thing.

"How you doin'? I heard your boyfriend fell off a horse."

Hamlin would hate this. Storm was glad he wasn't around to hear the scuttlebutt. "I'm okay, but he went back to O'ahu to see a doctor." She was going to hear it anyway.

"Too bad. You want to go out with me and my friends tonight?"

Storm bet it wouldn't be a dull evening. "I'm supposed to meet my aunt and uncle for dinner, but thanks. Any chance you're going into town this morning?"

"You bet. A container ship came in with the air conditioning compressor for the kitchen. I'm leaving in a few minutes. Wanna ride?"

"I could help you load it. After, could you drop me at the airport?"

"The guys at the dock will help me load it, but maybe you should come along." Delia winked at her. "No problem, the airport is on the way. You leaving tomorrow?" She sounded wistful.

"I thought I'd rent a car. The only rental places are at the airport."

"You're telling me." Delia arched a penciled brow. "Dusty using his truck?"

"I don't want to impose."

"Right." Delia threw some packages in the back seat. "Sure, I'll drop you."

Five minutes later, they were winding their way from Maunaloa town to Kaunakakai. Delia gunned the whining engine around a curve in the road. "That Dusty can be a moody SOB, can't he?"

Storm grimaced. "I asked him about Tia and the fire."

"Oof, bad combination."

"No joke." Storm squinted over at her. "How well do you know him?"

Delia put her dark glasses on and snapped her gum. "I know him."

Storm recognized the tough act. "I had the hots for him once, too."

"Once?"

"I didn't get to see him very often." She grimaced. "And he's a friend of my uncle's."

"Your uncle would have had a fit, right?"

Storm laughed. "Totally. What happened with you?"

Delia kept her eyes on the road. "We went out for a few months a couple of years ago, but we're not a good match."

"When I knew him, he was kind of a playboy."

A long moment passed and when Delia spoke, there was acquiescence in her voice. "Yeah, he's not the type to settle down."

"Did you know Tia?"

Delia nodded. "I met her when I first moved here. She was a hellion, you know. Marched to the beat of her own drum, so to speak. Drove Dusty crazy."

"Weren't you about the same age?"

"I'm two years older." Delia looked over at Storm. "Aren't you my age? I'm thirty-one."

"Me, too," Storm said. "So Tia and Dusty fought?"

"Big time." Delia let a few moments pass. "For a long time, I thought she went away."

"You don't think so anymore?"

"She would have turned up by now, wouldn't she? With a little boy and all that?"

"Seems like it," Storm agreed. A thought passed through Storm's mind. "Did Jenny ever go out with Dusty?"

Delia made a snorting noise. "Of course."

"She didn't have an easy life, either, from what I've heard."

"Guess not."

"Did Tia and Jenny know each other?"

"Sure." Delia looked over at Storm. "Jenny was trying to help Tia get a job with the local paper."

"Did Jenny date one of the editors?"

Delia laughed out loud. "Probably." Her expression grew thoughtful. "You know, I think she and Tanner were still together back then. Barely, though. I think the editor had covered one of her art shows."

They rode in comfortable silence for a while. Storm had to admit she was glad she wasn't a single woman on this island. "You ever think of moving to Honolulu?"

Delia shrugged. "Sometimes, but it's big and busy, and no one would care if I lost my job or was down in the dumps."

"It's not so bad," Storm said. "And you'd make new friends, lots of them. Better job opportunities, too."

"You've got a degree."

"Now I do, but I had a lot of jobs before that."

"You earn a lot, too, right?"

"I make ends meet."

Delia seemed to chew on that for a few minutes. "Are you going to look for the kid? That why you need a car?"

"What kid?" Storm asked, but a stab of dread went through her.

"Luke Williams. Your friend Tanner's son. You knew Jenny died, didn't you?"

"I heard about that, but I figured Luke was with Tanner."

"Not yet. Tanner was on the north shore when it happened." Delia's voice softened and she glanced at Storm. "Luke freaked out about his mother. They took him to the hospital, but he left."

"Where's Tanner now?" Storm asked. "I need to find him."

"I'd guess he's either on the north shore or out looking for Luke." Delia swung onto the airport road. "Forget about going to the docks with me. You probably want to pick up your car right away."

"Yeah, thanks."

By the time Storm was making her way out of the airport, still adjusting mirrors and opening windows to get rid of the smell of stale cigarette smoke, she'd decided to drop by the police station. The cop who'd come to see them last night at the Lodge seemed like a nice guy, and she wanted to talk to him again.

Storm walked into the small station and approached the front desk. No one was there, and she had to ring the bell on the counter before a short man wearing very thick glasses came around the corner. He gave her a big smile. "Those roosters still waking you up? We issued Mr. Koichi a warning already."

"No, I'm looking for Sergeant Niwa. Is he around?"

"Sorry, I got you confused with someone else." He peered through the glass that separated them, and she could see his name tag, which read *Jerry Sanchez.*

"He's out looking for that poor boy."

"Luke?" Storm asked. She'd never get away with this in Honolulu, but a flash of intuition told her the personal touch would serve better here. "He's my friend's son."

A shocked expression came over the little man's face. "Jenny's your friend?"

"Tanner, but I heard about Jenny. What a shame! I'd just met her."

"And the poor boy so sick!" The man clucked his tongue.

"He is?" When Delia had told her he was in the hospital, she'd made it sound like he'd needed care because of his mother.

"Yes, you didn't hear? Diabetes. Like me, except he's young and his is harder to control." He leaned toward the hole in the glass. "If he gets hypoglycemic, he's *pau*."

"You mean he'll die if he doesn't eat?"

"If his blood sugar drops. Gets worse if he has some shock to his system, like an injury. His mom's death was already a huge one." Sanchez's forehead creased and his brows met in the center. "He could just fall asleep and not wake up."

"That's terrible," Storm said. "I'm going to try and find Tanner. Maybe that will help."

"Where you going to look?"

"I'll start at Hawai'i EcoTours."

"If he's not there, try their storage hut out by Halawa."

"Okay, thanks. And if you see Sergeant Niwa, will you ask him to call me? Here's the number to my cell phone."

"It won't work when you get out of Kaunakakai," Sanchez said.

"Oh."

Sanchez shrugged. "Back to the good old days."

Out on the sidewalk, Storm stood in the sun, but it was too hot to think there, so she went to the car, which was a smoky oven. She burned her fingers on the chrome of the seat belt.

Luke's disappearance changed things. Both Tanner and Niwa would be looking for him. Probably Skelly and the brother, too. She didn't know the island well enough to guess where they'd go, either. And before she considered driving even a mile in this heat, she needed water.

Amos' Crack Seed store was only a couple blocks away, and though it wasn't air-conditioned, the ceiling fans stirred an anise-scented breeze and the darkness was welcome relief from the hot noon sun. It took several moments for Storm's eyes to adjust to the dimness.

She heard Rolly's voice before she saw him. "Did you see Jenny Williams the other day?"

Storm made out his hulking profile in the gloom at the back of the store. "Yes, and I heard about her death yesterday."

His eyes followed her as she made her way down an aisle. "And?" he asked softly.

"And what?"

"She was okay when you saw her?"

"Yes. I thought so, anyway."

"Was Tanner there?" He hadn't moved, and his voice was so low she had to strain to hear him. But he had her attention.

"I didn't see him." Storm stopped in front of the counter and regarded him. She decided not to mention the argument she'd overheard. "Do you know Tanner?"

"He loves his boy."

"How about Jenny?" Storm asked.

"She was nice to me." He smiled sadly.

"Was she nice to Tanner?"

"I don't think so." Rolly pushed air audibly through his nostrils. Storm tilted her head. "She was angry with him. He wouldn't control his disease."

"It's probably hard to do."

"You have to try." Rolly's voice was firm, as if he had firsthand knowledge of the effort Tanner should have put forth.

"I suppose." Storm didn't want to start an argument. In fact, his statements sounded oddly unsympathetic. She didn't know how to respond to him, so she walked to the cooler against the wall and pulled out two bottles of water and a packaged sandwich. "What do I owe you?"

Rolly didn't move. "You think I don't understand."

Storm stared at him.

"I've lost a hundred forty pounds. My insulin requirements are a third what they used to be."

That was about what Storm weighed. He'd lost the body weight of a whole person. "That's quite an accomplishment. You should be proud."

"Not yet." Rolly picked up her items and punched in the prices. "That's four dollars and eleven cents. I still have to lose a hundred fifty more."

"You're well on your way. Good luck." Storm handed him the money. He was harmless, she decided, but she didn't understand him, and she began to leave. She almost missed his parting words.

"Tell Tanner Luke's got his meds."

She turned. "Luke was here? Do you know where he is now?"

The huge man shrugged. "Nope."

"Did you ask where he was going?" She knew she was coming on strong, the big city lawyer type. Bad idea around here.

"No way, lady." Rolly looked affronted. He scooted his chair back further into the shadows.

"Okay. Thanks, yeah?" Storm said. "I'm glad you're Luke's friend."

Chapter Twenty-six

There was an old Firebird parked at Hawai'i EcoTours when Storm pulled into the drive. It didn't look like the typical rental car, so she hoped she was in luck and would find Skelly, Tanner, or anyone who could tell her where they were. The converted house was in a breathtaking oceanfront location, conducive to luring visitors on a water adventure, but she was too worried about Luke and Tanner to linger and enjoy it.

Storm scanned the hours of operation by the door, knocked lightly, and walked in. A heavyset guy with bad skin and a swollen black eye turned to her. He was on the phone with someone, but bobbed his head and held up a finger in the universal just-a-minute signal.

He finished the call quickly, remembered his black eye, and kept his head tilted so the good eye faced her. It made him look like a flounder. "Hello there." He gave her a wet-looking smile.

Not an opening to inspire confidence. Worse, his good eye had traveled from somewhere above her knees to her neck. It hadn't reached her face yet.

"I'm looking for Skelly Richards."

"And you are?"

Storm waited until his one eye met her glaring ones and she thought she saw his Adam's apple bob. Good. "Storm Kayama."

"So you're Tanner Williams' friend. The lawyer. I heard about you."

"And you are?"

"Connor Richards." He stood and held out his hand.

Storm shook the damp fingertips. "I was supposed to meet with Tanner. You know where he is?"

"What do you want with him?"

"He's an old high school friend and he asked me to get in touch."

Connor shrugged. "You're not the only one looking for him. Cops are, too." He leered and checked to see if this made an impression. He looked a little disappointed when Storm didn't react. "He might be in Halawa with the tourists he's taking out for us."

"You have any idea if Luke has shown up?"

Connor tried to smile at her, but couldn't quite pull it off. "You heard about that?"

"I'm Tanner's friend, remember?"

He stacked the papers up, matching the edges. "We figure he's probably gone to Tanner's cabin."

"But Tanner's with a group, right?"

"Luke'll be okay. The kid knows his way around."

Storm frowned. "He might be sick."

"I'm taking over this afternoon, so Tanner'll be at the cabin before dark."

"That's good. How about you? You know how to get to the cabin?"

"What do you want to know for?"

His swollen eye watered and Storm had the impression his tough act was all a bluff. For a brief instant, she felt sorry for him, and she softened her tone. "Tanner asked me to look into some things for him, and a lot has happened. I'm worried about Luke's health."

"You and everyone else." His shoulders dropped a bit, though he still didn't meet her eyes. "Still, Tanner doesn't like visitors."

"I wouldn't ask if I didn't think it was important for the boy. Tanner may not know how serious his illness is. Please, can you tell me how to get there?"

He slumped in his chair. "I heard the cabin's around Keawenui Bay. That's all I can say."

"Luke knows the way?"

"Sure. He's been there a lot." He fiddled with the stack of papers again, then pointed to a chair. "You want to have a seat? I can call the storage hut, see if Tanner or Skelly are there."

Storm sat on the edge of the chair seat and noticed that Connor seemed relieved to have an excuse to turn his head and hide the bruised side of his face. For such a bulked-up guy, he'd taken a beating. She wondered what the other guy looked like. On second thought, she'd always wondered what these over-muscled guys were compensating for.

"Hi Jimmy, your dad around?" Connor said into the phone and waited a few minutes. "Bob, you seen Tanner yet?" Pause. "Skelly or Dave Niwa there yet?" Pause. "Thanks, yeah?"

Connor hung up. "Bob said Tanner is pretty calm about Luke. Skelly dropped the group of tourists and is on his way back."

"How about Detective Niwa?"

"Not there yet. He left here about a half hour ago."

Storm stood up. "Thanks for the help."

Connor tried another smile. "You ought to come back and rent a kayak. I'll take you on a tour."

"Thanks, but I've got my hands full right now." Storm smiled at him. "But I've got a question for you."

"Yeah?" Connor looked a little too eager.

"Did you know Brock Liu?"

Connor couldn't hide the surprise on his face, and his skin appeared to grow more sallow. "Uh." His Adam's apple bobbed for sure this time. Storm waited.

"Yeah, sorta. I mean, I've met him."

"When was that?"

"I don't remember." Connor picked up the stack of papers and shuffled through them.

"You looking for a reservation?" Storm gestured to the stack of papers. "Do you know if he rented a kayak?"

He pushed the papers away. "These are today's clients. I'd have to look back in our records and see."

"Could you do that, please?"

Connor looked at his knuckles, which also looked bruised. He sighed. "I gave it to the cop."

"Detective Niwa? He asked you for it?"

"His partner."

"So when did Brock take the boat out?"

"Like two weeks ago. March 26." Connor peered up at her. "My brother doesn't like me talking about clients, so don't tell him I told you. Is Brock the dead guy in the woods?"

"I don't know. He'd been out there a while."

Connor's good eye widened. "You're one of the people who found him."

Storm nodded.

"Cool."

"No, it was gross."

He looked at her with new respect. Must have a very boring life, Storm thought.

"You sure you don't want to have a drink?"

"Can't, but thanks." She gave a wave and headed for the door, then turned back. "So what's the other guy look like?

"Huh?" He ducked his head and smiled. "Uh, he's in the hospital." The sad light in his eyes belied the stab at humor.

Outside the office, Storm dug her cell phone out of her handbag and dialed Hamlin again. Still no answer, and she left another message for him to call. Damn, where was he? She was going to be out of range for a while, too.

When she climbed into the rental car, she was glad she'd opened the windows and parked in the shade, because the sun was blasting overhead. She'd downed one of the bottles of water on the drive to the Richards brothers' office, but left a wrapped tuna sandwich sitting on the front seat. It was still there—no mynah birds had made off with it, but Storm hoped that wasn't because the mayonnaise had gone bad. She was hungry.

It tasted fine, and she ate it one-handed as she negotiated the winding road east to Halawa Bay. At times, the road was only a few feet from the ocean; the only time she couldn't see gentle waves lapping the shore was when a stand of trees or a house intervened. Homes were spread out, and there were no ostentatious stuccos, faux-haciendas, or trophy abodes. No condominiums at all. Not one. The sky was intensely blue, the sand blaring white, and palm fronds caressed one another in the breeze. From time to time, an outrigger canoe rested in the shade of a tree. Storm didn't see any people. It was mid-day, too hot for fishing or outdoor labor.

Fishponds in the style of the old Hawaiians were scattered along the shoreline, and some were quite large. The citizens needed these, she bet, because the drive to Kaunakakai would take an hour or more. Did the people commute, farm, have cottage industries, or live off welfare? Probably a combination. But she could see why they stood up for their lifestyle. Why the local people, of all different races, put bumper stickers on their cars that read, "Hawaiian Culture Not For Sale." She wondered how many lawyers lived here, and what kind of cases they handled.

The road climbed inland and soon she passed the park, which she'd heard was a place for people to catch rides, meet lovers, or buy drugs, and she slowed for a hairpin turn. Driveways on O'ahu were wider than this. Storm had slowed to about ten miles an hour, which was a good thing, because a pickup was coming around the next bend. The driver grinned, waved, and crunched onto a barely existent shoulder. Storm could have hand-fed biscuits to the dogs in the back of his truck.

The end of the road looked out onto the entire bay and valley, hundreds of feet below. The area at the end of the road had a wider shoulder, mainly because people had flattened the foliage, and Storm pulled the rental car as far off the pavement as she could, about three feet from the rear bumper of a police cruiser. She figured she was in good company, at least for avoiding a ticket.

It was a hike down a steep embankment through lantana and other thick ground cover to the sand, and then another trek across the crescent-shaped beach. In the distance, abutting the beach, a long hut with a thatched roof nestled under an overhang of *hau*, palms, and *keawe*. Skelly must have greased some palms to have his canoe house on that spot; she'd lay odds the area around the bay was state or private land, and there wasn't another commercial enterprise for miles.

The sand on the beach was hard-packed and fairly easy going, but Storm's progress came to a halt when she reached the river that bisected the bay. The mouth of the river had formed a delta, and the water was too deep to wade. A path wound inland along the banks of the river, probably maintained by Hawai'i EcoTours so they could bring their customers in. About ten minutes later, Storm discovered the temporary board bridge that had been set up at a narrow point.

Once on the other side, she headed *makai*, back to the ocean, and noticed four people milling around the boat shed. Two adults, one of them Dave Niwa, had observed her making her way across the hot sand. Niwa nodded a wary greeting. A tow-headed adolescent boy and girl were busy loading supplies into an outrigger canoe that sat on the beach. When she got closer, they grinned and approached.

"I'm Bob Crowder." The other adult, a tall, tanned man with thinning sandy hair, held out his hand. "These are my kids, Jimmy and Sara. They help out when they get their school work done, earn a little extra spending money."

Niwa greeted her with a handshake. He looked a little pale. "You get around, Ms. Kayama."

"Trying to keep my word to a friend. Tanner Williams and I went to high school together. He asked me to look in on his son, and I just heard the boy checked himself out of the hospital. Did Tanner leave? I was hoping to talk to him."

"He took a group of visitors to tonight's campsite, but one of the Richards boys'll go later this afternoon to relieve him," Crowder said. He jutted his chin toward the boy and girl, who were busy balancing what looked like a hibachi, making sure it was secure and in the center of the shallow boat, next to a large cooler.

Storm looked at Niwa. "Did you see him?"

"Nope." He didn't look happy.

"Do you know if Luke turned up?" Storm directed this question to both men.

Bob Crowder shook his head from side to side and Niwa's frown deepened.

"Dave, Luke's a really smart kid," Crowder said. "We've got to trust him. Tanner does."

"He's also a sick kid, and Tanner may not know how serious his condition is." Niwa wiped sweat from his forehead with an impatient gesture. "Plus, Tanner's illness can make him distracted, or out-of-touch with what the rest of us consider proper behavior. Like taking care of his son."

The web of crow's-feet around Crowder's eyes deepened. "I'll call you if I see or hear anything of him."

"Call me the minute Tanner gets back."

"I will."

"Tell him I'll have a ride waiting for him—and, I hope, Luke."

"How's he coming back?" Storm eyed the outrigger canoe. "Can he paddle that by himself?" It had four seats, and supplies were packed under all but the rear one.

"Sure, especially when the bay's nice and calm like this," Crowder said.

"What's the surf report?"

"He can handle it." Crowder seemed to be reassuring himself as well as Niwa.

Niwa shook his head again, and looked toward the path that led across the bay and to the road. "I'd better head back."

"Wait, let me give you some cold water," Crowder said. "Jimmy, run and get a couple bottles, will you?" The young man scampered into the hut, and the group could hear the slapping of cooler lids and the rattle of ice.

Storm turned toward Crowder. "I'm also looking into Brock Liu's disappearance on behalf of his father. He has proof Brock rented a kayak from you."

Crowder dug a toe into the sand. "Skelly asked me the same question." He intercepted the cold, dripping water bottles from his son and handed one each to Storm and Niwa. "He didn't go out from here. When I checked the rental slips, it looked like he was taking a kayak from the main office. We take boats back and forth, so I keep track."

"Any chance one of your kids could have outfitted him?" Storm asked.

"No way," he said. "They're not allowed to let boats go out without my attendance. I have to be here." He squinted at her. "March 26, right?"

"That's the date I was told," she said. Crowder seemed like an honest guy, but Storm had been fooled before. "Could he have taken one on his own?"

Crowder frowned. "He'd have to be pretty sneaky about it."

She glanced over at Niwa, who leaned against a nearby tree as if he needed the support. He'd downed most of the water. Crowder's son noticed the detective's thirst, and was back with another bottle before Storm could begin on hers. She thought Niwa looked paler than he had when she'd arrived. "Detective Niwa, I'll walk out with you."

Bob Crowder had been eyeing the policeman with concern, and he looked relieved at her suggestion. Storm and Niwa waved their thanks to the Crowder family and headed across the beach toward the river. The sand, a fine mixture of black lava, silica, seashells, and coral, absorbed heat, and though Storm wore sneakers, she kicked up hot little rooster tails that stung the backs of her legs. Niwa wore long pants, which might have been worse in terms of dealing with the heat. Halfway across the beach, he was breathing heavily and when they were almost to the river, he slowed down and burped. "Haven't had much sleep the last couple of days," he said, and rubbed at his stomach.

"Your stomach bothering you?"

"A bit. Hope I'm not getting the flu." He grimaced. "I don't have time."

"You feeling nauseated?"

"I'll be okay."

Storm took that as a yes. "I hate it when that happens." She had a strong feeling if she questioned him any more, he'd just deny any problem. She didn't need to ask if he was short of breath. He was breathing a lot harder than she was, and they hadn't started climbing yet.

They reached the path along the river and made the turn toward the little bridge and the mountains. Storm tried hard not to keep looking over at him.

"Want to rest a minute? It's shadier here." She sat under a hau tree, making sure to leave the place with the best shade for him.

He lowered himself with a groan. "I wanted to talk to you about some things."

"I wanted to talk to you, too. I went to Jenny Williams' house the afternoon before she was killed."

"That's what I heard. I figured it was you, by the description."

"Hard to keep a secret in a small town."

Niwa sighed. "Seems like someone's working at it, though."

"Do you get the feeling it's an old secret?"

Niwa regarded her. "My wife had the same reaction, and she's rarely wrong about these things." He looked at his watch and got slowly to his feet. "Let's walk and talk. What did you see at Jenny's house?"

He led the way across the bridge and along the narrow walkway back to the water.

As they walked, Storm told him about the argument she'd overheard. "I gathered she was fighting with Tanner, though she never said, and I didn't see him."

"Why did you go there?"

Storm explained her high school friendship with Tanner, that she hadn't seen him for ages, but that he'd seen her name in the paper and called. "He asked me to look in on his son."

"Tanner was upset by Luke's diabetes." They had reached the beach, and sweat ran in rivulets down the side of his face.

"Some other things, too. Right?"

Niwa nodded slowly. "It's hard to make judgments in cases like this."

They walked along quietly for a few moments. "I get the feeling you think Jenny was doing a pretty good job."

"Mostly." Niwa rubbed at his stomach. "I also heard she was seeing someone. That and Luke's recent diagnosis would have upset Tanner." He burped, then swallowed hard. His steps faltered.

"You okay?"

"I think I'm coming down with something, dammit."

This had to be a big admission. Storm handed him her water bottle. "Let's rest a minute."

Hot sunlight baked the top of her dark hair and burned the back of her neck. She was probably turning the color of a rare steak, but Niwa was gray.

She was thirsty, too, but she had water in the car and knew she'd make the climb up the steep, winding path to the road without too much trouble. Niwa was another matter, and he was too big a man for her to move if he couldn't make it under his own power. She eyed the sinuous path's rise through the thick underbrush.

Niwa took a few sips from the bottle, then leaned over and put his hands on his knees. He took deep, careful breaths, and after a few minutes, stood upright. His color was marginally better. He drank a little more. "Let's go."

Storm followed Niwa up the hill and with each step wondered what she would do if he fell. His breath wheezed and the back of his uniform shirt was soaking wet. So was his hair, and she couldn't see his face, but the color of the skin on the back of his neck wasn't pretty. He was getting up the hill on sheer will power.

Five feet from the top, he caught the toe of his boot in a twist of *kauna'oa* vines and went down like a gut-shot bison. He hit the ground with a grunt and crash before Storm could cover the few feet between them.

"Detective Niwa," she shouted and scrambled up the incline to his side. At least he was conscious and trying to struggle to his hands and knees. "Wait, get up slowly. It's too hot." She grabbed an arm and helped him up.

"Sorry." He gasped for air and kept his head down, arms braced on his legs. "Dizzy."

"Take your time. No hurry."

"Excuse—" His voice came out weak, but he lurched away from Storm into the thigh-high foliage around them, where he made a gagging sound, followed by the gurgling rush of vomit.

Storm winced and stepped a few feet away, trying to give the man some privacy. But she'd seen the start of what he'd thrown up, and it was red. Bright red, like blood.

He staggered out of the tangled plant life and tripped again. This time Storm caught his outstretched arms.

"I'm driving," she said, and let him lean on her as he tottered the mercifully short distance up the last part of the slope and across the road. Storm unlocked the passenger-side door and let him fall into the front seat.

"Put on the seatbelt." She ran around to the other side, started the car and rolled down all four electric windows simultaneously, as the car was nearly baking temperature.

She pulled a three-point U-turn and scattered gravel from the side of the road as she bumped onto the pavement.

"Slow down," Niwa mumbled, and she did, because a car rounded a blind turn and nearly took her side-view mirror with it. The jackass driving gave her stink-eye.

Fifteen minutes later, Storm had chewed the inside of her lower lip until she could taste blood and increased her average speed from ten miles an hour on the hairpin turns to almost twenty-five on the marginally straighter road. Thank God no one else was out driving. In another fifteen minutes, she was doing sixty in a thirty-five zone. Where the devil were the cops when you needed them?

Except for an occasional moan, Niwa didn't open his eyes. Fortunately, he would grunt an acknowledgment to Storm's periodic frantic questions. "You okay?" she'd blurt every ten minutes or so. She wasn't sure what "Unnnh" meant, except that he was conscious.

Storm had never been to the Moloka'i Hospital, but found it with only one wrong turn because Kaunakakai was a small town and Niwa revived enough to say two words: "Left here."

She slowed to thirty miles an hour across the parking lot, which drew the anxious glances of three families and the middle finger from one old fellow with a walker. When she jerked to a stop near the front door, she leaped from the car and left both Niwa's and her doors open in her rush to get the detective inside.

The receptionist's eyes went wide as silver dollars when Storm and Niwa stumbled through the front doors, and she called for help. A husky male nurse hustled to Niwa's side, and about ten seconds later a tall man in coke-bottle thick glasses, a long white coat, and the posture of someone leaning into hurricane force winds soared around the corner like a giant seagull. When he got close enough, Storm saw the embroidery over his breast pocket. *Alan Goldbaum, M.D.*

"Gurney, stat!" Goldbaum shouted down the corridor in a voice that rattled windows, and with utmost care he eased Niwa from Storm's grasp and helped him onto the gurney that had materialized from smoke.

"Hey, Alan," Niwa whispered.

"Dave, you putz," Goldbaum said, and Storm saw him give Niwa's hand a gentle squeeze on their way down the hall.

Chapter Twenty-seven

Tanner got to Halawa a couple hours ahead of Skelly and the tour group and used the camp shower behind the canoe shed. By the time Skelly arrived with the two families from Michigan, nine people in all, Tanner felt presentable and fairly calm. He'd taken his medicine, and he frequently rubbed his fingers over the note in the pocket of his cargo shorts. Luke had let him know he would spend the night in Kaunakakai, and that he felt okay and had access to insulin. He'd written "see you soon," which meant he would be at the cabin by sundown. If he'd written "see you later," it would mean the next day. Some time ago, he and Luke worked out a simple code so that they could arrange outings Jenny didn't approve of.

Tanner always locked the cabin when he wasn't there. He even had a couple of indicators set up to let him know if anyone had been snooping around, but Luke knew all about them, and he was the only other person to know where the key was hidden. Tanner had a small generator so that the refrigerator and some of his equipment would work, and since Luke's diagnosis, he always kept a stock of insulin and some basic food supplies on hand.

Tanner helped Bob Crowder instruct the families on how to operate their kayaks safely and made sure all the younger kids were carefully paired with adults. The visitors seemed enthusiastic and willing to dive into the fun—or water, whatever was needed. Every now and then, Tanner would get a prima donna, someone whose acrylic nails would prevent her from paddling, or who had a fit when his Blackberry didn't connect with the office. He couldn't figure out what people like that were doing away from the Four Seasons, let alone on Moloka'i.

This group looked like fun, and two of the boys were about Luke's age. If this worked the way he planned, he and Luke could meet up with them again on Sunday afternoon. Providing Luke felt okay. He'd have to play that by ear.

The paddle around the point went well, with only the sixteen-year-old girls capsizing and splashing happily around in the calm, blue water while they worked to right their boat. The boys wanted to join them, and Tanner told them to go ahead; he even encouraged the adults to go for a swim. Tanner had his own boat, which was filled with supplies, and he offered to hold the swimmers' kayaks, as he didn't want the boats to drift apart.

He was nearly as delighted as the swimmers to see three green sea turtles pop their heads warily out of the water to take a look at the commotion. Tanner knew they lived in the vicinity, and had hoped they'd show up. Two were big, probably forty or fifty years old. Even the small one was close to two feet across.

Sometimes on the trips, he saw humpback whales from a distance, but they visited Hawai'i in the winter when the surf was often too big to paddle through, even for experienced boaters. Most of them left by the end of March, though Tanner always kept an eye out for stragglers, maybe a mother who was waiting for her calf to mature before making the long trek to Alaska. Porpoises were another thrilling surprise that visitors loved. So did Tanner, but he didn't see any that day.

The last thing Luke did before going to bed was to poke his finger and test his blood sugar with the device he'd lifted from the hospital. He did it first thing Saturday morning, too. The nurse had told him he needed one of his own, and she'd instructed him as to the range his blood sugar should fall into. When all this was over, he'd take the gadget back to the hospital. He supposed he'd still be using it if he was in the hospital, so he wasn't depriving anyone else of the contraption. Though he guessed hospital personnel wouldn't see it that way. He hoped he could explain later.

Luke was more concerned with how he was going to get to Halawa this time around. In the past, he'd hitchhiked, which was easy. Lots of people were willing to give a kid a ride, and many of them were neighbors or friends of his mom or dad. Except now he knew one of them had killed his mother. And that person believed Luke could identify him. Lord, he wished that were true.

When Luke woke up in the gray of early dawn, he sat up slowly to check how he felt that morning. He'd slept soundly, safely tucked away in Rolly's little apartment. He hadn't even known exactly where Rolly lived, and was pleasantly surprised to find he had a small clean place above the store, toward the back so that it wasn't obvious from the street.

Now he listened for signs that Rolly might be up. He wanted to thank him, though they'd talked last night. They'd discussed what Luke had seen, and how he was going to get to Halawa and when he needed to leave. Rolly didn't have a car, and rarely drove. Normally, Luke would hitchhike to the end of the road, then hike down and back into the valley. The cabin was a good two hours beyond the bay.

Rolly had provided Luke with a backpack and a sweatshirt that must have belonged to a relative or someone, because though it was large on Luke, Rolly couldn't have put an arm in a sleeve. He'd packed various supplies: four or five vials of insulin, sandwiches, snacks, and plenty of water and sports drinks for the trip.

But most of all, Rolly worried about how Luke didn't know whose shadowy figure he'd seen. "Close your eyes and remember. Tell me what you see," Rolly said, his ubiquitous glass of ice water sweating in his huge hand.

Luke did, glad to have someone to share his sorrow and fear. He ignored his tear-stung eyes, as did Rolly, and tried to make his face the expressionless mask Rolly used. "He was big."

"You sure it was a man? There are some big women."

"The only woman this big is Aunty Makalani Pili'au," Luke said. "And the shadow was taller, but not as wide." He held his arms out to show Rolly.

Rolly pushed his glasses up with his forefinger. "Aunty Makalani never hurt anyone her whole life. She only teaches hula, heals people with dance."

"I know. Mom took classes for a while, but she stopped."

"Why'd she stop?"

"I dunno. No time, I guess." Luke shrugged. "She was going out with someone then. Uncle Dusty, I think."

Rolly nodded. "Hula takes a lot of time, you do it right. Now, close your eyes and think."

Luke took a deep breath and suppressed a shudder. "The window let in some light from outside, but the corner by the door was dark. He disappeared there."

"You saw him move?"

Luke nodded, his eyes still closed.

"Was he holding anything?"

Luke sat absolutely still. "He held a white or light colored cloth. Like clothing."

"Good." Rolly took a drink of water. "You saw your mom, right?"

Luke couldn't stop a few tears from escaping, and Rolly acted like he didn't see them. "Yes," he whispered. "On the floor."

"Any of her clothing missing?"

"No." The word strangled in Luke's throat.

"Okay. What was this guy wearing?"

"I don't know." Luke slumped. "He was dark, except when the light came through the blinds."

"If you had to guess, what do you think he was doing with that cloth?"

Now Luke's voice shook, and not even his self-control could stop it. "There was a lot of blood. I didn't know until I went up to her, but now I can't stop thinking about it."

"Was the cloth just hanging there, like a rag? Like he was wiping up?"

"Not exactly." Luke's eyes popped open. "It looked hard, like he was covering something."

"Good. Close your eyes again." Rolly gave Luke a moment to compose himself. "What else you see?"

"Sunglasses on top of his head."

"Good, anything else?"

Luke's voice came out in a whisper. "A strip of light from the window went across him. He's got a tattoo. Like a tribal one."

"Where?"

"On his arm, his biceps." Luke's voice shook.

"Good, Luke. Open your eyes now."

Luke turned his head so that Rolly wouldn't see him wipe a cheek dry.

"I been thinking," Rolly said, and tipped his bottle for a long swallow. "You gotta catch a ride with some tourist tomorrow. Whoever did this is local, so you need to ride with someone from off-island." He pointed to his water. "Helps me lose weight, you know? I try and drink twelve glasses minimum a day."

"Yeah." Luke's head bobbed gratefully. "You're doing good, man."

"But I pee all day." Rolly smiled, and Luke thought that it was the first time he'd ever seen Rolly's face change. "It's not the diabetes, either."

Chapter Twenty-eight

Storm got four words out before the Emergency Room crew whisked Niwa away. "He threw up blood."

Goldbaum's brown eyes, sharp behind the thick lenses, focused on her face. "I'll bet he did," he said softly, and marched down the hall into his own private head wind, his white coat like a sail.

Storm stood for a few seconds, then wandered into the parking lot, where she'd left the car with the engine running and both doors open. If she did that in Honolulu it would be in a chop shop inside ten minutes. The car still sat there, but someone had turned the engine off and laid the keys on the roof. No one was around, though, so she couldn't thank the person, let alone apologize for her rude arrival.

Storm dropped into the front seat and sagged. Now that her role in getting Niwa to the hospital was over, she was drained. The fact of his collapse and the urgent reaction of the hospital staff sank in, too. Up to this point, she'd hoped it was the flu or something he ate. But no, whatever he had was bad, and she was troubled.

She barely knew the guy, and she liked him. Liked the way he worried over Luke like a dad would, and the way he put Luke's welfare before his own. Storm was concerned about Luke, too. How could Tanner take a group of tourists out when his son was missing? He was the real dad, and he didn't seem to put his sick son's wellbeing first, dammit.

Jenny's tired demeanor came back to her, and Storm wondered if she'd borne the responsibility of parenthood alone. Storm wanted to be angry at Tanner; it would have given her more energy. But she just felt sad and lonely, and she wanted to talk to Hamlin.

During the frantic trip back from Halawa, her handbag had slid under the front seat, and she leaned over to retrieve it and her cell phone. He answered after the second ring. "Ian? I'm so glad you're there." She let out a pent-up breath she didn't know she'd been holding. "How's the shoulder?"

"You should see the sling the doctor's got me in."

"Does it make your arm feel better?"

"Yes, and he told me the numbness will go away. But I may need surgery to keep it from dislocating again."

"Oh, no. When will you know?"

"In a few weeks, I guess."

"Did you get some rest this afternoon?"

He sighed. "I wish. Sergeant Niwa called Devon Liu around noon. The body was Brock's."

"Poor Mr. Liu. He called you when he found out?"

"His assistant did. I guess the old guy is taking it hard."

"It's too early to have a cause of death, isn't it?"

"Not if you're Devon Liu. He sent a private helicopter to pick up the body and take it to Maui for the post-mortem. Looks like he died from blunt trauma to the head."

"Is he dropping the lawsuit against Hawai'i EcoTours?"

"Not yet. He's still convinced they're involved."

"Could the head wound have been caused by a paddle?"

"Not unless it was metal. The ME found something embedded in his skull, and they think part of the weapon broke off. It's bronze with traces of other substances. Wax was one of them."

"Bronze?" Storm was quiet for a moment. "Like a sculpture?"

"Could be. Wax is used as part of the casting process."

"Did he and Jenny Williams know each other?"

"Why Jenny?"

"I heard she was a sculptor."

"No kidding." Hamlin let a beat pass. "Everyone knows everyone else on that island, right?"

"If they've been around for a while. Hamlin, remember that nice cop who—"

"Damn, I've got a call coming in. It's probably Liu or his assistant. Sorry, I'll call you later." He disconnected.

Storm let her phone drop in her lap. He hadn't done much to ease her loneliness. On the other hand, he'd dropped an interesting piece of information. If Jenny had something to do with Brock's bludgeoning, the investigation could end. She'd have to dig tactfully into how well they'd known each other.

Storm remembered that Jenny had died of a head injury, too. She wondered what the ME said about that one. What she'd been hit with, time of death, and her blood alcohol level, since Storm had seen her drinking earlier. Lambert had implied she drank often.

Storm wanted to talk to Lambert again, anyway. Her gut feeling on the guy was that he was smart, and not likely to lash out without careful thought. Storm had the advantage of being a fellow Hawaiian, too. She picked up her phone again, and dialed the Lodge.

"Aunt Maile, how was the outing to Phallic Rock?"

"Glad I'm not likely to get pregnant," Aunt Maile said. "It's a very realistic likeness. And BIG, goodness me."

Storm grinned. She should have called Aunt Maile in the first place. Phallic Rock was an important site for Hawaiian spirituality, and women who had fertility problems still made offerings and spent the night on the soft ironwood needles that surrounded the giant stone phallus. It was supposed to be quite effective; Storm had friends who swore by it. She didn't want to go within five miles of the thing—not yet.

"I want to hear all about it. What time do you and Uncle Keone want to have dinner?"

"He's napping right now, so not for a couple of hours yet. Where are you?"

"I'm in Kaunakakai, but I want to drive out to see Lambert Poele. It's five now; if I'm not back at the Lodge by seven-thirty, come looking for me."

"You sure you're safe?" Aunt Maile's voice sharpened.

"That was a joke. He doesn't seem like a bad guy."

"What about the sorcery manuscripts?"

"He's got a ton of Hawaiian history and lore. I don't think he's doing sorcery."

"Keep your cell phone in your pocket."

"I will," Storm said, and hung up. Though Poele had been friendly enough the last visit, she would follow Aunt Maile's advice.

She didn't want to call ahead and give him time to think about all the reasons she might want to talk to him, so she was relieved to see Poele's rusting old pickup on the lawn and the four-legged greeting committee trotting toward her. The bleating of the goats and bumping noise of her car on the dirt drive alerted him, too. Before she had the car turned off, he'd descended the steps to his home, wiping his mouth on the back of one hand. It looked like she'd interrupted his dinner, and Storm was glad she'd stopped for some *pipi kaula* and beer before she left Kaunakakai.

"To what do I owe the pleasure?" Poele asked, but he didn't sound happy. He wore a tank top and Storm could see the tribal tattoo that banded his upper arm. The colors were deep hued and the skin around it somewhat inflamed.

"Sorry to interrupt." She pulled the twelve-pack and package of dried beef jerky out of the back seat.

He looked mollified when he caught sight of the gifts. "Hey, thanks."

"Want me to put this in your ice chest?" She offered the beer to him.

"Bring it inside. I'll put it in the fridge." He turned, gesturing for her to follow. Storm had the sudden feeling other women visited him the same way, and remembered his sly expression when they'd talked about Jenny. Her cheeks flushed. She'd make sure there was no misunderstanding on that front.

The smell of hot dogs, rice, and ketchup filled the little house, and Storm again got the sense that although he was a bit of a flirt, he led a self-imposed solitary life. He pulled two beers out of the carton Storm had brought. He handed one to her and gestured to the sitting room. "Have a chair. I'll be right back." He returned in a moment, carrying the other beer.

Storm was standing in front of his crowded bookshelves. "Is this hula dancer one of Jenny's sculptures?"

"He's not a hula dancer. You'd recognize it if I hadn't knocked it over and broken off part of the lasso. That's Maui roping Kalā, the sun. Remember that legend?"

"Oh, yeah." Storm thought of Hamlin's description of the murder weapon and swallowed hard.

Poele pointed to the lamp by his reading chair. The shade was bent into a baroque oval. "Had a little too much to drink one night." He picked up the heavy sculpture and ran his hand gently over it. Regret carved deep lines along the sides of his tanned face. "I don't care about the lamp, but this really bums me out. She was going to fix it, too." He placed it carefully back on the shelf and shook his head. "Now she can't."

"That's really too bad." Storm watched him carefully. "She gave it to you?"

"Yeah." He looked away and sat down in his reading chair. "Someday, maybe I'll get it repaired, but right now I...well, it doesn't seem right to have someone else work on it."

"I bet." She wanted to change the subject and gestured to his arm. "Is that a new tattoo?" she asked.

His dark eyes danced. "Yeah, you like it?"

"Does the design have a specific meaning?"

"Did you know the word tattoo comes from the Polynesian term *tatau*?" He popped open his beer. "These designs have been found on Tongan pottery shards that date back to 1300 B.C."

"Really?" Storm liked that idea. "So tattoos really do have a basis in Polynesian history?"

"Definitely. Hawaiian history, too."

"Were they a sign that a person belonged to a certain tribe?"

"Sometimes. Others were used to signify a person's *'aumakua,* some to show a life passage."

"So is yours an *'aumakua*? Or does it have some other purpose?"

"Nope." He took a swallow from his bottle. "You must have driven up here to talk to me about something important."

Storm picked at the label on her bottle. "Yes, I've got a few questions."

"About Hawaiian history, or more recent stuff?" He squinted at her.

"A bit of both. When Hamlin and I visited you yesterday, I noticed your interest in Hawaiian culture, and you were once a leader in Hawaiian activism." He winced at this, but Storm kept going. "Keeping Hawaiian culture strong is important to me. A couple days ago, I sat on a bench with the message, 'Just visit, but go home,' carved in it. What's going on around here?"

Poele rested his beer on his knee. "The push to develop will never stop. There are plans for a luxury residential development, out where we take our kids, go fishing." He pointed in the direction of the sea and his outstanding view. "Two hundred multimillion dollar homes. Can you see this? A gated community on an island that doesn't have traffic lights, where no one locks the doors to our houses?"

Storm nodded sadly. "It would change everything."

"It's not just the fact that it's in my neighborhood. Did you hear some visitor threw a package at a clerk at Friendly Market the other day?"

"You're kidding."

"It wasn't the right brand, whatever that is." His voice rose. "We don't want people like that around. We don't want sewage treatment plants and cell phone towers on sacred land."

"I can understand."

"You been to Maui lately?"

"Uh, yeah. Got stuck in a traffic jam, too. But Moloka'i people, your people, are doing a good job of vocalizing the kinds of changes you're willing to live with. I heard Moloka'i Ranch was transferring control of 65,000 acres to the community."

Poele snorted. "True, but the community doesn't always agree, does it?"

"I know," Storm agreed. "We can't get our own people together on the issue of sovereignty."

"Look at it historically, since that's why you came." He gave her a half smile that said he knew better and continued anyway. "Hawaiian chiefs used to rule over huge pie-shaped chunks of land called *ahupua'a*. Hawaiians believed land was the gods' domain, and the chiefs held communion with the gods. But when Europeans came, chiefs began to owe certain powerful commoners for favors. Certain businessmen were given chunks of land as a 'mark of personal esteem.' Pay-offs." Poele shook his head with disgust.

"Human nature doesn't change much, does it?" Storm said. "So what can we do? How do you keep your lifestyle, and still live in the twenty-first century?"

"That's the million-dollar question, isn't it?" Poele's voice was rueful.

Storm got up, went to the fridge and got two more beers.

"Thanks," Poele said, and put his empty down with the others collecting on the floor beside his chair.

Storm took a long pull on her own beer. The issue of progress was one that bothered her. It wasn't easy to discuss with Hamlin, who considered development inevitable and potentially profitable. Nor was it by any means a local concept, because Storm's best friend Leila, a fair-skinned redhead originally from the Midwest, was even more resistant than Storm to the idea of development at the expense of culture and environment. Leila recycled everything in her bakery, plus she drove a converted diesel car that ran on recycled vegetable oil. It smelled like fried potatoes.

Storm pulled herself back to Poele, who also seemed to be lost in his own thoughts. "You led a protest against development ten years ago," she said softly.

Poele heaved a heavy sigh. "Yeah, and it haunts me still." He stared out the front window, though all Storm could see was a handful of grazing goats.

"You regret the fire or the protest?"

His eyes, now more focused, came back to meet hers. He tipped back his beer and finished it before he responded. "The fire."

"What happened that night?"

A long moment passed. "I can't talk about it."

"Legally?"

"Nah, I don't care about that," he snorted, and dropped his empty bottle on the growing pile. He got up, went into the kitchen, and came back with two more beers. "You're a slow drinker, eh?"

"I've got to drive."

"You don't have to." He gave her a sly half smile.

"Yeah, I do."

"That Hamlin didn't seem like your type."

"He's a great guy."

"Suit yourself." Poele shrugged.

"So why can't you talk about it?" She didn't have to mention the word 'fire.' It loomed large in her mind, and she was certain it was huge in his.

He took a swallow of beer and burped softly. "I made a vow."

"To the person who set it?"

"No." The thousand-yard stare had returned to his eyes. "Well, I don't think so, anyway."

Storm frowned. He was the one accused of setting the fire, and he'd given her an unanticipated answer, one that sounded sincere and somewhat puzzled. He didn't know who did set it? That wasn't what she expected. And the question seemed to have vaulted him into some distant memory. The muscles in his jaw bunched, and his eyes glazed with what looked like remorse. Not so much guilt, but profound regret.

Storm watched him carefully. He might also be an excellent actor, and he had a likely murder weapon sitting within arm's reach. How good was she at reading another person's feelings? She was having a hard enough time with Hamlin's, and she knew him intimately. And knowing her own feelings? Never mind.

The little house was hot; no air stirred the grubby-looking cotton curtains at the front window. Unlike most people, he was immune to gaps in conversation. Several minutes passed, and she was the first to break the silence.

"How well do you know Makani's dad?"

Poele pulled himself back to the present with a lurch and tossed off the question with a shrug. "Never met the guy."

"He didn't see Makani?"

"What do I know?" His dark eyes glittered beneath half-closed lids. "Sounds like you're doing background checks on us."

"I'm trying to figure out people's relationships to each other."

Poele snorted. "You still trying to find out what happened to Brock Liu?"

"Yeah. His dad's going to sue Hawai'i EcoTours, you know."

"Christ." Poele shook his head with disgust and downed half of his beer.

"Do you know if Jenny knew him?"

"Sure."

"Sure, she knew him?"

Poele nodded his response.

"Did he hit her like he hit Delia?"

Poele's answer was so low Storm had to strain to hear him. "I think she was the only woman he couldn't intimidate."

"Good for Jenny," Storm said, and meant it.

"Yeah, but I've been thinking about this since I got to know her better. Maybe she figured she didn't have anything else to lose." Poele sounded sad. "Except for Luke, of course—and she kept Liu away from him."

"Did she act hopeless?"

"Maybe that's what it was. She acted like she didn't expect anything from a man." He dropped his empty bottle next to his chair. "Like she didn't give a fuck anymore."

His last words were nearly a whisper, and Storm had the feeling the conversation was waning. Poele's eyelids looked heavy and the glazed look was staying in his eyes longer. Sadly, Storm didn't think it was all due to beer; the questions she'd posed had seemed to take a toll. She needed to ask another big one, though.

"Do you think there was a relationship between the fire and Tia's disappearance?" Her voice was soft. She worried the question might shut him down the way it had Dusty, but Poele just shook his head slowly from side to side. Several moments passed before he answered.

"I'll never know for sure, will I?" He popped the top on the new bottle, but didn't look up. "But I think so."

"It must have been horrible for you and Dusty," Storm said.

Poele looked up sharply, but Storm only took another drink of beer, and he followed suit. "None of us can imagine the loss of a child. I was worried about him for a long time. A handful of us made sure someone dropped by every day, especially in the evenings."

"Having Makani around probably helped."

"Probably saved him. Makani worships the ground he walks on. At least Dusty felt needed."

"He and Tia were close?"

To Storm's surprise, Poele smiled wistfully. "He and Tia were a lot alike. Strongly opinionated, so they butted heads." He took a long pull from his beer. "Yes, they were close."

"He talked a little bit about her disappearance. I know he adored your son."

Poele paused, and the silence that elapsed told Storm a secret. Makani had told her the truth, even though Dusty believed—or hoped, Storm wasn't sure which—that Tommy was Poele's son.

Poele's eyes slid to hers, and he took a drink. "Tommy was Alika's son. Hell, I was trying to adopt him. He was my son as far as I was concerned."

No one spoke for a minute, then Poele spoke again. "How strong is blood? Is it stronger than friendship?"

He took another drink, and dropped the bottle onto the pile with a clank that jarred them both.

"Brotherhood isn't built on blood alone," Storm said softly.

"You're right on that one, sister."

Chapter Twenty-nine

Rolly handed Luke a full backpack. "I know it's heavy, little brother. Better you stop and rest than be without food, medicine, or fluids. Diabetics have to take more care than other people."

Luke was used to walking, and he was a mile or two out of town in the cool morning air before a rental car stopped to give him a ride. The visitors, a friendly man and woman from O'ahu, were only going as far as one of the beach parks along the way, but Luke was happy to get farther down the road. They offered to take him the rest of the way in a couple of hours, but Luke didn't want to wait around.

He walked steadily and put out his thumb when he saw cars approaching. In places the road was curvy, and he often could hear the vehicles before he could see them, which made him jumpy. Rolly's advice had resonated with him, and the memory of the man looming over his mother was clearer than ever since their conversation. The image was still faceless, though, and scarier because of it.

Luke was on a shaded bend in the lane of oncoming traffic when he heard the rumble of an approaching auto, and he walked backward, thumb out, facing its approach. The faded red Jeep Wagoneer was scarcely around the corner when Luke recognized it as Connor Richards' car. Connor saw him, too.

He leaned out the window and shouted, "Luke, Jesus! The whole island is looking for you!"

Luke took one look at the beefy arm in the window frame and the swollen black eye in the florid face and bolted. He jumped onto the shoulder of the road, skidded into a ditch filled with muddy water, and scrambled on all fours up a three or four-foot embankment clotted with thick foliage.

Connor squealed to a halt in the middle of the road. "Luke! Stop!" he screamed, his voice cracking with effort.

Luke scrambled faster. In his effort to scale the muddy embankment, he slipped and planted his hand squarely on the broken remains of a beer bottle some reveler had tossed from a car window.

Connor saw the flush of vivid blood and heard Luke's cry of pain before the boy crashed through the giant philodendrons and into bank of trees beyond. The last image Connor had of the boy was of Luke's hand in his mouth, blood running in two bright rivulets down his arm.

"Holy shit," Connor said aloud. Was panic a side-effect of the boy's illness, or had he just scared the kid away? He slumped in his seat and gripped his head between his hands. He was the reason for Luke's terror, no doubt about it.

Connor got out of the car, leaving it in the middle of the road, and walked to the shoulder where Luke had disappeared. "Hey Luke, I won't hurt you. Let me help," he shouted at the shrubbery. His voice shook a little bit.

Connor climbed back into the car, which smelled of his own sweat, an odor that seemed rancid even to him. A moan of self-loathing escaped him. He'd gone almost a day without a dose of Anadrol, and his buddies had warned him about the withdrawal. They said it was important, though he was going to have to gut it out through mood swings, depression, and physical weakness. They also told him his personal and social skills weren't the only things that needed a break. His heart, liver, and gonads did, too.

The confrontation with Skelly had pushed Connor to this self-awareness. But when he thought about it, he knew he'd done some things he wished he hadn't. In fact, he shuddered at some of the things he remembered, and worried about those he didn't.

No wonder his brother held him at arm's length, no longer trusted him, and had begun to exclude him from the tight circle of friends they'd grown up with. He knew about the recent oath, too. And Skelly hadn't been the one to tell him about it, which really hurt. One of the guys at the gym had been talking, and they'd hushed when he passed by.

And now this kid was terrified of him. How could he undo the damage he'd caused?

Luke pushed through the trees. Was Connor the shadowy monster? He didn't know. But he did know the guy was bad news, that he had a nasty temper that exploded without warning, and worse, that he'd once had a fight with his mother. Luke had seen it. Connor had taken a swing at her, but she'd grabbed her sculpture of Maui lassoing the sun, a heavy bronze statue that people admired. She'd had that slimy creep backpedaling in a hurry. It was a good memory.

Luke's breathing was returning to normal. He was thirsty, his hand hurt, and he needed to check his blood sugar soon. The cut was still oozing, and looked pretty deep. Connor really was a pecker-head, he thought.

The ocean glimmered through the trees, and he walked over sprawling hala roots to get to a clearing where he could sit in partial shade and have a snack. He dug through the backpack and got out some items. Rolly, what a friend. Luke knew he owed him. There was a package of tissues, which he could wrap around the cut until he got to the cabin, where his dad could take care of it. He also got out a sandwich and a drink, leaned back against a tree trunk and told himself to relax. He not only needed to recoup some energy, he had to let Connor get away, though Luke worried a bit that the jerk would call for help, and it would be someone else Luke didn't want to see.

He smiled at the memory of how his mom had hefted that statue of hers. Luke knew she was proud of the stone and glass table in their living room, but didn't like the statue much.

"You should go back to your art," her friends would tell her.

"Someone's got to pay the bills," she'd snarl, and that person wouldn't bring the subject up again.

Some of his mother's comments brought a flood of emotion he couldn't sort out. Embarrassment for her and his father, whom he loved and who Luke worried might be kind of a loser. He recoiled from thinking that might be true, no matter what his mother said. Uncle Skelly, of course, thought his dad was a genius, but Luke wasn't sure if Skelly was a good judge. Skelly was a nice enough guy, but he didn't always have control over his own life. After all, Tanner had to help with the business all the time, and look at his stupid brother.

Luke took a bite of the sandwich and closed his eyes, trying to fit Connor into the silhouette of the man he'd seen in his living room. There was something different about Connor though, something that didn't quite fit, but who could tell? It had been dark, except for the bands of light from outside, almost like one of those optical illusion games. Plus the guy had been bent over, so Luke wasn't sure how tall he was, just that he looked big and strong. Connor certainly fit that description. But he'd been wearing a T-shirt when he'd stopped on the road, so Luke couldn't tell if he had the tattoo.

Luke finished off his lunch and peeked at the seeping wound in his hand. Hey, he didn't have to prick his finger this time. He'd just use the stuff that was still oozing from the wound. Not too much blood anymore, but enough to put on the little slide that fed the monitor. The cut was starting to throb, and Luke didn't want to think about how far he still had to go. He wrapped a clean T-shirt around it and tied it as tightly as he could.

His blood sugar was in an acceptable range, but he sure was tired. He packed his food, medicine, and gear back into the pack, got slowly to his feet and worked his arms into the straps. The sun was high and hot and he needed to get this trip behind him.

Luke walked for about ten minutes before a car stopped. It was a car he recognized, which wasn't so good, but he knew Mrs. Olivetti, and she was safe. It was too late to run for the bushes.

She rolled down the window on the passenger side. "Luke, everyone's looking for you."

"Hi, Mrs. Olivetti. Who's everyone?" Luke peered into the car. Mrs. Olivetti worked at the pharmacy with Mrs. Niwa. She was a nice lady, but kind of a busybody, and Luke was afraid she'd insist on taking him back to Kaunakakai.

She leaned over the front seat and pushed open the passenger side door. "You okay, honey? You look pale. Luke, your doctor is all worried. And the poor Niwas, well, they—"

"Have you seen Sergeant Niwa? I want to talk to him."

"He's in the hospital. Bleeding ulcer." She tutted and shook her head from side to side. "You better get in, dear. Good lord, what happened to your hand?"

Luke didn't answer her question. Instead, he grabbed the corner of the open door for support. "He's in the hospital?"

"He's a sick man, from what I heard. Maybe you better call him."

"I will. Where you going?"

"I'm going to visit Mrs. Shima. She had a hysterectomy, and I've got a pot of chicken curry for the family."

The aroma filled the car, and Luke's mouth watered. "Where's she live?"

Mrs. Olivetti frowned at him. "You're just full of questions. A little past Puko'o. Where you going?"

"I'm meeting my dad at Halawa Bay."

"That's a good idea, hon. You need someone to take care of you. What happened to your hand?"

"I fell and scraped it, but it's okay. I didn't want dirt to get on it, so I wrapped a shirt around it."

"You sure you don't want to see the doctor?"

"Dad will take me if it needs it. He's waiting for me."

"You sure? I heard he was taking out some people for the Richards brothers."

"That was earlier." Luke didn't want to say more. His plans would be all over the island. Plus, she'd undoubtedly protest the fact that he had to hike into the forest.

The lines between Mrs. Olivetti's eyes deepened again, this time in apparent thought. "Okay. I don't have to be back until five. I'll drop you at the bay."

"That's really thoughtful of you."

"Get in, honey."

Mrs. Olivetti asked him a few questions, carefully avoiding the death of his mother. Her remarks seemed solicitous and careful, and Luke got the feeling she was struggling to make conversation. Before long, the heat of the car and the soft background music on the radio made his eyelids heavy. Luke leaned his head against the window. Before he succumbed to sleep, he was certain he spied an expression of relief cross Mrs. Olivetti's face.

The next thing he knew, a gentle hand on his shoulder woke him. "Luke, you got a good rest. We're here."

Luke pried open his eyes. His mouth was sticky and stale, strands of hair clung damply to his forehead, and his head ached. The curry didn't smell so good anymore. "Thanks, Mrs. Olivetti."

"You sure you feel okay?"

"Yeah, I'll be fine. You really helped me out."

"I don't see anyone down there." She squinted through the windshield. "Is someone in that hut down there?"

"Yeah, they're probably just staying out of the sun."

"Good idea. You better do that, too."

Luke made sure he had his backpack situated and got out of the car. "Thanks again," he said.

She'd done a three-point turn on the narrow road before he even started down the path. Probably forgot what a long drive it was, and was worried she'd be late in getting the curry to Mrs. Shima's. But she saved him a lot of trouble, and he was grateful. As soon as she was out of sight, Luke got one of the sports drinks Rolly had packed for him and gulped the entire bottle. A wave of nausea convulsed his throat soon after, but he fought it. His body needed the fluid and the electrolytes. He had to keep going.

Chapter Thirty

Storm left Poele sitting in his easy chair with another beer in his hand and at least six empties beside him. She'd opened a second, but had merely sipped at it. When she announced that she had to leave to meet her aunt and uncle for dinner, he'd flapped his hand in a feeble dismissal and resumed his stare out the front window. It reflected his despair back into the room.

Back in the car, Storm bumped down the dirt lane and tried to remember what part of their conversation had precipitated his melancholy. She thought it was the topic of the fire, followed by the referral to a vow. Then he posed his question of blood and brotherhood. By the time she asked about Tia's disappearance, he was buried in dark memories.

Even with her knowledge of the manuscripts in the bedroom—and she'd intended to bring those up, but hadn't had the chance—he didn't strike her as a murderous type. Cocky and flippant. But evil? Poele didn't have the twisted malevolence and immorality she'd seen in the man who'd imprisoned her and killed others in an ocean cave a few months ago. The memory made her shiver, despite the warm evening. But, she asked herself, was evil a prerequisite for murder? Not necessarily, she thought. Self-righteousness, anger, greed, desperation, and a writhing swarm of other motivations could push a person to murder.

Would she—could she—recognize a murderer? Could anyone? She had her doubts, but the solitude of the dirt road, with its canopy of distant, glittering stars overhead may have evoked these views.

She reached the paved road with a wave of relief. Thoughts like that were counter-productive, and induced self-doubt instead of results. Only about fifteen minutes to meeting her aunt and uncle. An hour with the dour Poele, and she couldn't wait to bask in their affectionate and uncomplicated company. The thought of affection and selflessness reminded her of Niwa.

Storm checked her cell phone and found, to her delight, that she had three bars of reception. Information gave her the number to Moloka'i General Hospital, where she hoped to talk to a floor nurse about Niwa's condition. To her surprise, the operator connected her directly to his room.

"This is Caroline."

"Mrs. Niwa?"

"Yes, who's this?"

When Storm gave her name, the first words out of Caroline Niwa's mouth were those of gratitude for the help Storm had given her husband.

"How is he?" Storm asked.

"Pretty good, thanks to Dr. Goldbaum and you. When you told Dr. Goldbaum about Dave vomiting blood, he suspected an ulcer and called for a series of tests, including a gastroscopy. Dave's got to stay in the hospital a few more days, then see a specialist in Honolulu. But he's going to be okay, that's the important thing."

Caroline's voice became muffled for a minute, and Storm figured Caroline had her hand over the receiver. Storm made out the words, "Rest...tomorrow." Then Caroline's voice said something like, "For crying out loud," and Niwa's voice came on the line.

"Mahalo for your help today."

"You're welcome. How're you feeling?"

"A lot better." His words came out low and slow. "But that could be the sedative they're giving me."

"Do you know if Luke showed up?"

His tone sharpened to cop mode. "My partner and others are looking for him." Then he softened a bit. "Look, we don't want you to end up in here, too."

"I'm just trying to find Tanner."

"Right. And I'm a hick cop."

"No way," Storm said, and meant it. "But I'm worried. Why did the boy leave the hospital so suddenly?"

"We're looking into that." There was a grim note to his voice. He hadn't meant to, but he'd given Storm a big piece of information with that statement. He suspected Jenny had been killed, instead of supposing she'd hit her head because she'd been drinking. And he was concerned that Luke could be running from someone, a person who was with Jenny or was responsible for her death.

"Thanks, Sergeant Niwa. Get better soon."

"And Storm? If you hear anything, call me."

Storm heard Caroline's voice in the background.

"Okay, dear. Or my partner, Steve Nishijima."

The lights of the Lodge beckoned with a warm amber glow as she bumped into the parking lot. While Storm gathered her purse and locked the car, someone called her name, and she turned to see Delia jogging across the pavement.

"Did you find him?" Delia asked.

"Luke? No, have you heard anything?"

"Yes, Connor saw him on the road to Halawa."

"Good! Did he pick him up and take him to the hospital?"

Delia swung her head from side to side and panted. "No, Luke ran away."

"Oh, no."

"Connor said he got out of the car and shouted at him, but he wouldn't stop. He says Luke cut his hand, too."

Storm frowned. "When was this?"

"Before noon, maybe around ten?"

Connor, the stupid ass, hadn't said a thing about it when she'd talked to him in the office. "Have you seen Connor lately?"

"No, but he called." Delia wore a big smile at that pronouncement.

Storm had seen that bright-eyed hopefulness in some of her other women friends. "Are you dating him?"

"No…well, we used to go out. He's really trying to change."

With some effort, Storm clamped her mouth shut. Delia seemed like one of those nice people who pick losers for partners, and would have a list of excuses for anyone who told her this. She'd have to find out on her own, unfortunately.

"I saw him earlier today and one eye was black and nearly swollen shut," Storm said. "I'd run from him, too, if I were a kid."

"He had a black eye?" Delia's eyebrows climbed out of sight under her bangs. Her voice rose with them. "No one would dare hassle him."

"Someone did more than that." Storm turned to leave. "Where was Luke when Connor saw him?"

"Not far from their office."

"Thanks for telling me, Delia." Storm turned and headed for the dining room, dialing the number for the police station and trying to remember the name of Niwa's partner. She sensed Delia still watching.

"Steve Nishijima, please."

The man who answered put her on hold for a few moments. "He's not in. Want to leave a message?"

Storm left her mobile number and room number, then pulled open the heavy double door to the Lodge. Connor said Luke was a smart kid, and so did Bob Crowder, who had kids of his own. Storm hoped this was true, and told herself Nishijima didn't answer his extension because he was out looking. That was the only way she was going to enjoy dinner.

When she got to the table, Aunt Maile and Uncle Keone had just given their cocktail requests to the waitress.

"Could you add a glass of merlot to that order, please?" Storm asked the departing server.

Uncle Keone, Aunt Maile, and Storm exchanged hugs and Storm dropped into the dining chair. Subdued lights and candles made the room glow with comfort.

Aunt Maile regarded Storm's subdued demeanor. "Did you see Lambert Poele?"

Storm nodded. "Seems that Brock Liu and Jenny had a relationship. She had a fling with Dusty, too."

"I wonder when?" Uncle Keone mused.

"I imagine it's hard to be a single woman here," Storm said.

"Small towns can be tough on the unattached," Aunt Maile said.

The waitress brought their drinks and Aunt Maile leaned in, her eyes shining with amusement. Storm could tell she was trying to cheer her up. "I met up with an old friend."

"You did?" Storm took a sip of her wine.

"We used to talk about all kinds of things in our high school days. She was always *kolohe*." Maile grinned.

"She's still mischievous," Uncle Keone said dryly. "Those comments about the big *ule*. I nearly blushed."

"You were red as a hibiscus."

"Not."

"Uh huh."

A smile pulled at Storm's lips. So that's why her aunt had been so amused by Phallic Rock. "She lives here?"

"Moved to Moloka'i about twenty years ago."

"What's she do? Is she a *kahuna lā'au lapa'au*, like you?"

"No, she dabbles." Maile dropped her voice. "She's also done some light sorcery, mostly as a *kahuna ho'o ulu lā hui.*"

"That figures," said Keone with a snort.

"What's that?" asked Storm at the same time.

Maile ignored her husband. "She's a specialist in getting women pregnant."

"It's an excuse for raunchy dancing," Keone said.

"Hush, you." Aunt Maile slapped his arm and he nearly spilled his beer. "See why women have to keep some things secret? Men do not understand. They just want to unzip and—"

Storm was snorting into her wine glass by this time. "Uncle Keone, I never heard you complain about lusty dancing before."

Aunt Maile gave him a look. "She's old enough to hear about the Stoplight, you know."

"The Stoplight?" Storm's voice rose with surprise. "Wasn't that the bar on Kapiolani Boulevard with the strippers who wrote birthday cards, gave change, and peeled eggs without using their hands?"

The conversational buzz at nearby tables was dropping.

Keone was scarlet to the roots of his grey hair. "Hey, I didn't know what it was 'til I got in there. Dusty took us there on a trip to Honolulu."

"Blame it on Dusty." Storm shook her head. "Naughty boys in the big city."

Keone pointed at his wife. "She was there, too."

Storm peered over at her aunt. Was that a blush blossoming up her neck, across her cheeks and forehead? She was nearly as red as Keone.

"I didn't know, either."

"Is that place still open?" asked Keone.

"No, it closed down years ago," said a man at a nearby table.

A new waiter brought the tray with their entrées. Storm figured he'd hijacked the food from their waitress on the way out of the kitchen. "I heard there's one in Pearl City now. You know anything about that?"

Aunt Maile's eyes were the size of her bread plate. "Not!"

"I just wondered," said the waiter. He scooted back to the kitchen with the speed and dexterity of a slalom racer.

It was more than Storm could take. She choked on the effort of swallowing her laughter. Uncle Keone was making some pretty interesting sounds, too, a cross between a cackle and a squeak. But it was Aunt Maile threw back her head and let rip with a hoot that resounded through the room.

The other tables might have chuckled along and gone back to their meals, except that Aunt Maile knocked her glass of ice water into Uncle Keone's lap and his amusement turned into a gurgled yelp.

People at the tables around them were either laughing outright or gazing into each other's eyes. The man on the other side blotted his face with a napkin while his female companion slowly licked chocolate from a strawberry.

"Ahem!" Keone cleared his voice and anyone who was still leaning their way went back to eating. Fastidiously. "What do you two want to do tomorrow?"

He had already piled both Storm's and Maile's napkins onto his wet lap. Their first waitress, who glared a squinty stink-eye toward the kitchen, arrived with clean, dry napkins.

"Any chance of another ride?" Storm asked, trying to help Keone turn the conversation to a more acceptable topic.

"I was thinking the same thing. I mean, no offense to Hamlin or anything, but we could cover a bit more ground than we did on Friday and see a different part of the island."

"Sounds good to me," Aunt Maile said, and borrowed a napkin to blot at her forehead.

"Dusty will let us trailer them if you want to ride somewhere else than here on the west end."

Storm perked up. Even through the silliness of the last several minutes, thoughts of Luke had teased at the corners of her mind. Nor had Tanner called, although he not only knew she was on the island, the coconut wireless had probably informed him that she'd visited Jenny not long before she died. And that bothered her.

Had Jenny's death put him in a mental state where he didn't want to be around other people? Granted, she'd only asked a few people, but the ones she'd talked to said he was out with tourists. This sounded cavalier for the day after his wife was killed. Unless he had something to do with it.

"Could we trailer them to Halawa Bay, where the road ends?" she asked.

"I suppose," Keone said. "I'll have to check on where the private land is, so we don't trespass. There are some traditional kalo terraces back there."

"I'd like to see that," said Aunt Maile. "People don't often grow taro the old way anymore."

"You're thinking about Luke Williams, aren't you?" Keone asked.

"A bit. I wouldn't mind getting a look at where Tanner has his place."

"If we can find it, or get to it."

"I understand," Storm said. "Say, this lobster paella is to die for. Anyone want a taste?"

"Sure, I'll swap you a bite of my blackened ahi," Aunt Maile said.

"I already finished my lamb chops," Keone said, and the women began to laugh again.

After dessert and coffee the three meandered out of the restaurant and paused in the great room to say goodnight. Right before they split to go separate ways, Storm stopped.

"I almost forgot. Aunt Maile, you were telling me something about your friend, the sex therapist."

"Not a sex therapist, a pregnancy kahuna. I thought she would be a safe person to ask about the manuscripts you saw at Poele's. So I asked her about sorcerers who could pray someone to death. She not only knew about it, she told me there was a local family whose members were said to be kāhuna kuni."

"Fire prayers?"

Maile nodded and dropped the level of her voice. "The family's name was Kekapu."

A chill crept over Storm. "That's Makani's last name. But ten years ago, he was just a teenager."

"She told me a hand-picked young man would study with an older kahuna to learn the chants. Sometimes they needed an item that belonged to the person to whom they directed the chant."

"Does the sorcerer have to be at the site of the fire?"

"Not necessarily. And they often had to chant over a period of time to bring about a change."

"I need to call Hamlin," Storm whispered.

Maile and Keone dropped Storm at her room and walked on to theirs, a few doors down the sidewalk. Once inside, Storm turned on all the lights. The maid had folded what clothes she'd left around and laid them on the neatly made bed, and the room looked empty without Hamlin's things. A rush of loneliness filled her.

Hamlin had said he'd call back, and Storm dug out her mobile phone to check. Sure enough, there was a message from him. Bothered by static on the phone, she walked out onto the small lanai off the bedroom and reclined on one of the lounge chairs to listen to it. She got better reception, plus she could see the brilliant dusting of stars in the sky.

Hamlin's voice was professional. "Storm, call me. Liu's assistant called, and she said Brock Liu knew who started the fire." She could hear him draw a tense breath. "There's no statute of limitations on murder, you know."

Chapter Thirty-one

Just in case Mrs. Olivetti stopped to watch, Luke walked across the sand to the boat house. Bob Crowder had closed up for the day, and Luke lingered on the far side of the structure for a few minutes. Then he made his way back across the beach, to the same path Storm and Niwa had taken twenty-four hours earlier. Like them, he turned inland from the bay, but where they headed up the embankment to the road, Luke kept going deeper into the valley, where trees blocked the trade winds and the air hovered like a physical presence, muggy and still.

For over an hour, he sweated and picked his way over tangled roots and small streams. The path was often muddy and he slipped and grabbed at tree trunks to keep from falling. Often he had to use both hands, and he punctuated his progress with grunts and an occasional cry of pain. His injured hand throbbed in time with his footsteps. Or maybe it was the other way around and he stepped to its beat, because when he stopped, the wound kept its own tender percussion.

Over time, the trail became harder to make out. The dense foliage grew quickly, and the path was rarely used. With an eye to the future, Tanner had cut tiny notches into certain tree trunks to guide Luke if he ever needed to make the trip alone. This was Luke's first time, and he now questioned his earlier confidence. It had seemed easy when Tanner had been there. Maybe he should have let Mrs. Olivetti take him back to the hospital, where he could have talked to Detective Niwa.

Luke's eyes ached with the effort of seeking the inconspicuous marks, which were five or six feet apart in the thick jungle. Knowing his dad's need for seclusion, this was an act of trust meant for Luke alone, and the boy was proud and grateful. But between every mark, he had to stop and check his route. If not for the notches, he would have been lost long ago.

Luke was tiring quickly. He had to stop and eat, drink, and test his blood sugar several times along the way. When his blood sugar dropped, he became weak and lightheaded. If he pressed through this, he began to stumble over even the small roots that twisted over the trail. At one point, his vision darkened, and he sat down in the mud to eat an energy bar from Rolly's supplies.

Without realizing it, he dozed off for a while. He wasn't sure how long he was asleep, but he felt a bit better when he woke up. But the nap didn't stop the throbbing in his hand. It didn't help that the shirt he was using as a bandage was bulky and made the wound hot and sweaty. Still, Luke figured it was better than getting dirt in the cut.

The walk took Luke over two hours. By the time he got to the cabin, he was thirsty and exhausted. The sun was an oblique shimmer that poked shafts of light through holes in the thick canopy of trees. While droplets of moisture danced in the beams, the leaves alongside the rays lost their individual nature and melded into green-black tarpaulins.

Stumbling, Luke made it to the far side of the building where his father hid the key to the front door in a specific crack in the wall. Holding himself up against the side of the cabin, he slipped his fingers into the split between the boards. He could scarcely respond to the sound of footsteps behind him.

"Luke, thank God you're here." Tanner drew the boy to him. He wore a flannel shirt over a T-shirt, as the setting sun had begun to take back its warmth from the forest floor. Luke snuggled to him, weak with relief.

"How you feeling, son?" Tanner asked.

"Tired."

"I've got soup heating. Let's get you warmed up."

Tanner helped Luke take off his shoes before he stepped into the little house. It had been months since Luke had been at the place, and it seemed tidier than ever. Tanner had laid some kind of ceramic tile throughout the cabin's front room and kitchen. It was white, as were the immaculate rugs that he'd placed with careful symmetry in relation to the two chairs and low coffee table.

"Sit down," Tanner said, and knelt before Luke to remove his socks and put some cleaner, warmer socks on his feet.

Luke leaned back. "Where's my backpack? I need to check my blood sugar."

"It's a little muddy, so I left it outside on the steps. You want it now, or can you have a bit of soup first?" Without waiting for an answer, Tanner walked into the kitchen to give the pot a stir. One burner on the gas stove was turned up high. "It's almost ready," he said.

Luke watched through half-open lids.

"What happened to your hand?" Tanner asked.

"I fell and cut it." Luke was so tired he could hardly speak, and his words were a little slurred. He let his eyes drift closed in the warmth and comfort of his father's home. He'd made it, and he could let go of all his worries, at least for a few hours. Maybe he'd even tell his dad about the shadow in the living room.

"I'd better take a look at that." Tanner rummaged in a cupboard and came up with a bottle of hydrogen peroxide and some cotton balls. He took off the flannel shirt and sat before his son.

Tanner removed the bag, unwound the gauze, and grunted. "How'd you do this?"

Luke didn't bother to open his eyes. "Fell on a hill. I was trying to get away—" He yelped at the sting of the peroxide Tanner had poured over the cut and opened his eyes to watch the injury foam.

"Sorry about the sting," Tanner said. "We've got to disinfect it, though."

But Luke had gasped again, and didn't answer. A tattoo peeked from the sleeve of his father's T-shirt, and Luke could see a geometric design like the one he'd seen on the shadowy figure in the stripes of moonlight.

"That still hurt?" Tanner looked up at him. "You okay? You look kind of queasy."

"Yeah." Luke's voice came out in a rasp. "I'm okay." He cleared his throat. "When did you get that tattoo?" He pointed at his dad's arm.

"Oh, that. A few days ago." Tanner looked a little embarrassed.

"Why?"

Tanner kept cleaning Luke's wound. "It's a friendship thing. I made an oath not to talk about it, though. You know about oaths? They're even stronger than a promise, otherwise I'd tell you." He spread ointment on the cut, and glanced up at Luke, who had shrunk back into the chair. "Sorry, I bet that hurt." Tanner unwound a swath of sterile gauze from a roll. "About the oath, though. You'll understand when you get a little older."

"It's like a vow." Luke's voice was strong and drew Tanner's attention.

"Right, good for you." Tanner squinted at his son. "You ever made one?"

Luke nodded.

"Can you tell me about it?"

"No."

"Good boy," Tanner said, but Luke saw regret flutter through his eyes. Tanner concentrated on gently wrapping the gauze around Luke's cut hand.

Luke didn't speak, either. It was to his mother that he'd made the vow, and it had happened only a few months ago, when he'd found a postcard from Chicago on the kitchen table. Grief for his mother filled him with a rush, and it threatened to overflow, but he could not let that happen, not in front of his dad.

The situation came back to him as if it had occurred that morning. He'd asked where Chicago was, and the *People* magazine Jenny had been reading slid from her hands.

"Please, love, don't ever tell anyone about it."

"Okay, Mom." But she'd heard the questions in his voice.

"Will you promise from the bottom of your heart?"

"Okay," he'd said, and he meant it. Now he thought about his words. From the bottom of his heart, that was a vow, wasn't it? And even though she was gone, he knew he'd keep it. Especially now.

His dad was wrapping a bandage around the cut with tender care, and hadn't seemed to notice that Luke's reaction was to the tattoo and not the pain of his injury. Luke closed his eyes and forced himself to recall the figure silhouetted in his living room. It scared him still. It was all he could do not to pull his hand from his father's grasp.

Luke's heart beat so hard and fast, it seemed to flutter his eardrums. He could hardly believe his father hadn't noticed. A tear slipped from beneath Luke's right eyelid, and he stopped himself from wiping it away. Instead he turned his head.

"This really hurts, doesn't it?"

"A little," Luke lied. It didn't. If it did, it was surpassed by the emotional restraint he was using.

The figure that had bent over his mother was big and strong, he knew that. Was it shorter than his dad? He wasn't sure. Tanner seemed taller than most of the men Luke knew. He cracked open his eyes to check. He couldn't tell.

But his dad would never have done this. Would he? Luke hated himself for even letting the thought enter his mind. He watched the care with which his father tended his injury and felt shame redden his cheeks.

But apprehension wouldn't leave him alone, and it prodded him until he faced an awareness he'd tried hard to ignore. What Tanner had told him about the vow had revealed something. His father had made a promise to at least one friend, and Luke believed one of them killed his mother. Tanner didn't have that many close friends. Luke guessed he knew them all.

Nasty suspicions again tapped at his mind. Had Tanner's vow something to do with his mom's death? His father wouldn't protect her killer, would he?

Luke shivered. Even if his dad didn't know it yet, he'd made a vow of friendship and silence with Jenny's murderer. So what would his father do when the man came for Luke? Who would Tanner believe if it came to Luke's word against an adult's, an adult who was a sworn friend?

Chapter Thirty-two

Jenny Williams reached for someone out of sight. She leaned toward this person, her mouth open and eyes wide. Storm sat in Jenny's living room, on the worn sofa with her feet up on the big stone and glass coffee table. It was a party, and a pile of beer bottles was growing beside her. She wasn't drunk, but she was laughing. And she wasn't reacting to Jenny's plea for help. Instead, she observed the others who were there, talking and interacting with each other. No one responded and Storm wondered why this was, but she didn't do anything about it. She even looked around for Luke, who didn't seem to be in the room. Storm knew that Jenny, though she was surrounded by people, was alone and terrified. And Storm took another drink of her beer.

She woke with a start, drenched with sweat. A soft bird call sounded. Storm peeked at the clock by the bed, which said two forty-five. Birds shouldn't be up yet. Yet she recognized the *'alae*'s call.

The idea that the mudhen was sounding a warning again bothered her, but Storm had been raised at the knee of a kahuna, in this case a teacher of Hawaiian myths and lore. Aunt Maile, hopefully snoring peacefully in her own room, would advise Storm to go back to the dream. She needed to find the reason for it, both from within herself and from any outside forces. Aunt Maile would tell Storm her subconscious was trying to pass along information, something she needed to know.

Storm shivered. Don't move, she told herself, or you'll lose the connection to the dream. She took a breath, closed her eyes, and placed herself back on the sofa in Jenny's living room. Poele sat in a chair across the room, next to the sculpture of Maui, which sat on the bookshelves next to him. His eyes were glassy with grief. Makani sat next to him, crying, while someone popped a beer open in the kitchen.

Tanner sat close to Storm on the couch, but acted like he hadn't seen her. He didn't look at anyone else, either. Instead, he frowned down at the cluttered surface of the coffee table and twisted his hands together as if he were holding them under a faucet.

There was a beautiful woman across the room who wore hospital scrubs like the ones Jenny had been in when she'd come to the door on Thursday afternoon. So long ago. Storm's mind fled the dream to figure out what day it was. It was Sunday, very early, three days since Jenny had died.

Storm didn't know the pretty woman, nor did she recognize the man sitting next to her, who touched her hand lovingly when she spoke. There was an odor Storm recognized, though she couldn't place it. Not a good one, either. Rancid and penetrating.

The scent didn't come from the affectionate couple, from Tanner, or from Poele's direction. Lambert's eyes were swollen and bloodshot, and though they met Storm's and tried to communicate something, Storm didn't know what. They always returned to Jenny, who wasn't paying attention. Jenny watched someone outside the front door, someone who either couldn't or wouldn't come in.

The next Storm knew, a halo of daylight was peeking around the drapes, and she woke again with a jerk, this time because she was worried she'd be late for breakfast. She'd agreed to meet Aunt Maile and Uncle Keone at six-thirty so they could get an early start on their ride.

She jumped out of bed, did the least she could in terms of morning rituals, and jogged over to the dining hall. Aunt Maile and Uncle Keone already had a table and were sharing the Sunday *Honolulu Star-Bulletin*.

"Good morning," Aunt Maile said. She took a drink of her coffee and Storm resisted the urge to grab it from her. She still felt fuzzy with sleep, while Aunt Maile looked fresh and rested.

"Have you been here long?" Storm asked instead, and snagged the mug at the empty place setting. She loved it when restaurants left an entire carafe of strong, hot coffee on the table.

"Five minutes." Uncle Keone looked up from the paper. "You look tired."

Storm thought about sharing her dream, but decided she'd mull it over a bit longer before she put it into words. She explained the other reasons she hadn't slept well. "I'm worrying about Luke Williams. And I couldn't get hold of Hamlin last night."

"Hamlin probably went to bed early and turned off his phone," Aunt Maile said. "You could call the police to check on the boy."

"I'll do that right now," Storm said. "If the waiter comes before I'm back, order me the taro pancakes." She took her coffee cup with her when she left the table to make the call.

Outside the dining room, she dialed Hamlin, who answered on the first ring.

"How're you feeling?" she asked.

"Better. Did you get my message last night?"

"Yes, who told you Brock Liu knew who started the fire?"

"Devon Liu's assistant."

"Brock told him? Why didn't he say anything before this?"

"Her name's Alyssa Bennet, and Brock mailed her a letter. It got here yesterday."

"So it was sent Wednesday or Thursday?"

"The postmark is from Kaunakakai on Thursday."

"Brock had been dead about two weeks already. You think he told someone to mail it if he didn't show up at a specified time? What does it say? Have you seen it?"

"I think so, I don't know, and no." Hamlin cleared his throat. "Let me tell you what I do know. It seems Brock and Alyssa had a thing going."

"Why am I not surprised?"

"Yeah, well, Alyssa will only tell me the part of the letter that mentions sorcery. It's apparently like the stuff you saw at Lambert Poele's."

"So who's the sorcerer?"

"Don't know yet. She didn't have the letter when we met with Liu yesterday because she didn't want him to know about it until we have more information. We're meeting in an hour, and I told her to bring the letter, or at least the pertinent pages."

"Aunt Maile got some information that the fire sorcerer's name is Kekapu."

"Sounds familiar."

"It's Makani's last name."

There was a stunned silence on the line. "Holy shit."

"My reaction, too. See if that corresponds to Alyssa's information."

"Makani would have only been, what, sixteen, seventeen?"

"That's what I figure."

"I wonder if the sorcerer has to be on the site to start a fire."

"I already asked Aunt Maile about that, and she doesn't think so. It's done by chanting, perhaps over a period of time, and the chanter may need a possession or part of the intended victim."

"You mean like hair or fingernails? Storm, I just don't buy this whole premise. Alika Liu died of smoke inhalation. He got trapped and overwhelmed by the fire."

"I'm just repeating what I've heard, and the part that matters to me is that someone is still willing to commit murder to keep anyone from finding out who lit the fire or why. You can take or leave the sorcery aspects, except as possible clues to help you answer the who and why." She thought for a moment. "We know the police already looked into arson. Have you seen any of those reports?"

"Devon Liu got all the evidence collected back then, which is pretty skinny. No one knows how it got started, though the inspector believed it began in the living room, where the drapes caught first and spread across the ceiling. There were no apparent signs of accelerants or faulty wiring. The house was frame and about thirty years old, so the wood would have been dry and flammable. That's part of the reason Poele was never indicted. No evidence."

Storm heard the question in his voice. "What are you thinking?"

"I wondered if you could ask the local guys what they saw and if they conducted interviews. You know, what they didn't write in the reports. That guy Niwa might talk to you."

"He's in the hospital, and it's serious."

"Damn. What happened to him?"

"A bleeding ulcer."

"Don't tell me that's caused by sorcery."

Hamlin was joking, but the comment made Storm think twice.

"I doubt it," she said.

A long moment passed before Hamlin spoke. "Storm, you don't want to raise people's suspicions. Just talk to the cops. Don't go to anyone else. Please?"

"Okay," Storm said. It was good advice. As it was, he'd have a fit if he knew she'd gone back to Poele's. That outing could stay a secret until this was over. "Aunt Maile and Uncle Keone are with me, remember?"

"Make sure Aunt Maile stays close by. Keone and you are cut from the same cloth."

Storm chuckled. "I'll tell him."

This time, Hamlin laughed. "He'll be flattered."

"Oh, sure."

Storm was still grinning as she searched for the number to Moloka'i Hospital on her call log. "Do you know if Sergeant David Niwa is up yet?"

"I'll connect you to the nursing station," the operator said.

The nurse who answered was friendly and informative. "He's not in his room now. Could I take a message?"

"I'll call back, thanks." Storm hung up and called Iinformation for the police station. She asked for Detective Steve Nishijima.

"Nishijima here," he answered.

Storm explained that she was a friend of Tanner's, and that she was concerned about Luke. "My mother died when I was about the same age," she said. "Plus, I heard he was diabetic."

"We had a call from a woman last night who picked up the boy and drove him to Halawa Bay to meet his father."

"Do you know how to get hold of Tanner? I'd like to make sure Luke got there."

"He didn't give you a number?"

"Only to Hawai'i EcoTours, but I haven't been able to catch him." It was likely Connor didn't pass along her message. She decided right then to ask Uncle Keone to stop at the Hawai'i EcoTours office on their drive to Halawa Bay.

"That's our phone contact, too."

"Do you know where his cabin is located?"

There was a pause on the line, and Nishijima's tone was cooler when he answered. "Not exactly."

And Storm knew she'd reached the end of that line of questioning, at least until she met him face to face. Maybe she should have started with questions about the fire, but she didn't think he'd tell an unknown person about a cold case from ten years ago. No, she was going to have to try and talk to Niwa in person.

She went back into the restaurant and found Aunt Maile drinking her coffee and reading the paper alone.

"Where's Uncle Keone?" Storm asked.

"He saw Dusty walk by, probably getting a cup of coffee, and he went out to talk to him about using a horse trailer for the ride."

By the time the waitress had set down the plates, Uncle Keone had returned, and he looked disgruntled. "He acted sort of secretive. After all these years, Dusty could at least tell me if he's got a date." Keone doctored the levels of cream and sugar in his replenished coffee mug and took a sip. "Then he told me Makani would try to hook us up with a trailer. Like he wasn't sure."

"Maybe he's getting more discreet with age," Aunt Maile said.

Keone looked at her dubiously and bit into a piece of toast. "I know he's got a horse trailer. I've used it before, and I've loaned him mine four or five times."

"Maybe it's with Makani," Storm said.

"Yeah, maybe," Keone said again, but he didn't sound happy. His irritation didn't affect his appetite, though, and a smile spread across his face when he bit into his omelet.

Chapter Thirty-three

Lambert Poele stood inside the industrial-sized refrigerator in his barn and scrutinized the label on one of the cartons stacked against the wall. He shoved his reading glasses up his nose and handed the box to Dusty Rodriguez.

"Jesus, these are heavy. How many are there?" Dusty asked.

"Twenty-eight all together. Orders are good. I may have to get some more goats."

He picked up another, checked it off on a clipboard, and handed it to Skelly Richards. All three men were sweating.

Skelly grunted with the weight Poele deposited in his arms. "I thought you had new goats."

Poele peered at him over the reading glasses. "They're three months old, and two are males. I'm glad you run a tour business."

Skelly rolled his eyes. "I didn't have all the information."

Dusty laughed out loud and shifted the box in his arms.

Poele clapped Skelly, then Dusty, on the shoulders and grinned. "I appreciate the help." He bent to pick up his own carton.

"What are friends for?" Dusty said, and headed out the door. No one talked as they walked the ten yards or so to the horse trailer, which was backed as close as Dusty could safely get it. The barn sat on a rise and had a great view out to the ocean, but someone had placed a ring of big lava rocks around it.

"The fuck is with these rocks?" Skelly asked, and wiped his streaming face with the back of his hand. It left a dirty smudge.

"Safety." Poele's voice was short. "It's a Hawaiian thing."

Skelly just grunted.

Dusty situated his box in the front horse stall, then stacked Skelly's and Poele's boxes beside it, and the three men went back for the next load.

"Did you get your truck running yet?" Dusty asked Poele.

"It's sputtering along, but I wouldn't trust it with this load." He handed over two more boxes, and followed with a third. "I owe you guys."

"You need a new starter," Dusty said after the next trip. He held out his arms for the next carton. "Makani's good with engines. We'll help you install it."

"Where is he this morning?" Skelly asked. His face was red and he didn't look happy.

"Hey, Sunday's busy," Dusty said. "Someone's got to get the tourists saddled up, take care of the horses."

"Sunday's busy for everyone. I've got things to do, too." Skelly gave Poele a sidelong glance. "So, is he with us or not?"

Poele didn't acknowledge the look and both he and Dusty ignored the comment. Poele checked off three more boxes, handed one each to Dusty and Skelly, and led the group out to the truck.

Back at the barn, he consulted his clipboard. "Four more trips oughta do it." Poele put the board down and looked over the labels on the remaining cartons. When he handed a box to Skelly, he said, "The boy's young. Don't worry, he's with us."

"Yeah, how can you be sure?" Skelly asked.

"He is." Poele's eyes over his glasses were hard, and they flicked between Dusty, who scowled silently, and Skelly. "I meant it when I said I appreciate the help." His eyes settled on Skelly. "We thought you were with a tour group this weekend."

"That's what I meant about Sundays being busy for all of us. Business is good." Skelly took a box from him. "Connor's got the tour group this morning."

"No shit. You trust him with kids and all that gear?" Dusty asked.

"Of course," Skelly snapped, then seemed to reconsider his tone. "He's shaping up. He's off the drugs."

"For real?" Poele asked. "Where's Tanner?"

Skelly scratched at his arm. "He has to meet his son."

Poele grunted. Dusty went for appeasement. "That's great, man. And how's Tanner doing these days?"

"He's okay, but he and Luke are kind of broke up over Jenny's death," Skelly said.

"I thought Tanner hated her."

"Not hate. That's too strong a word," Skelly said. "They couldn't live together, that's for sure, but they agreed on their kid."

"How's the boy doing?" Poele asked. "Must be really hard on him. He's sick, isn't he?"

Skelly shrugged. "Diabetes, but he's good at taking his meds. Hey, how many more boxes you got there?"

The men finished the last load and Poele invited them in for a drink. He popped the top on a longneck and handed it to Dusty, who waved it off.

"It's not eight yet. I'll take some water, though."

Skelly took the beer. "I'm not proud."

"It's not pride, I've got to drive this load into town, then get back to the ranch." Dusty sounded a touch defensive.

"Hey, no problem." Poele handed him a glass of ice water. "I appreciate your dropping the load at the docks."

"Let's get that truck of yours fixed." Dusty downed his glass of water.

Skelly watched Poele dig through a line of beers to pull out a Coke. "You got more beer than food in there."

"That woman came over last night and brought half a case."

"Woman?" Skelly snorted. "You made a quick recovery."

"Huh?" Dusty lowered his glass.

Poele raised an eyebrow at Skelly. "It wasn't like that. She had some questions about Hawaiian history."

"Who did?" Skelly and Dusty asked together.

"The lawyer from Honolulu. She's half Hawaiian." He gestured toward the sitting room, where the three of them took seats. Right before he dropped into his chair, Poele caught sight of his sculpture and a shadow crossed over his face. "She thought

Maui was a hula dancer." His eyebrows met in a frown. "And it's all I've got left of Jenny."

"You're lucky Skelly got it back to you before the crime tape went up," Dusty said.

"Yeah, I guess." Poele looked at his friend. "How'd you do that?"

Skelly suddenly looked very sheepish.

"You never got it dropped off, did you?" Poele asked, but there was no anger in his voice.

"I forgot for a few days, then Connor borrowed my car."

Poele shook his head slowly. "Connor, again." He shrugged. "Well, none of us expected what happened." He looked around. "Did we?"

"Hell, no," Dusty said, and Skelly echoed his words.

"Like I thought," Poele said. "So now I've got to get it fixed."

"She used to send stuff to the Big Island for bronze casting." Skelly got up and went over to the piece. "How'd it break?"

"Dunno," Poele said. "I think I knocked it over the night I tripped over the lamp." He pointed at the misshapen, dented shade.

"You gotta ease off the beers, buddy," Skelly said.

"He's working on it." Dusty pointed to Poele's Coke and stood up to leave. "I'd better get your cheese to the docks."

"And watch out for Honolulu attorneys asking questions," Skelly added.

Dusty looked back. "Yeah, what did she want to know?"

"History, just history," Poele said.

All three men stood up and Poele walked with his friends to the door. When he closed it behind them, he wore a thoughtful expression.

◇◇◇

Luke found himself on clean white sheets under a warm blanket on the pull-out sofa in the living room. The shutters were closed, but sunlight streamed through the kitchen windows and spilled a warm glow through the house. He smelled coffee brewing, and knew his father was already up and making breakfast.

The last thing he remembered was Tanner bringing the glucose monitoring kit to him and watching him to make sure his blood sugar was in an acceptable range. He must have fallen asleep soon after, because he didn't even remember moving from the chair to the bed.

Luke stretched lazily, then sat up, his eyes wide open. Thursday night, after he'd called 911, Luke had run to his mom's room. Just inside the open door, he'd stopped to take in the unmade bed, the clothes she'd left strewn across it, a couple of pairs of shoes kicked in the direction of the closet, the scent of her soap and powder in the air. He knew what he was looking for, but the sensuous assault had stopped him as surely as a shove to the chest.

After a moment, he pushed on, nearly frantic with the knowledge that he'd failed to protect her. There was one thing he could still do, and that was to keep a promise he'd made.

For years, he'd known about his mother's secret hiding spot inside a big book she cherished on sculptor Louise Nevelson. He figured she knew he knew, though neither of them ever mentioned it. His parents' marriage license was in the book, too. When his father had first left, Luke would get it out and look at it, hoping that if he made wishes while he held it, they would hold more power.

The night she died, he left the marriage license behind, but he took the postcard with the Chicago postmark and put it inside the book he was reading for his English class. He was supposed to have read Chapters Ten and Eleven of *From the Mixed-up Files of Mrs. Basil E. Frankweiler* for Friday's class, but he'd never made it to school that day. It was a paperback, not much bigger than the card he'd stuck between its pages, and it was the only book he'd put in his backpack.

Last night, when his dad retrieved the blood monitoring kit, the card had crossed his mind, but he'd been too tired to do anything about it. But now he needed to check on the contents of his pack.

Luke stood up, noticed that his father had not only undressed him, but put him in too-big but clean pajamas.

Tanner peeked around the kitchen door. "How're you feeling?"

"Better. I'm starved."

"That's good, I'm cooking. Get dressed and come sit down."

"Dad, is my bag around here? I've got some stuff in it."

Tanner pointed at a chair in the living room. "Over there. I took your insulin out and put it in the fridge."

"Is the glucose kit in there?"

"Sure."

The first thing Luke did was to remove the kit and set it aside. When he heard his dad's steps go back to the kitchen, he withdrew the paperback novel. The postcard was still there.

Chapter Thirty-four

After breakfast, Storm went back to her room to change into the boots she'd deemed too dusty to wear to the dining room. She stuffed her mobile phone, a bottle of water, and a light jacket into her fanny pack. At the last moment, she crammed in an Almond Joy bar, too. Not that she'd need it after that big breakfast.

She bustled out the door and scanned the walkway. Aunt Maile and Uncle Keone weren't in sight yet, but Delia was, and she gave a wave.

"Any news on the boy?" Delia yelled from across the parking lot.

Storm walked over to her. "No, you heard anything?"

"No, but Connor's going to a camp down past Halawa today and said he'd keep an eye out for him."

Great, Luke would go tearing in the opposite direction again. Storm changed tactics. "Did you know Jenny Williams very well?"

Delia shrugged. "I hate to speak ill of the dead, but she wasn't all that friendly to me. Maybe it's cuz we both dated Dusty. People say she was a good artist. A good mother, too. It's sad."

"Poor Luke."

"Yeah. The last few years, she stopped making art, drank more, and seemed more and more unhappy."

"You ever see any of her work?"

Delia looked thoughtful. "Sure, you can see it here and there. She had a show about ten years ago and sold some, plus I heard she gave some to friends."

"You know anybody who has any of it?"

"The bank has a humpback whale and her calf. It's really big. I love that piece." Delia thought a bit more. "Lambert Poele has one, too. I saw it in the back of Connor's car. He was supposed to drop it off at Jenny's because something broke off it."

"When was this?"

"Couple weeks ago. I mean, I don't know when she gave it to him—that's when it was in the car."

"I see," Storm said, then added, just in case Delia wondered why she was asking, "I was interested in picking up a piece myself."

"Good luck," Delia said with a laugh. "Doesn't it get real expensive when the artist dies?"

"Yeah, maybe. I'll let you know," Storm said, and headed up the road toward the barn.

She watched the puffs of dust her feet sent up on the crushed coral as her mind turned over Delia's information. How many broken sculptures could there be on this island, anyway? And was it in Connor's or Skelly's hands when Brock disappeared? From their kayaking establishment, no less. Which was a little too convenient in Storm's view, though she'd often heard her police friends talk about the stupidity of criminals. Problem was, Skelly Richards didn't sound stupid. He'd overcome personal obstacles and built a thriving business in a place where financial success was difficult to achieve.

She hadn't met the man yet, but it was time. From her short observation, he appeared to be the person who'd best emerged from the ashes of a decade-old fire and death. He just didn't seem like the kind of guy who would leave an incriminating weapon in the trunk of his car. Question was, was Skelly the kind of man who bashed in another guy's head? Or a woman's head, for that matter? Storm couldn't answer those questions. Not yet, anyway.

When she got to the barn, Makani and a young woman were tying horses along the paddock rail and laying out baskets of grooming tools. They didn't look as if they'd been told that Keone, Maile, and she wanted to trailer three horses.

"Hi there," Storm said, and Makani looked up with a cheerful smile. "Any chance we could saddle three horses for a ride?"

"Uh, I guess." Storm's hunch was right. Makani hadn't been warned of their plans. "Your aunt and uncle going, too?"

"Yes, but we were wondering if you might let us trailer them to state land around Halawa Bay."

Now Makani looked outright startled. "It's Dusty's day off and I have to stay here for other guests."

"We can take them alone. Uncle Keone talked to Dusty about it this morning."

"He did? But Dusty's using his trailer today."

"I think he mentioned that, and he thought you might have one here we could use."

Makani laid a curry comb in a basket of grooming tools. "I guess you could use mine. I mean, we wouldn't do it for anyone, in fact almost no one. But your uncle just bought some brood mares for Parker Ranch, and he's interested in a couple of our ropers."

"He's on the way up from the Lodge. You could talk to him about it," Storm said. She walked over to the horse he was working on. The woman she'd seen earlier had disappeared into one of the stalls, where Storm could hear the scrape of a shovel or pitchfork. "I'll help you groom."

"I'm not supposed to let guests—"

"I know, but I'm not a regular guest and you look like you could use a hand." Storm picked up a hoof pick and approached the first horse in the line of animals Makani had tied to the paddock rail.

"Thanks, we're short handed. A few of our non-rental horses need exercise, too. When would you be back?"

"We won't get there until ten or eleven. Maybe around six, or about dusk?"

"I guess that'll work. I'll give you my mobile number in case you have any trouble." He paused. "Except cell phones don't work down there."

"I noticed that already." Storm spoke into the horse's left forefoot, where she dug out the stable debris. The ranch took good care of their horses; they were newly shod, and she could tell they were brushed and their hooves were cleaned often. She liked Makani and Dusty for that fact, and she moved easily from the horse's front feet to its rear ones. Because the job was done frequently, it didn't take as long as it might have, and before long she reached for a curry comb.

When she did, she found Makani watching her. "You know your way around the stable," he said. "I knew you rode well, but I wasn't sure about the dirty work."

"It's all part of having horses, and I enjoy this part, too."

He was quiet a minute, and carefully straightened a twist in his horse's halter. "Do you know Kathy Matayoshi?"

"Sure, we surf together. I haven't seen her for a month or so."

A slow flush spread over his cheeks. "I'm going to see her next weekend. She told me you guys were friends."

"You're dating?"

His face reddened further and he nodded. "She was a guest at the Ranch about a year ago and we've been trying to see each other every few weeks. She's going to teach me to surf. There aren't as many good breaks here as on O'ahu. I'm *hōlona*, a real beginner."

"Awesome. Can I come, too?"

Makani grinned at her. "Kathy was going to give you a call. Especially since I told her I'd met you."

"I'll check the surf reports when I get back. That'll be fun." She worked on a knot in the horse's tail and after a few minutes, she asked, "Say, where's Dusty this morning? We saw him briefly, but he didn't have time to join us for breakfast."

"He's running errands, mostly for Lambert Poele. His truck is on the fritz—still. Hand me that sponge, will ya?"

Storm got a sponge from the basket and held it out to him. Makani reached over the appaloosa he was grooming, which Storm recognized as the one she'd admired before. "Is that Moonlight?"

"Yup, he's one of the ropers your uncle likes." Makani strained to grab the sponge and a dark tattoo peeked from the sleeve of his white T-shirt. It looked a lot like Poele's, plus she could see a similar halo of redness around the dark pattern.

"That a new tattoo?" she asked.

"Yeah." Makani pulled his sleeve down. "Some friends talked me into it." He shrugged and ducked behind Moonlight. Storm worked on her horse quietly for a moment and pondered Makani's reaction. He didn't want to talk about it, which corresponded to Poele's reaction, though at least Poele had told her about the oath. She found it interesting that Makani was in on it. Storm would have given odds Dusty had a new tattoo, too.

"Could we take Moonlight today?" Storm asked.

Makani frowned. "He shies at stuff. Dusty thinks he needs more ring work."

"Okay. He's a beautiful horse, isn't he?"

"Yeah, I kinda hate to see him go." Makani rubbed Moonlight's ears, and the horse turned to rub his head on the young man's shirtfront.

"I can ask Uncle Keone to leave him with you for a while," Storm said.

Makani shrugged, but he couldn't hide the happy expression creeping across his face. "I'd like to work with him a bit longer."

"I'll ask him." Storm picked up the basket and walked to the next horse in line, a big roan. In the distance, she saw two figures walking along the coral road. Keone and Maile would arrive momentarily.

"Makani, does that tattoo have anything to do with the old protest group?"

Makani dropped the sponge, which splattered dust on Moonlight. The horse then shifted his weight, and placed a forefoot squarely on the sponge, which flattened and oozed soapy water.

"Now how did he know to do that?" Storm asked. She eyed the appaloosa, who seemed to be watching for a reaction from Makani. She stepped next to Moonlight and leaned her weight into his shoulder. Moonlight grunted, stepped off the sponge, and bent his head to snuffle Makani's hair when he picked it up. "This horse is teasing you."

"He does that," Makani mumbled, and tossed the dirty sponge into a bucket of water.

"My aunt and uncle are walking down the drive. What about the protest group, Makani?"

"It might have something to do with that." He looked around. "You can't tell anyone I told you about this."

"Don't worry, I won't."

Makani looked tormented. "Look, Storm, no one knows what happened that night. I swear. Dusty thinks Poele started the fire, but he'd turn himself in before he'd tell anyone." He shook his head. "But I heard Poele tell Skelly he'd take the rap before he'd say a word about Connor. Skelly thanked him over and over. Both of them thought Connor started the fire, see? And they didn't know I was listening, either."

"What about Alika? Anyone accuse him of starting it and underestimating how fast it would spread?"

Makani wouldn't meet her eyes. "I don't know."

"What was he really like, Makani? Was he as big an ass as Brock?"

Makani's face darkened. "Alika made Brock look nice. Except he was better looking. I think he got Tia pregnant on purpose. You should have heard him mock Dusty for trying to protect her."

"On purpose? Like she didn't consent—"

Makani shook his head violently. "I don't know for sure. Tia didn't tell anyone until she was about four months pregnant, and Dusty went crazy when he found out."

"Because she got pregnant?"

Makani's voice tightened. "He blamed her." Makani rested his head against Moonlight's shoulder, and the rest of his words came out muffled. "Then he told her to get an abortion."

"Oh, no," Storm said softly. "Did she ever tell him she was raped?"

"She tried."

Neither said anything for a long moment. Makani was the first to break the silence and his voice was low when he spoke. "The fire was bad. Tanner got worse after that night. He was always prone to ups and downs, but man, he really flipped out after the fire."

"You think he lit the fire and felt guilty?"

"No one ever talked about Tanner that way, but I don't know. He might have known about the rape." Makani swallowed hard. "He and Tia were friends. But it was Skelly, Connor, and Poele people suspected." He brushed the horse slowly and kept his head turned away from her.

"What did you think?"

Makani didn't say anything for a few moments. Keone's and Maile's footsteps approached, crunching in the gravel. Keone yelled a greeting and Storm waved over the back of her horse, then whispered to Makani, "Well?"

"I think Tanner might have known there would be a fire. It made him hyper, a little crazier." Though Makani rushed his words, Storm detected sadness in them.

"Then what happened?"

"Alika used to tease him, make fun of his neatness fetish. Tanner walks into a room and rearranges things. Maybe it's kind of funny, but no one except Alika would dare mock Tanner. It pissed Skelly off big time."

"How did Tanner react?"

Now Makani met her eyes, and his held puzzlement. "He laughed, but it was like he was laughing at himself. One time Tanner got this sad laugh after Alika teased him. Skelly went crazy. He jumped on Alika and started punching him. We had to pull him off. And what I remember was, there's Alika's nose streaming blood, but he just kept laughing. Like Skelly didn't matter. Tanner, neither."

"And what about Tia? What happened after Dusty found out she was pregnant?"

"She and Dusty were never the same. She finally moved in with Poele."

Chapter Thirty-five

Lambert Poele watched Dusty's truck bump down the dirt road. Skelly's overloaded Jeep Cherokee followed behind. They would caravan as far as the docks, where Dusty planned to drop the cartons of cheese and Skelly would go on to his office.

Skelly's business was doing great. The whole EcoTour idea was hot all over the country. Poele followed this kind of thing; it was how he got the idea to make and sell goat cheese. His friends might not know it, but Poele read at least three papers. He even got the Sunday *New York Times*. Sometimes it got to him on Monday, but he didn't care. He savored it all week.

Once the two vehicles were out of sight, Poele exited his house and strolled across his property, kicking a rock before him. He ignored the puffs of dust that arose. The goats had been penned during the cheese loading, or they'd have been underfoot. A dozen goats running around, butting and sniffing at Dusty and Skelly? No, that would not have been appreciated. Now he could let them out of the little paddock in the shade behind the barn. He liked them free to roam; their amusing, individual personalities kept him company. Jenny had teased him about how they were his best friends. She wanted him to get the truck fixed, too, he thought, and smiled sadly. She finally had wanted him to come to her house.

He'd let Storm think that Jenny had had an affair with Brock, but that wasn't exactly true. From what Poele could tell, Jenny had held him off. Yet Brock respected her. Poele had heard it in the man's voice, and marveled. It was the only thing he could find to admire in the slimy, promiscuous, ass-kissing little creep.

Brock had tried to suck up to Poele at first, by offering to loan him that big SUV and help with the truck repairs, but Poele saw through that ruse. It was obvious Brock wanted Poele's land, a measly four point eight acres, almost too dry for cattle. Goats weren't quite as picky. Prime view, though, which was why the Liu family wanted it. They'd irrigate, and develop the resort plan that was merely delayed by Alika's death ten years ago.

Poele hadn't trusted any member of the Liu family for a long time. He'd been the one to discover Alika's treachery, though none of the others wanted to believe him at first. It happened because Alika kept him waiting, as usual. Alika had been playing one of his little power games, keeping Poele waiting outside while Alika showered or something, not that Alika would ask any of the group in for a drink, even water. So when Poele heard Devon Liu's voice come tinnily over Alika's answering machine, he'd listened just for something to do.

"We got the results to the Hakina/Kaheu survey. Call me, son, I want a report."

The old man's voice had carried, and Poele, who heard every word, knew right away Alika was scouting real estate for his father's developments. Hakina/Kaheu was the land adjacent to the Ranch, the very development the group was protesting. Alika Liu was a fucking traitor.

Unlike Alika, Brock had no pretenses about his aim to enlarge the family empire. But Poele could only take so much, and when he'd reached his limit and threatened to pound Brock's sorry ass into the ground, then burn him at the stake—maybe he shouldn't have made that fire reference—Liu had sneered that nothing better happen to him because Jenny Williams had proof, and he could trust her.

Poele figured Brock was making a reference to the fire, and he'd already walked those hot coals once in his life. The police had made it very clear they thought he was responsible for the fire. All they needed was more evidence against him, and the idea that Brock might have something made Poele skittish.

Meanwhile, Jenny didn't admire Brock, but she didn't hate him, either. Most annoying to Poele was that she wouldn't tell Poele what Brock's "proof" was. She told him she didn't know yet herself, because it was sealed up. But then she said he didn't have anything to be worried about unless he lost his cool.

Which pissed Poele off, but Jenny knew how to calm him. She had a very special way of soothing Poele's feelings. Kind of wrapped herself around him, with every means she could.

Poele pulled open the wide gate of the paddock and let the goats mill around him, looking for pats and treats. He had grass pellets and pretzels in his pockets, and they worked their velvet noses into his hands until he smiled. The smile faded when he recalled how he and Jenny had hidden her car in this same paddock one night. At that point, she didn't want gossip about their relationship spreading like a brush fire. So they'd sat out here under the stars, talking and making love under the full moon until they couldn't stand the hard ground any longer and had gone to his bed.

He'd fallen into a sound sleep, and thought she had, too. Still, she left around four in the morning because she wanted to be home when Luke got up for school. She was discreet that way. It made Poele feel excluded, but she was a very good mother to the boy. If only she'd stayed away from Brock, he thought, and his throat tightened.

Poele wandered back to his house with a few goats still nuzzling at him, though he paid no attention by this time. Skelly was right about one thing; he was drinking too much. He just didn't want to think about some of the events of the past week, but it wasn't going to get any better until he picked off the scab and let the pus out.

The night Jenny stayed was the night he tripped over the lamp. He'd gone to the kitchen to get her some ice water and himself a beer, and it seemed like the lamp was sitting farther out from his chair than usual. He'd cracked his toe, sworn, and turned on the hall light to take a look at what he'd crashed into. Then he'd merely sworn again and set the lamp upright to get it out of the way and get back to Jenny.

Later that morning, after he'd risen early and milked the goats, he'd hitched into town for some groceries. It had been a busy day, and he'd had a few beers for lunch while he was in Kaunakakai.

But reality wouldn't leave him alone, would it? He hadn't moved that lamp. Hell, he never moved anything around here. For years, he hadn't examined his life or anyone else's. He barely talked to people, except to restaurants who wanted his cheese and the occasional woman who took him on as a social rehabilitation project. He hadn't even asked for Jenny, but the universe kept tapping him on the shoulder.

Poele stumbled over a tuft of grass the goats had left. Jenny's death was the tap on the shoulder he couldn't ignore. He'd lost, again, what he should have held dear.

This persistent obstinacy of his undermined his life. He'd managed not to see the sculpture until he'd plopped into his reading chair with a couple beers in hand and a few more nearby on ice. And there was Maui, on his side and without his rope. His big, hammer-like hands were out-flung in an ambiguous gesture, while his muscular legs flexed with effort. Storm Kayama was right. He looked like a hula dancer. Not that hula was bad, it just wasn't what Jenny had intended. When he'd called Jenny to tell her, she'd laughed before saying she'd fix it.

A few days later, Skelly dropped by and offered to take it to her. He was on his way to Jenny's to pick up some medicine for Luke. Tanner wanted him to keep an extra supply at the office. Poele had the feeling Skelly hoped he might butter her up with the sculpture errand so she'd be more apt to give in to Tanner's request for insulin.

Poele opened his front door slowly and stood inside while his eyes adjusted to the dim light. Then he shook his head sadly, dug through a kitchen drawer for a tattered address book, and dialed a phone number.

◇◇◇

Makani's truck was nicer than Dusty's. It was a much newer model, with no rust holes and a big diesel engine that towed the three-horse trailer with steady power. Uncle Keone took the wheel, with Aunt Maile in the middle of the wide bench seat, and Storm by the window.

"Do you mind if we go by the grocery and hospital?" Storm asked.

"Is Detective Niwa still there?" Aunt Maile asked.

"Yes, he was getting tests when I called this morning."

"Anyplace else you want to go before we head to the bay?" asked Uncle Keone.

Storm grinned. She wasn't getting anything by these two. "Skelly Richards' business. It's on the way, and it'll take me five minutes."

Storm put together a fruit basket at the market, then had her aunt and uncle drop her at the hospital while they went to get gas for the truck. The receptionist at the information desk gave Storm directions to Niwa's room.

He was alone, sitting up with his glasses perched on his nose, and it took him a second or two to register that someone had walked into the room. He was reading Jan Burke's *Kidnapped*.

Storm offered the basket. "I thought chocolate might be frowned on."

"Hey, thanks. You musta read my doctor's mind." Niwa put a finger in the book to hold his place. "What are you up to?"

"I got a call last night from Ian Hamlin, who told me Devon Liu's assistant got a letter from Brock Liu. It's postmarked last Thursday. We think Jenny Williams mailed it."

"No kidding." Niwa sat up straighter. "Jesus, I wonder if someone killed her because he knew she had it. Or had information, anyway. What did it say?"

"Hamlin's got a meeting with the assistant today, but I'm sure it's about the fire on the Ranch."

Niwa raised one eyebrow. "Interesting. You don't look surprised, either."

"It all seems to go back to the fire, or Alika Liu's death."

"I've been seeing the same trend." Niwa reached out for the phone by his bed. "You mind sharing this news with my partner?"

"Not at all, but my aunt and uncle are waiting for me in the parking lot. We're going riding down at Halawa Bay."

He frowned at her. "Does this have anything to do with Tanner's cabin?"

"I wouldn't mind seeing if Luke is safe."

"Do you know where the cabin is?"

"Not really. Do you?"

Niwa looked at her over his glasses. "Not exactly. And the only reason I'm telling you any of this is because Tanner called you to look after his boy." He pushed a button on his bed that made him sit up straighter. "You have to go inland about a mile from the bay, then take a right when you get to a fork in the path. Problem is, I'm sure the trail will change again, and I don't know where. Tanner can get there from either Keawenui or Halawa Bay, so I'd go east if I were you. Some of this is guessing on my part, and if you get to the cliffs on the north shore, you've gone too far."

"I've got a question about the fire, too," Storm said. "Did you ever hear anything about a kahuna kuni, a person who starts a fire by sorcery?" But she could tell before the last words were out of her mouth that she didn't need to explain the term to him.

"Tell you what," he said, and shifted his weight in the bed. "I'll tell you that when I hear who's mentioned in Jenny's letter."

Storm glared at him for a moment, dug her mobile phone out of her fanny pack, and dialed Hamlin. He didn't answer, which disappointed but didn't surprise her, and she left a message for him to call both her mobile phone and Detective Niwa at the hospital.

"C'mon, you'll know soon," Storm pleaded.

Niwa shook his head. "It's a murder investigation. And I don't want you going near these people."

"I'm already near them. It's a small island." She paused. "I heard the weapon that killed Jenny Williams corresponds to the one that killed Brock Liu. Can you tell me if that's true?"

"Not going there." The pupils of Niwa's eyes contracted and bored into Storm's. "And neither are you. The less you know, the better off you'll be."

"Hah." Storm didn't believe that for a minute. "You know any good tattoo artists?"

Now Niwa's eyes popped wide. "You getting a tattoo?"

"I'm thinking about a souvenir." For a short moment, she contemplated telling him that she already had one. There was a little *pua'a*, her *'aumakua* and guardian animal spirit, on her left cheek. The one her bikini barely covered. "It's the style," she said instead.

"You kids. You don't think they're going to fade and sag, but it's nature's way. Just wait." He glowered at her. "Try Body, Ink. They say he's the best."

"Where's his shop?"

"I'm gonna hate myself for this. It's a block from Kanemitu's Bakery."

Storm moved toward the door. "You'll probably hear from Hamlin before I do. Get better soon."

"Thanks for the fruit," Niwa said grumpily. He picked up his book and flipped through for the page he'd lost.

Aunt Maile and Uncle Keone were indeed in the parking lot. Somewhere they'd found a Honolulu paper and were sharing it in the cab of the truck.

"Sorry to keep you waiting," Storm said as she climbed in.

"Only five minutes, no problem," Keone said. "On to the Hawai'i EcoTours office?"

"I thought of something else," Storm said, which made both Keone and Maile turn their heads in tandem.

"Yes?" Uncle Keone said.

"A couple blocks from here should be a tattoo parlor. I wondered if we could stop for just a minute."

"It takes longer than a minute," Aunt Maile said. "And one is enough."

"I'm not getting another tattoo. Not today, anyway. I've got a quick question."

Body, Ink turned out to be right up the street, and Storm hopped out of the truck while Keone pulled to the curb. The little store was dark, though, and a sign on the door said CLOSED.

It was nine o'clock on a Sunday morning. Not surprising that it wasn't open, Storm thought, but she desperately wanted to ask the owner if Makani, Poele, and Dusty, if she wasn't mistaken, had gotten their tattoos here. Maybe the artist would tell her whose idea it was, or who made the first appointment. She didn't have any paper in her fanny pack, but she found a pen and wrote the phone number posted on the door across the back of her hand.

◇◇◇

Jerry Sanchez wasn't home, and Poele didn't want to leave a message. He thought for a moment, then dialed the police station. Jerry picked up.

"I told you not to call me here," Jerry whispered.

"Talk normal. You're going to attract attention."

"Hello, Maui Police Department, Island of Moloka'i," Jerry intoned.

"Cut the crap, Jerry. I have one quick question, you answer yes or no."

"If you weren't my cousin, I wouldn't do this," Jerry whispered again.

Poele paused. "Not even because I'm a nice guy?"

Jerry made a gagging noise. "Get to the point, Lambert."

"Now it's going to be two questions."

"Shit."

"Have the police identified the weapon that killed Jenny Williams?"

"No."

"Have they found parts of it in her skull?"

"Yes." Jerry spoke very quietly and drew the word out.

Poele waited.

"How'd you—"

"It's not shaped like an ordinary tool, is it?"

"That's three. Where'd you get this information?"

"Tell Aunty Bea I'm going to miss dinner Friday night. I gotta get my truck fixed." Poele hung up.

Chapter Thirty-six

"Ready?" asked Keone, who was watching out the window of the truck.

"Let's roll," Storm said. "I'm itching to ride."

A horse nickered in response and Keone grinned. "You get one more stop."

It was nearly ten when they got to the cut-off past Kamalo, and both Aunt Maile and Uncle Keone remarked what a lovely site the Richards brothers had chosen for their business. A van with the Hawai'i EcoTours logo painted on the side was parked outside the converted house. Its doors stood open as if someone were busy loading it.

"I won't be long," Storm promised.

"It's shady, there's a breeze, and we've got the Sunday paper," Aunt Maile said.

Skelly Richards swiveled his office chair toward the screened front door before Storm had a chance to knock. He was big, over six feet tall, and had the body of an aging linebacker. His mat of dark, curly hair made him loom even larger. Dark glasses perched on top of his head, nestled in the thick hair.

"Finally, the great Storm Kayama," he said with a sardonic smile.

"Uh oh," Storm said, and opened the door. She stuck out her hand. "Which greatness am I known for this time? Hope it's my great jokes, not my great forgetfulness or some other mistake."

Skelly shook her hand and raised an eyebrow. "Tanner speaks highly of you."

"It's been a while, but he helped me a lot in our high school days."

"He's a brilliant man." He pointed at a chair. "Have a seat."

Storm perched on the edge of the chair. "I always thought so, too."

"What brings you out this direction? You interested in a tour?" Skelly let his eyes move around her face, but avoided the full body scan his brother had given her. Storm had the feeling he'd done it, but was slicker than Connor. He'd most likely given her the up and down before she got to the front door.

"I wondered if you knew where Tanner was."

"It's been a real bad weekend for him. He took my people out Saturday morning, but we made sure we relieved him yesterday afternoon. I presume he's at his cabin."

"Is Connor with your tourists?"

Skelly's eyes flared. "That's right, you met my brother. Yeah, he's had a rough time, too, but he's coming around." He dropped the pretense of the smile. "I'm one of those guys who believe in second chances, you know? People screw up, they shouldn't have their lives ruined." His hands formed fists as he spoke these words.

"We all screw up, don't we?" Storm said, trying to quell what looked like a brewing storm. "Do you know how to get to Tanner's cabin? I'd like to see him, and check on the boy."

Skelly frowned. "Connor and I helped him get the generator back there, but we swore not to tell anyone." His dark eyes met Storm's. "Tanner does some special work at his place. He's doing research for a big pharmaceutical company, and he doesn't want anyone going out there, messing with his equipment."

When Tanner had called her at the office last week, he'd told her he had inquiries from natural supplement manufacturers for his seaweed extracts. Skelly was exaggerating, but probably out of pride for his friend. Storm decided she could be charitable about that point.

"You may know he called me to look after Luke. That's all I'm going to do."

"Luke should be with him by now. My brother saw him hitchhiking yesterday."

"But he had a long walk after he reached the bay. Do we know if he made it?"

"Tanner would have radioed if he hadn't. We would have gone in to help."

"He has a two-way?"

"Sure, we use 'em all the time. You have to be ready to get a visitor out of the wilderness quickly. For example, if an allergic person got a bee sting."

Or if you wanted to track someone who threatened you or your friends, Storm thought. "I see what you mean."

Skelly was smart, he planned ahead, and he was not going to reveal how to get to Tanner's cabin. Storm changed tactics. "I'm also looking into the death of Brock Liu for his father."

"Yeah, I heard the son-of-a-bitch wants to sue me." Skelly's mouth twisted into a bitter sneer.

"Hey, I'm just doing my job." Storm held up a hand. "Being straight will help your position."

"It wasn't an accident, and it didn't happen because of our negligence." Skelly bit off his words, angry but in control.

Storm kept her voice low and calm. "I agree, but I need to collect information about what did occur. Otherwise, you *could* get blamed. He apparently rented one of your kayaks."

"He did, and he was supposed to pick it up here. Wanted to check some family land near Kalaeloa Lighthouse." Skelly put extra emphasis on the words *family land*. "I waited around most of the morning, but he never showed." He slapped the desk to emphasize his frustration. "That guy's a pain in the ass. Or he was. Sorry if I seem harsh, but it's the truth. Ask anyone."

"That helps," Storm said. "I can take that back to the lawyer representing Devon Liu."

"That's not you?" Skelly flexed his hands and leaned back in his chair.

"No, I told you. I'm not legal counsel for anyone in this case. I'm an independent consultant, I'd guess you'd say."

"An investigator?"

"Not even that," said Storm.

"Glad to hear it," Skelly said, and gave her what looked like the first genuine smile of the interview.

"I've got a couple of questions to satisfy my own curiosity. I've known and admired both Tanner and Dusty since my teens. I wasn't having an easy time of it back then, either, so these guys were important to me."

Skelly grinned at this news, and Storm took a deep breath. "Did Tanner get worse after the fire?"

Skelly turned his chair to look out the window toward the ocean, and Storm could see the muscles bunching along his jaw line. She poised herself to dash for the door when he exhaled explosively, then dropped his head into his hands. "Yeah," he said in a muffled voice.

"You have any idea why?" Storm's voice was gentle.

"Those were bad times." Skelly raised his head and Storm could see that his eyes were red, though there was no evidence of tears, and his face was a mask of control. She waited.

"No one was supposed to get hurt in that fire. We thought Alika was a prick—some of us more than others—but you've got to believe me." His head turned to her and she was reminded of a bull, docile for the moment but unpredictable.

"What happened?"

He narrowed his eyes at her. "It's over. We've all paid, especially Tanner."

"I'm not blaming." Storm leaned toward him. "But I don't think it's over. Do you?"

"You mean Tanner's mental health?"

"That's one way. How about Connor?"

"My brother is a fuckup, but he's a follower. And he's finally getting his act together." His eyes flashed a warning.

"I'm glad to hear it," Storm said. "You happen to know if he passed my message to call along to Tanner? I asked him when I dropped by yesterday."

Skelly's shoulders dropped a notch. "How 'bout I radio him later?"

"That's okay. He may have told him. I heard Tanner has a hard time calling people."

"That's true." Skelly looked at his knuckles, and Storm noticed for the first time that some of them were swollen, and the back of his right hand had a long scratch. He looked up at Storm and held her gaze. "Some of us have had our problems, like I said. It's better if the outside world lets us work them out."

"The world's a small place these days."

"In case you haven't noticed, since you're from Honolulu, it's different here." A tiny muscle twitched under his left eye, though his face was impassive. "A few of us have been dogged by suspicion, even here, for ten years. Every now and then someone has the courage to ask a question about the past, but usually not. And that's worse, because they don't meet my eye, and then they talk behind my back." He clenched his fists. "And I'm not alone."

"I'm sorry." She didn't have to remind him that when she said it wasn't over, that's what she meant. Others lived with it, too, and at what cost? It was time for her to go.

"Hey, thanks for your time." She held out her hand. "Good luck."

Skelly took her hand briefly and let it drop. Storm could feel his eyes on her as she left. The screen door made a sighing noise when its springs eased it closed.

Skelly sat without moving until the truck and horse trailer made its careful U-turn in his wide lot and turned onto the highway. Then he picked up the phone and hit speed-dial.

"She's leaving here now." He listened to the reply.

Chapter Thirty-seven

Storm was quiet on the drive to Halawa Bay. She could tell that Aunt Maile and Uncle Keone noticed her reticence, but she didn't want to explain her thoughts right then, and they apparently understood. Though her eyes flicked past the pristine, aquamarine shoreline, she didn't see the white sand beaches and black lava rock, often next to each other in extraordinary contrast. At any other time, she'd have been fascinated at another chance to examine the calm, clear, manmade coves of igneous rock, fishponds in the ancient Hawaiian tradition. Moloka'i was the only place where large fishponds, constructed as they were a thousand years ago, dotted twenty-some miles of prime coastal real estate. On most of the world's inhabited islands, oceanfront land was too expensive to lie open and unencumbered. This was what Moloka'i people wanted so desperately to preserve, Storm thought. These open expanses of fine white sand and sparkling reef, uneroded by private sea walls, and accessible to whoever ambled along to relax, hunt shells, or cast a fishing line. No one would think to come up and say, "Move along, you can't do this. It's private property." This was what Poele and his friends fought for.

An hour passed before Aunt Maile said, "Maybe it would help to think out loud."

"I'm spinning my wheels."

"It has to do with the fire sorcerer?" Uncle Keone asked.

"Maybe." Storm frowned. "It all goes back to the fire, whether it was started by a sorcerer or not."

"If you knew who started it, would you know who killed Brock Liu and Jenny Williams?" he asked. "And is it the same person?"

"It would help. From the information Hamlin got from the ME, their deaths appear to have been caused by the same weapon. And I think it's Poele's sculpture." She thought for a moment. "But I don't know if the killer is the same person who started the fire."

"The sculpture was in Poele's hands, right?" Uncle Keone asked.

"Not necessarily." Storm explained how Skelly and Connor had possession of the sculpture, too.

"Maybe it broke when he clobbered Brock Liu," Uncle Keone said. "Then he gave it to the Richards brothers for an alibi."

"Then why did one of the Richards brothers, or both of them, for that matter, kill Jenny Williams?" Storm said, though as she said the words, she recalled the letter Jenny mailed to Alyssa Bennet. She told her aunt and uncle about it, which plunged the trio into minutes of quiet thought.

Aunt Maile broke the silence. "It could be any of the three."

"If Poele killed Liu, would he use a gift from his lover? Which could be easily traced to him? The guy sits alone up there and reads. He's not stupid," Storm said.

"Let's go back to whoever started the fire," Aunt Maile said.

"The fire sorcerer connection is tempting, but it points to Makani, and of all the people I've talked to, he's been the most cooperative," Storm said. "Not so much about the fire itself, but about the people involved and their relationships to each other. For example, he told me Tanner had his breakdown after the fire. And that fits with when Jenny quit doing her sculpture and got a job at the hospital. This made her angry and bitter."

"You think Tanner killed Jenny?" Uncle Keone asked.

"I don't want to, but it's a possibility."

Aunt Maile said, "That makes four possibilities. Five, if you think Makani started the fire."

Storm chewed a hangnail on her thumb. "It bothers me that Skelly seems closer to Tanner than his own brother."

"You get that impression from Makani or from the visit you just made to Skelly?" Keone asked.

"They're childhood friends, aren't they? Connor's a couple years younger," Aunt Maile added.

"Both," Storm said in response to Keone's question, then included Aunt Maile's comment in her next thought. "I think Skelly gave Connor his black eye. Plus, Makani and Poele both alluded to Skelly's and Connor's estrangement." She reflected a moment. "But something is eating Poele. He had a relationship with Jenny, and though he's a bit of a flirt, I think he truly cared about her." She related his distress over the broken sculpture.

"Maybe that's from guilt, not sadness. Can you tell the difference?" Uncle Keone asked.

"Good question." Storm shook her head. "I've just come full circle, haven't I?"

They rode along in silence for a while, then Storm spoke again. "Makani made me think that no one really knows who lit the fire."

"And what about Dusty's daughter?" Aunt Maile contemplated out loud. "Is her disappearance tied to the fire?"

"I think it is," Storm said.

"That devastated him," Uncle Keone added.

"So did the fact that she was having Alika Liu's baby."

"Really?" Keone asked.

"Really what?" Aunt Maile asked. "The fact that she was pregnant or that it was Alika's?"

Keone chewed on the side of his cheek. "He never told me it was Alika's."

"I hope he didn't take it out on Tia," Aunt Maile said. "She didn't do anything he hadn't done a couple hundred times."

"Yeah, well. Women pay a higher price." Uncle Keone's eyes flicked sideways to see if his wife might hit the roof of the cab.

She glowered. "Makes me spit fire, though it's true."

"Watch out." Storm's hand shot up to point out a blind curve, where a large white van was rounding the corner. The road had been growing progressively narrower over the last few miles, and there wasn't room for the two large vehicles to pass each other. The driver of the white van waved and pulled off onto the shoulder.

As they pulled abreast, Uncle Keone had to creep onto the shoulder himself just to keep the side-view mirrors from scraping. He gripped the steering wheel in his effort to hold the vehicle steady while he judged the inch of space between the trucks.

Storm peered over at the driver of the van. "Thanks, Connor," she shouted. "Wait a sec."

Uncle Keone pulled ahead a few feet and looked with surprise at his niece. "Another stop?"

"If you don't mind," Storm said, and opened the passenger door, nearly banging it against a boulder. She crab-walked part of the way and climbed over several rocks to get to the back of the trailer, where the van had stopped.

Connor had his door open, and was talking to the people inside, who looked out curiously. "Hi, Storm."

One of the kids in the back seat levered his window open. "We're making him go slow so he doesn't hit another rock."

Storm caught the flush that rose from Connor's neck. His black eye was less swollen, but also more green and purple than it had been yesterday. The split lip wasn't nearly as noticeable.

"That how you got that shiner?" she asked Connor, but she could tell from his brief and wordless nod he knew that she knew how he got it.

"You going riding?" he asked.

"We thought we'd go to Halawa Stream and back in the valley a ways. How you doing? Did you see Tanner?"

"Sure, I took over from him yesterday afternoon. We had a great time." With that, he looked toward the van, as if for confirmation. The people all looked satisfied. And curious.

Storm took a step toward the front of the van, where they'd have a bit more privacy. His eyes looked more alert and his skin was clearer. A good sign he was weaning himself off the steroids.

"You know if Luke got there?" Storm asked.

"No, but Tanner left in a hurry. He was worried."

"Connor, how do we get to the cabin?"

"I don't know. I've only been there once, and I'm not that good at directions." He shoved a rock around with the toe of his shoe.

"I'm not going to bother Tanner. I just want to see if he and Luke need help. Luke could be really sick."

"He cut his hand badly, too. There was a lot of blood." Connor let the air hiss through his teeth as he seemed to reach a decision, then he heaved a sigh. "From the bay, there's one path leading into the valley. A couple of miles in, you'll get to a fork. Go right. The path is going to get narrower, until it's just a game trail. Hunters use it—and Tanner, but he makes sure it stays overgrown." He met her eyes. "It's going to be tough going at that point on horseback. You may have to tie them up and go on foot." He kicked the rock hard. "Storm, you can't tell anyone I told you this. Not ever."

"I won't," Storm said. "I promise."

Connor's eyes bored into hers. "Try to keep in mind where the ocean is and head east. There are tiny little notches cut in some of the tree trunks, but you've got to be looking for them."

"You're not bad with directions, are you?"

"No."

"Hey, Connor?"

He looked at her with sad eyes, full of doubt.

"Whose idea was it for those guys to all get tattoos?"

"My brother's." Connor's voice was so low she could barely hear him.

"You don't have one, do you?"

"No," he said, and turned away. He got back in the van without looking at her, but his hand rose in the open window as he drove off. The tourists waved with more enthusiasm.

Chapter Thirty-eight

Luke gave himself an insulin dose after breakfast, helped wash the dishes, then went back to the sofa. Tanner had already put away the bedding, and Luke looked around for the blanket he'd used. A chill had come over him. He couldn't find the blanket and Tanner was outside checking the tanks where he cultivated and dried seaweed samples, so Luke dug through his backpack and put on another shirt. He also got out his copy of *From the Mixed-up Files of Mrs. Basil E. Frankweiler.* He liked the book, and he might as well do his homework. In fact, he'd probably missed the weekend assignment. He shivered again and curled into the arm of the couch.

Luke was having a hard time concentrating, despite the fact that he loved the descriptions of the museum where Claudia and Jamie, the characters in his book, were hiding. So different from his life. Maybe he should write a story about a rainforest. He was pondering how to work an evil, tattooed character into his own novel and shivering with the thought when his father's hand on his forehead woke him up.

"You're burning hot." Tanner loomed above him, frowning. "I've got to look at that hand again. Stay here."

Like he was going anywhere. Unh unh, no way, he was just too tired. And his head ached, though the hand didn't hurt much at all. Or at least not as bad as his head did, especially right behind his eyeballs, which throbbed like his hand had yesterday.

Tanner woke him up again. "Stick this under your tongue." He jammed an old, mercury-type thermometer in before Luke could even get his mouth open, and Luke gave a grunt of protest. Tanner rummaged through Luke's backpack, which elicited a louder complaint. "Where's your glucose kit? Oh, here."

Luke's eyes popped open when his dad poked his finger. "Ow."

"Sorry, I should probably let you do that. Son, can you stay awake long enough to help me use this?"

Luke peered at it, but the numbers were blurry. He squinted, and Tanner turned the gadget so that the boy could see better. Luke still couldn't see the numbers very well. Looked like 48 mg/dl, but that must be 148 mg/dl. He'd just had breakfast, hadn't he?

"What time is it?" Luke mumbled.

"You had breakfast two hours ago. I didn't want to wake you up."

"What's that number say?" Luke asked.

"Forty-eight. What's it supposed to be?"

Luke blinked a few times and his dad grabbed his chin to look into his eyes. He then took Luke's injured hand in his and unwound the gauze bandage.

Tanner was being a little rough, Luke thought. His hands were shaking a bit, too. But Luke's mom had told him that it was okay when his dad's hands shook because it meant he was taking his medicine, so Luke let his eyes close again. Medicine was necessary, and Luke was careful about his. Took his insulin just like the doctor told him, on time and the right dose.

Tanner poured a lot of peroxide over his cut and Luke jerked at the sting. The wound was foaming like the beers Skelly liked to drink. Luke used to get to pour for him. He hadn't done that for a long time, though.

"This doesn't look too good," Tanner said, more to himself than to Luke. "Hey, son? What's your blood sugar supposed to be?"

Luke forced his eyes open. His voice sounded slurred, even to him. "One-thirty to one-fifty. I think." He made himself think for a moment. "I ate two hours ago, right?"

Tanner didn't answer. Luke peeked at his father and noticed that his eyes looked big and dark against his white face. His hair looked messed up, too, which struck Luke as funny.

Tanner got up and ran into the kitchen. He came back with a glass of orange juice. "Can you drink this?" Tanner held it to Luke's lips. "All of it."

"I'm not hungry. My head aches."

"Luke, your blood sugar is too low. We've got to get to the doctor."

"Call her. I want to take a nap."

His dad left him alone for a few minutes, but Luke could hear him banging around the house. A few cupboard doors rattled, then he came back.

"Luke, please. Put your backpack on."

"C'mon, Dad, let me sleep."

"No, now." Tanner spoke sharply. "And eat this." He handed Luke a granola bar. This time Luke recognized the edge in his father's tone as fear instead of impatience or anger. He took a bite of the bar while his dad worked his arms into the straps of the newly stuffed pack.

Tanner toggled a switch on a radio, and Luke watched his father shake his head with disgust. "Shit, the battery's dead. I should have plugged it in last night." Tanner almost never swore, and his voice cracked, almost as if he wanted to cry. He gave Luke's shoulders a gentle shake. "I'm going to carry you piggy-back. You understand? Your job is to hold on. If you need to stop, you tell me."

Chapter Thirty-nine

Uncle Keone parked the horse trailer at the end of the road. A couple of other cars lined the shoulder, too, probably fishermen and hikers, but the people were no longer in sight. Storm hopped out of the truck, with Aunt Maile close behind. The two women walked around to the back of the trailer while Keone locked up the cab.

Storm clucked her tongue. "We're here, fellas." A horse nickered in response, and she opened the gate. Three alert heads turned toward them. Moonlight was the closest.

"Hey, buddy. I thought you weren't coming. You'd better not get spooky and dump one of us."

Uncle Keone walked up. "Dusty's been working him on the lunge line, dangling all kinds of stuff in front of him. Grocery bags, rubbish bin lids. He should be okay."

Keone had been around horses his entire life, and he still worked with them. More than she did, so Storm knew better than to question. She also knew that no one, no matter how much experience he or she had, was exempt from Murphy's Law, especially where horses were concerned.

"Want me to ride him?" Storm asked, though she knew the answer.

"We're considering buying him for Parker Ranch, so I'd like to give him a try. Maybe we can swap when we turn around."

"Makani wants to train him more."

Uncle Keone didn't say anything, but Storm caught the flash of annoyance in his eyes when he led Moonlight out of the trailer. She was butting into his *kuleana*, and he was proud of his expertise.

Storm gave a shrug and went after the second horse. He'd forget in about two seconds as long as she didn't raise the topic again. She'd tried. Not that she was any better rider than either her aunt or uncle, but she was younger and she'd rather have her own tailbone get bruised than one of theirs.

Aunt Maile rummaged in the bed of the pickup right behind the cab where they'd stowed the tack. "Okay, I've got three bridles, three saddle pads, and two saddles. What's up? Storm, did you help load this stuff?"

"Yeah, and I could have sworn I saw three saddles back there. Check and see if it slid under the trailer overhang."

Keone spoke up. "Makani muttered something about a broken girth after he got that phone call. Damn, I wonder if he got distracted and forgot to put a replacement in."

"No saddle under the trailer," Aunt Maile said. She blotted sweat from her face with a handkerchief. "Whew, it's hot up here."

Keone had tied Moonlight to the side of the trailer and Storm tied a big chestnut with white forelegs next to him. She went into the trailer after the third horse, a buckskin, which she led out. "Isn't this the horse Hamlin rode the other day?"

"Looks like it," said Keone.

"You think he's spooky?"

"Hard to tell," Keone said. "One of us might have been able to hold him, but you never know."

Aunt Maile walked over carrying two saddle pads. "What are we going to do?"

"I'll take one bareback," Storm said. "I'm used to it." She turned to Uncle Keone. "Which do you think, the chestnut or the buckskin?"

He shrugged. "Six or a half-dozen."

"That's what I figured."

"Take the chestnut. We'll canter across the beach and see how she behaves," Aunt Maile said.

"We can always swap saddles," Uncle Keone said. "The important thing is we don't want you getting hurt."

"Me either," Storm said. "But I'm comfortable bareback."

"I know," Aunt Maile said.

The first thing the trio did was pick their way down the sharp slope from the road to the beach, and Storm remembered right away that the hardest part of riding bareback was going up or down steep hills. Normally, a rider would lean back when descending a hill and forward on the way up, but a bareback rider has to keep from sliding. Storm had to use her thighs and calves like vices to keep from sliding onto the horse's neck. Naturally, the chestnut interpreted this as a signal to pick up the pace. Storm was glad the mare, whose name was Poppy, was behind Uncle Keone and Aunt Maile on their mounts.

"What are you giggling about?" Uncle Keone turned around to watch Storm.

"She's responsive. I like that."

"Storm's bouncing all over the place," Aunt Maile added.

"Not," Storm said, and gathered herself. "Let's run." This time, when Storm squeezed Poppy's sides, she let the horse go. Poppy had a smooth gait, and Storm kept the reins loose while she gave the horse a little more pressure with her left leg. To her delight, Poppy veered right, toward the water. Storm let up with the left leg and used the right. Poppy went left.

"I like this horse," she declared as she shot past Uncle Keone. Moonlight tossed his head and added a hop or two, asking to be let go. Uncle Keone looked back at his wife, who nodded.

None of them had to do anything to encourage the horses. All three galloped across the wide beach and all three people wore big smiles. Storm led the group and pulled up when Bob Crowder came out of the boat house to see what all the noise was about. Storm pulled Poppy to a stop.

"Howzit," Bob said. He shaded his eyes with his hand. "How's the cop doing? Someone told me you got him to the hospital just in time. A bleeding ulcer, was it?"

"He's getting better," Storm said. "He was in a lot of pain that day, and I was worried."

"Me, too. He's a good guy."

"I think so too." Keone and Maile were riding up and Storm turned to greet them. "We'll see you soon," she said with a wave at Bob.

Storm pointed to the trail that led inland, and they followed.

Keone eyed Poppy. "You like that horse?"

"More and more. How's Moonlight?"

"He's good." Keone still watched the mare.

A half-hour later, Poppy splashed into Halawa Stream without hesitation, and all three let their horses drink from the cold water.

"See if she'll balk when you ask her to cross," Keone said. He, like Storm and Aunt Maile, knew that some horses would hesitate to cross water and needed another horse to take the lead, especially if the stream was fast moving. The crossing in front of Storm was about a foot deep and burbled swiftly over a rocky bed, a good test.

Storm gave Poppy a gentle squeeze. Whenever she was on a new horse, Storm would at first give the animal the gentlest of commands. Poppy responded right away and picked her way across the stones. Moonlight and Aunt Maile's buckskin followed.

The trail went deeper into the valley, winding a parallel path to the stream. At one point, the group came to a fork in the path, and Storm told Uncle Keone, who led, to go right. Before long, they emerged from the forest into a clearing. A sagging fence, which from time to time leaned on trees for support, paralleled the path for as far as they could see. Inside was a series of beautifully maintained and terraced kalo patches.

"They farm taro the old way," Aunt Maile said. "A labor of love."

A tidy one-room cabin, surrounded by about eight lolling cats, sat adjacent to the taro farm.

Storm eyed the little house. "Tanner is farther in, from what Niwa told me."

"We've gone about a mile," Uncle Keone said. "No electrical service, and I don't see a generator, either."

"Tanner has a generator. I heard he does some research on seaweeds at his place."

"Do I hear a waterfall?" Aunt Maile asked.

"Must be Moalua Falls," Keone said. "If we're lucky, we'll see it from the trail."

"Isn't that where the *mo'o* lives?" Storm asked.

"That's the legend. You have to put a ti leaf in the water. If it floats, the lizard will leave you alone."

"I'd rather go swimming back at the beach," Storm said, and Aunt Maile agreed.

Keone looked over his shoulder at the two women. "That does sound good. We'll do that before we trailer the horses for the ride back."

About a quarter of a mile farther, the pounding of another waterfall sounded, even through the dense foliage of the forest.

"That's Hipuapua Falls," Keone said. "It's about twice the height of Moalua."

"Any evil lizards?" Storm asked, and Keone laughed.

In a mile or two, the trail began to narrow and climb. Up to this point, the horses had negotiated mud puddles, half-buried boulders, and tangled roots without any problem, but Storm, who could feel Poppy's muscles working, sensed the horse gather herself to push ahead. Storm leaned forward to help with the incline, gripping the horse's sides with her legs.

Before long, Storm stopped Poppy at a fork in the path. She looked back at Aunt Maile, who was next in line. "This is the second fork, where Connor said to turn right."

"We're heading up the side of the valley toward the cliffs," Keone said.

"Do you trust Connor?" asked Aunt Maile.

Storm paused, but only for a moment. "Yes, I do."

"We'll be careful," said Keone. "We're still a ways from the cliffs."

"From the descriptions I've heard, we'll get to the cabin before we get to the cliffs."

"The path is going to get steeper and rockier, and some of the drop-offs will be concealed in the undergrowth," Maile pointed out. "You okay, Storm?"

"Tomorrow I'm going to feel muscles I didn't know I had," Storm admitted, but she didn't want to turn back. Though she remembered Hamlin's warnings about not taking chances, she wanted to know if Luke was all right. Hamlin would be happy to hear that Aunt Maile was along on this adventure.

"Look." Storm pointed to a tree. "There's a notch. We're on the right track."

"Hold up a minute," Uncle Keone said.

Storm stopped Poppy and turned to watch Uncle Keone get off his horse. He wrapped Moonlight's reins loosely around a tree and put a gentle hand on Poppy's rump so that he could squeeze by. He walked ten or twenty feet ahead and bent to inspect the path.

"Shoe prints. Looks like a pair of sneakers," Keone said.

"How big?" Storm asked.

"Yours or Maile's size, maybe a bit bigger."

"Twelve-year-old boy size?" Storm couldn't keep the hope from her voice.

He placed his own boot lightly beside one of them. "Smaller than my feet. Who else would be walking back here?"

Storm could think of a few characters, but she didn't say anything.

Keone made his way back to Moonlight and mounted. "What do you both say? If we head back, we can ride along the beach some more, maybe go for a swim."

Aunt Maile looked at her niece. "Storm, it's your call. You know, if the path gets any steeper and narrower, we're going to have to tie the horses and walk."

"I don't want to make you two go in on foot."

For a brief moment, she considered telling them to turn around and going on alone. Only a brief moment though. Not only would going in alone be foolhardy, it would bring Hamlin's wrath. Taking a horse into wilderness was like swimming alone. People did it. And it was a lousy idea. Neither Aunt Maile nor Uncle Keone would leave her.

"I say we go on for ten or fifteen minutes." Uncle Keone looked at his wife, then back to Storm. "Who knows, the cabin could be a hundred yards away. But when the path narrows, we turn around."

"Okay," Storm said. She saw the doubt cross Maile's face, but her aunt slowly nodded.

"Ten minutes," Aunt Maile said.

Storm urged Poppy forward. A six-foot wall of moss-covered rock edged the narrow trail on Storm's right while to the left, the dense ground cover fell steeply. Jagged lava rock boulders poked through the foliage.

They hadn't gone far before the mare's ears pointed forward and the horse gave a quick snort of warning. Storm squinted into the dense forest. Perhaps Poppy was reacting to one of the birds that twittered overhead. Except the birds had been present all along, and now they were quiet.

Chapter Forty

"What is it, Storm?" Aunt Maile called out.

"I don't know, Poppy senses something." As if to confirm her words, a shudder ran through the mare. Without prompting, Poppy stopped, her ears pricked forward and her head high.

The sound of thudding footfalls and the rustle of disturbed foliage came from ahead. Poppy stamped a forefoot and whinnied a warning.

"Someone's coming," Storm shouted.

"Can you turn?" Uncle Keone asked. He looked back at his wife. "Maile, you may have to back up."

Aunt Maile was already urging her horse to reverse, and the buckskin looked glad to have direction. Not far behind them, the path widened and Aunt Maile aimed for a place where she could make a safe turn.

"Is it another horse?" she asked.

"Sounds like a person running," Storm said.

The wall of lava rock to her right was so close she could brush it with her elbow. She had maybe eighteen inches to her left before the thick ground cover dropped precipitously.

Storm gathered the reins and rested the right one against Poppy's neck. The horse responded instantly by sitting back on her haunches and pivoting on her hind legs. Poppy hadn't wanted to step into the deep foliage, either. Surprised at the mare's tight response, Storm grabbed a chunk of mane and caught herself before she slid off Poppy's rear.

Now the rushing steps were very close, around the next curve in the trail. And Storm and Poppy were blocked by Moonlight, who was near panic.

Uncle Keone was planted deep in the saddle in an attempt to transmit weighty calm to the animal, and he had the reins short and low. Still, the horse was too excited to give his rider all his attention. The appaloosa stamped both front feet, and added a nervous hop to his frantic efforts to break loose and run. That option spelled disaster for the horse, and likely the rider. Moonlight's dark eyes, ringed with white sclera, rolled in the direction of the oncoming clatter.

Storm looked back. She was more certain than ever the slapping steps were human. But what maniac would come hurtling down a track as muddy and steep as this one?

Then she heard a man's voice, muttering as if he were carrying out a secret, yet desperate, negotiation with a greater power.

"Tanner," she shouted.

Tanner pulled up, and both his wide eyes and the fact that he carried a passenger on his back reminded Storm of Moonlight.

"What's wrong?"

"He's sick. I've got to get by." Tanner barely looked at her, and headed for the ground cover Poppy had so neatly avoided.

"Stop, I'll help you." Storm's voice was sharp. There must be a drop-off hidden there. The undergrowth was so dense, it could easily hide a precipice. Enough to break an ankle or collar bone.

He glared up at her, and she could see tear tracks in the dust on his face. "Storm, Christ almighty. Move." His voice begged.

Storm reached out an arm. She could see that Uncle Keone finally had Moonlight calmed and turned around. Aunt Maile waited at the next turn. "We'll carry you out. We can go faster."

"I don't ride. Please, he needs help."

Storm could see that. The boy's head flopped on Tanner's shoulder and his lips were bloodless, almost as white as his face. His left hand was heavily bandaged; the fingers poked out like sea urchin spines.

"We're faster than you are, Tanner. Bob Crowder can call an ambulance from the boathouse. Give him to me."

Tanner looked at her for a half a second. In that time, he made a decision, and turned so Storm could get a grip on Luke's left arm. Tanner eased the boy off his back and lifted him to slump in front of Storm. The boy moaned. "You can do this?" His voice shook.

"I've carried bigger things than Luke," Storm said. That was true, but it had been a long time, and it had never been anything as important as a sick child. But she knew the horses would be much faster than a man who was both under extreme duress and carrying a hundred-pound burden. She wrapped her right arm tightly around the boy's waist.

"Get up behind me," Uncle Keone said to Tanner, and reached out to the man.

"No," Tanner said, and backed away.

Uncle Keone looked back at Storm and raised an eyebrow.

"Let's go," she said.

Aunt Maile set the initial pace at a fast walk, while Tanner brought up the rear. He had to jog to keep up with the four-footed animals, and his breathing quickly became labored. Every now and then, on a steep part of the path, he slipped close enough to Poppy's rump that she flicked her tail in warning. She didn't like him so close, with his sliding, pounding footsteps and ragged breaths punctuated with muttered pleas, but she kept on, steady and alert.

When the trail widened at the fork, Aunt Maile increased the group's speed to a trot. Twenty feet farther, Storm heard Tanner fall with a crash that made Poppy tense.

Storm looked back. "Tanner, are you hurt?" He curled in the mud and grabbed an ankle. His mouth gaped with pain.

"Aunt Maile, stop," Storm yelled.

"No, go on. Go on," Tanner cried. He waved a hand to shoo her on.

Uncle Keone pulled Moonlight off the trail, dismounted, and walked toward Tanner. Storm knew her uncle would take care of Tanner, probably by loading him onto Moonlight, and she waved Aunt Maile on. Poppy caught up to the buckskin, and the two horses trotted swiftly along the path. Storm tightened her grip on Luke, who stirred at the bumpy gait.

"Luke? Are you awake?" He didn't look back at her or answer, but she saw his fingers curl around clumps of Poppy's mane. "We're helping your dad get you to the doctor."

She figured it was a good thing to reassure the kid. How scary would it be to wake up and find yourself bouncing along on horseback? Storm let the reins, which she'd tied together, drape over Poppy's neck, and dug in her fanny pack. She drew out the chocolate bar and handed it to the boy.

"Eat this if you can," she said, and was gratified to see Luke try to keep his bandaged hand entwined in Poppy's mane while the other wrestled with the wrapper. Storm kept her right arm wrapped tightly around the boy and picked up the reins with her left hand.

"Straighten your legs," she added. "It'll help keep you from sliding side to side."

Poppy didn't react to the shifting weight of her passengers, but the horse's ears flicked and she turned her head to regard something in the woods. Probably the waterfall, Storm thought. They had to be getting close to Hipuapua Falls.

Aunt Maile turned back toward Storm, a puzzled expression on her face. "Did you hear that?" she asked.

"What?" Storm asked.

"Pig hunters?" Aunt Maile said, just as the buckskin tossed his head and leaped sideways. Storm watched her aunt catch herself and struggle to calm the lunging horse.

Poppy snorted with alarm, and Storm tried to slide her hand forward on the reins, but holding on to Luke made the task more difficult. "Easy, girl. Easy."

Storm had a bad feeling about what the horses were picking up. Aunt Maile was coaxing her horse, which had balked in the path, when a sharp crack snapped through the trees. The buckskin leaped forward. Poppy jumped, too, and rolled her eyes back, in the direction the sound had come.

Storm clutched and pulled at the reins. "Whoa, whoa."

Luke slid to one side, dropped the remains of the candy bar, and grabbed the mare's mane in both hands. He was definitely awake now. Storm could see the clench of his jaw in his effort to hold on.

Poppy obeyed, though she twitched to be released. For a few seconds, Storm could hear the buckskin's galloping hooves, then nothing.

A small voice interrupted Storm's thoughts. "Was that a gun?"

"I think so." Storm whispered the words.

Poppy's twitching subsided to trembles and she stood quietly with her head high. She'd be off like a shot at the slightest sign from her rider. But Storm wondered if that wasn't what someone expected.

And who was that someone? Could the gun have come from local pig hunters? Pig hunters in Hawai'i usually used dogs, and she would have heard the dogs' baying before the hunters fired a shot.

"Is someone chasing you?" she asked Luke in a soft voice.

"Maybe." He looked around. "I think so."

"Who is it?"

"I don't know." She could hardly hear his answer. "But he killed my mom."

"Hold tight."

They needed to get behind a thick stand of trees or a boulder. Where was the shooter now? Ahead of her or behind? She thought the shot was from a rifle, though she wasn't sure. If she were shooting in the woods, that's probably what she'd use. With a scope, she thought, and squelched a burble of panic.

Storm tightened her legs on Poppy's sides and the horse moved forward. Fortunately, the ground was soft and the mare's hooves made little noise. Storm thought of the galloping racket Aunt Maile's horse had made when he took off and swallowed hard. She wanted to cry out to her aunt, make sure she was all right. She also hoped, and was immediately ashamed of the impulse, that the shooter had followed the running horse. She bit her lip, hard.

A copse of trees loomed ahead, and Storm stopped Poppy when they got behind the makeshift shield. Just long enough to ask Luke questions, and think about what to do next.

"How're you feeling?" she asked the boy.

"Shaky, but a little better. The chocolate helped."

"Didn't your dad feed you?"

"Sure, he did." The defensive note in Luke's voice was unmistakable. No boy wants to believe his dad is mistaken, or has fallen in the eyes of others. She'd have to remember this.

"Can you tell me who's chasing you?"

"I didn't see him well enough." Luke sounded very sad.

"Did you tell the police?"

Luke shook his head. Storm waited, and a few long moments later, the boy spoke. "I was staying with the Niwas. You know them?"

"Yes, they're nice people."

Luke seemed happy that she agreed. "I thought I'd get to talk to Uncle David, I mean, Detective Niwa, but Aunty Caroline took me to the hospital."

"What happened?"

"My blood sugar gets low when I get hurt or tired. The doctor always wants to check it and make sure I'm eating right and taking my insulin shots."

"You need one now?"

Luke grimaced. "I don't know. Dad's got my backpack."

Storm had guessed this was the case; the boy didn't seem to be carrying anything. "So what happened at the hospital?"

"The doctor adjusted my insulin and gave me some tests. She wanted me to spend the night."

"So why'd you leave?"

"I was scared. The guy in my living room saw me."

"Can you describe him at all?"

"He was bending over my mom, and it was dark, except for the light coming through the blinds." The boy's voice shook. "He had a tattoo."

"You couldn't see his face or what he was wearing?"

Luke just shook his head.

"You remember where the tattoo was?" Storm was sure she already knew the answer to that question, and it was no surprise when Luke pointed to his upper arm.

But his next words were, "Dad told me it was a vow."

"Does your dad have a tattoo, too?" Storm kept her voice even and warm, without a hint of outrage.

Luke just nodded.

"I don't blame you for leaving the hospital," Storm said. "I probably would have, too. Did your dad protect you?"

Luke rushed to answer. "He doesn't know who did it."

Storm looked behind. Speaking of Tanner, she'd really like to talk to him. Shouldn't he and Uncle Keone be coming along? A terrible fear went through her. What if Tanner had faked his turned ankle? It would have been so easy to do. With all her heart, she hoped Aunt Maile had made it back to the beach, and that the buckskin's dash along the winding path had kept them both safe. She also prayed Aunt Maile had been able to call the police.

Storm let Poppy walk ahead, and she thought about Tanner. Luke was quiet, too, and his face was sad and thoughtful. Jesus, Tanner wouldn't fire at his son, would he? She was sure he hadn't been faking his concern when he'd handed over the sick child. No, the father's quest for medical help was sincere.

But maybe the riders had messed up his grand plan. Maybe he thought he could stop them and take the boy in on his own, as he'd originally planned. That didn't sound right, either. Nor could he have fit a rifle in the backpack. Though it didn't have to be a rifle. But Tanner had called her in the first place because he was worried about Luke. She didn't think he'd have fired a gun of any kind in the direction of his son.

So that left who else? Connor knew exactly where they were, though Skelly could have figured it out. And she'd told everyone she could think of they were going riding, let alone they'd hauled a big horse trailer for two hours on the only eastbound road on the island. The Goodyear blimp would have been less conspicuous.

Chapter Forty-one

There was nothing Storm could do when Poppy clopped across the stream except flinch at the noise. She also felt a twinge of guilt for pulling the mare's head up when she lowered it to drink, but they didn't have time for Poppy to dawdle in the stream. Storm was nearly vibrating with anxiety, and Luke's knuckles were white in the mare's mane. Poppy's head bobbed in surprise at the urging pressure on her sides, but she splashed on through the water.

Nor was the path on the other side, strewn with round river rocks, a quiet passage. Storm began to consider a trick she'd only read about, which was to wrap cloth around a horse's hooves to mute the unmistakable clip-clop. She was just about to remove her T-shirt and tear it into strips, then ask Luke for his, when they rounded a bend in the trail.

Poppy nickered a greeting. But neither Storm nor Luke welcomed the man who stood before them. Storm felt the boy shrink against her.

Lambert Poele held a rifle in one hand and held the other hand before him in a stop gesture. He wore a long-sleeved cotton shirt and matching pants in a green camouflage pattern. Sweat had darkened the shirt to a mottled black. His long, disheveled hair and mud-streaked skin looked as if he'd been hunting for hours.

"At last," he said.

Neither Storm nor Luke said a word. Storm's mind raced to remember if she'd given Poppy a signal to pivot on her hind legs or if the horse had done it on her own. She wasn't sure. All she knew was they had to do it again.

Maybe they could get behind some trees before he got that rifle up and aimed. Maybe he'd hesitate to fire. Maybe he hadn't chambered a round.

Storm sat closer to Luke and hoped he'd pick up on her body language. She wanted to warn him, and ask him to hold on tighter. He must have felt her tension, because his fingers gathered in larger hunks of Poppy's mane. He also straightened his legs, seeking a better seat, but didn't have the experience to do it with stealth.

Poele let out a yell, "No!"

At the same time, Storm squeezed with her legs, harder with the right one, and simultaneously laid the right rein against Poppy's neck to turn her hard into the narrowest part of the path.

Poppy did it. She whirled. It was an unexpected move for Luke, who yelped with alarm and began to slide backward. Storm did, too, even though she knew what was coming.

Before she was even upright, the horse bolted down the path, in the direction they'd just come. This sent Luke even farther toward the horse's rear end.

"Lie down," Storm shouted. Luke would have to lie forward, which would put his weight up, and nearer the mare's shoulders. Storm hoped he'd be able to drag himself forward with his grip in Poppy's mane. Meanwhile, she grabbed with every muscle in her legs and tried to do the same, flattening Luke to the horse's back.

Luke's slide had pushed Storm back to where Poppy's rump slanted downward, and her leg muscles, spent from holding on during the upward, twisting ride into the forest, could no longer grip the mare's sleek sides. There she was, back near the animal's tail, just like she'd done with Butterfly half a lifetime ago. But back then she'd been sixteen, her legs were accustomed to riding, and most important, she'd been able to grab the saddle strings.

Here, she had only the reins and Luke. If she held on, she would drag the boy off with her. So she let go, and hoped she could roll off the path to a place that didn't plummet her onto rocks six feet below.

At the same time, another gunshot ricocheted through the trees. It even seemed to echo, but that could have been the crack of her head and shoulder when she hit the ground.

Darkness gathered in her vision, while a searing pain pierced her upper chest. Storm lay in the mud, where she gasped like a gaffed tuna and sobbed with the knowledge of her miserable failure to protect Luke.

Chapter Forty-two

She must have blacked out, because Detective Niwa's face swam into Storm's view. He was pale, and looked about ten pounds thinner than he had two days ago.

"Am I in the hospital? Am I shot?" she asked him, and realized he wasn't wearing the blue gown she'd seen him in that morning.

"You're still in the forest," he said, and put a gentle hand on her shoulder. "Try not to move. I think you broke your collarbone."

"Where's Luke?" Storm still struggled to sit up, and gritted her teeth against the pain.

"If you don't stay quiet, you're going to push that bone through the skin. Then we'll have real problems."

Storm ignored him and used her good arm to push herself into a sitting position. "Where's Luke? And Aunt Maile?"

"Christ," Niwa muttered, but this time he helped her by supporting her back.

What was *he* swearing for? Her head pounded and her chest hurt so bad she could hardly breathe. "What happened? Where are Aunt Maile and Uncle Keone?"

"Good thing I coached Little League all those years." He took a big handkerchief from his pants pocket and folded it into a triangle.

"Wear this." He gently worked the makeshift sling over Storm's head.

He wasn't answering any of her questions. "Where's Poele?" she shouted. "He's got a gun."

He lowered himself to a seat on a rock. "Poele dashed off after the boy and the horse. Probably scaring them worse. My partner is right behind. It's a regular high-speed chase, Abbot and Costello style." He didn't smile when he said it. "I hope that kid doesn't fall off."

"Me too."

"Can't Nishijima bring him down?"

"Who? The horse?"

"No, Poele." Storm wanted to scream with frustration. Pain, fear, and the knowledge of her failure to get the boy to safety were pushing her to the breaking point.

"He's trying to help."

Storm stared at him. "No, he's looking for Luke because Luke saw him the night Jenny died."

"It wasn't Poele he saw."

"The murder weapon's the sculpture, you know."

"We know. Poele brought it in." He squinted down the path. "Problem is, we thought Connor used it. You know, to hit Brock Liu."

"I don't think so." Storm took as deep a breath as she could and tried to gather her thoughts.

"Me either, now," Niwa said. "He called, told us you were on the way in here. Of course, I knew that." Niwa winced in what looked like self-reproach. "I was still looking in the wrong direction."

"Did Hamlin tell you what was in the letter? Who Brock accused of starting the fire?"

"It was Makani. And Nishijima went to talk to him. He was up at the ranch when Connor's call came in."

"Jesus, it *was* Makani." Storm wished she didn't feel so fuzzy. But how could Makani be here, in the forest? "He couldn't be after Luke, could he? He was with a new foal when Jenny died. Plus, how could he beat us here, and why didn't he stop us at the ranch?"

"Makani's not back there." Niwa looked down the path into the forest.

He tried to explain. "Nishijima talked to Makani after you left. Makani takes responsibility for starting the fire. He's carried that with him for ten years. He told us how bad Alika hurt Tia, and how he hated him for it. He thought Alika damaged his entire family."

"So he tried to kill him in a fire?"

Niwa nodded. "Seems his dad taught him some of the old chants before he moved to New Mexico."

"Was Makani at the scene of the fire?"

"No. The fire started about eleven-thirty on a Thursday night. Makani was studying for a test with a classmate. He was a junior in high school, and we found the other student, who verifies they were together. But Makani says he chanted every day for a week, and he's convinced the curse worked."

"What do you think?"

Niwa shrugged. "Who knows? I don't know how a court of law would look at it, either." He stared past her as if he looked for answers in the leaves of the trees. "Or whether they should."

Storm thought for a moment. "Could it have been Makani's dad? Where was he?"

"Seems Mr. Kekapu has been working with a Hopi shaman for the last fifteen years. Makani's gone to visit, but the older Kekapu hasn't been back since he left."

"Who do you think started the fire?" Storm asked.

"I don't know yet, but I still have some questions to ask." He met her eyes. "What I do know is they all say someone else did it. At first I thought it was a big cover up."

"Isn't it? Isn't that why they got the tattoos?"

Niwa shrugged. "I'm not so sure anymore. The tattoos, yeah. That's a sign of solidarity. But when you question them separately," Niwa met her eyes, "you get the feeling no one's sure about the fire. They all cover for someone different."

"Makani told me Dusty thought Poele did it. But then he said he overheard Poele talking about protecting Connor."

"Poele's still keeping a secret, but I have a hunch he'll share it when we get back into town." Niwa looked thoughtful. "I don't think he cares all that much about himself anymore."

"I think Connor suspects Skelly." Hadn't Makani said something about that? "Skelly gave him that black eye, you know."

A look of distress crossed Niwa's face. "Those boys have had troubles since their mom died eight or nine years ago."

"Makani tried to slow us down, didn't he? He only gave us two saddles, and—"

The crack of a rifle came from down the path. Niwa jumped to his feet. "Nishijima's got an AR-15, and that was a larger caliber rifle."

A second shot rang out, a higher-pitched sound than the first. Niwa spoke a quick command into the radio transmitter on his shoulder.

But the next noise stopped him mid-sentence. Storm's blood ran cold. A child's high, thin wail pierced the still air, and it went on for longer than either would have thought possible.

Niwa was out of sight before Storm could react. It was all she could do to get to her feet and take a few shaky steps. The howl had been a chilling lament of unfathomable pain. Had Luke been shot? Where were Uncle Keone and Tanner? Most of all, why had Niwa avoided telling her whom he and his partner were chasing?

She stood alone in the silent woods. The breeze had stopped and the leaves on the trees hung heavy and still. No birds twittered or called. The only sound was the nearby stream, but its babbling no longer seemed cheerful; instead, the water was one more obstacle in keeping her from the people she'd wanted and failed to protect. It was another reminder of her defeat.

It seemed that she stood there for hours. Finally, the throbbing of her broken clavicle forced her to lower herself onto the boulder Niwa had been using. Later, she'd guess that fifteen or twenty minutes elapsed, but it seemed an eternity.

Pain blunts the senses. Storm didn't hear the trudging footsteps until they were close. Her first thought—more of a hope—was that Uncle Keone and Luke were on the way. A half second later, she knew the heavy tread belonged to a human rather than horses. He crunched leaves and squished mud with an uneven gait.

"Detective Niwa?" She stood, not knowing whether to move in the direction he'd gone or dash the opposite way. Not that she could dash; she could barely get to her feet. The raw pain of grating bone was agony.

It was Dusty Rodriguez who limped around the bend in the trail. Like Poele, he wore a camouflage shirt that was soaked with sweat. His shirt tail hung out, and one leg of his jeans was dark with blood. He reached out to Storm.

"Dusty, what happened?" she asked, but she backed away. What was *he* doing out here? Niwa had said Poele was trying to help, but he hadn't told her Dusty was in the forest, too.

"I got caught in the crossfire. Damned cop aimed over me. Sights on his gun must be way off."

"Who was he shooting at?" She looked down at his leg. From his thigh down, the denim glistened with fresh blood. His left boot made a squishy noise. "Oh, God. You better put pressure on that."

Squish, clump, squish, clump. He made his way closer to the rock where she'd been sitting. "Good idea."

He almost fell trying to keep his injured leg straight and threw his arms out for support. One grabbed at a nearby tree and the other windmilled, looking for an anchor.

Instinctively, Storm took a step closer, and he grabbed her arm.

She yelped. "Ow."

"Just help me out a sec."

"I'm hurt, too," she said.

But Dusty yanked her toward him, and she stumbled from the stabbing shock to her injured arm and chest. He pulled her tight, until her face was smashed against his chest. She couldn't move, and her shoulder hurt like hell.

"Stop it. You're hurting me." Her voice was muffled against him.

The bitter stench of pain and desperation saturated his shirt. It was the odor from her dream, and it nearly choked her.

"Let go." She tried to turn her head, but he gripped her back like a vice. If she'd been uninjured, she would have pushed free in a second, but the broken collarbone kept her captive.

He didn't answer, and she could feel the muscles in his chest contract when he turned his head from side to side. He was looking for someone.

"Why are you doing this?" Pain pulsed in her ears and she fought the sensation that she might black out.

The slide of a rifle bolt clicked behind her. "Let her go," a voice said. A voice she'd heard, but didn't know well. Nishijima?

Dusty only intensified his grip. Tears of pain and betrayal stung her eyes. It was Dusty who'd hunted them.

"Why?" she said into his shirt front. "I always admired you."

"You should have left us alone." He spoke through gritted teeth and she felt a tremor pass through him. He was probably weakened by pain or the loss of blood.

Storm wanted to cry, but she knew she'd be better off trying to comfort or appease him. She had to convince him to let go.

"Are you worried about the letter?" Storm asked. He merely tightened his grip, and she gasped. "Are you protecting Makani?" Anything to make him talk. What pushed him to this act?

"It's too late." Dusty's voice was low and sad.

"Nobody believes Brock Liu."

"Let her go." Nishijima's voice came from a different copse of trees. He was moving closer.

Dusty turned toward the voice and reached under his shirt tail for the gun at his back. He leaned back against the rock for stability. The movement jerked Storm forward, off balance.

She lurched, the ends of her collarbone grating with a crushing pain that buckled her knees. Pain and terror blackened the edges of her vision and a wave of nausea swept over her. She slid to one side, and as she did, another shot rang out.

◇◇◇

The flurry of voices and crackling radio static awoke her. "She's conscious," a voice said.

"Check her vitals and get a mental status evaluation," said a voice from a radio. "What's your name?" someone said. "Do you know where you are?"

Storm forced her eyes open. A woman's face swam above her and Storm felt as if she were rocking from side to side. She closed her eyes to stop the spinning sensation. She was flat on her back, unable to lift either arm. The last thing she wanted to do was barf.

"My name's Storm," she said. Her mouth felt as if it were filled with dry pebbles. "Shot?" was the only other word she could utter.

"No, but you got that broken collarbone jammed pretty good. You know where you are?" the woman repeated.

"I'm thirsty." Storm could only whisper.

"Suck on this." The woman held an ice cube to her lips. Heaven. Storm wanted a tall glass of them.

"Honey girl?" came a warm, familiar voice.

"Aunt Maile? Where are we?" She could hear the slur in her voice and she kept her eyes closed. Too much movement. Urp.

"An ambulance."

"Tell 'em to stop that swaying." Storm tried to open her eyes again. No spinning, but that rocking was bad.

"Road'll straighten out in a minute or two," the ambulance woman said.

A few minutes later, Storm opened her eyes long enough to take a look around. Aunt Maile was next to her. She was strapped in, too.

An emergency medical tech sat between them, with a stethoscope around her neck. She checked the IV drip in Storm's arm and smiled. "Feeling any better?"

"A bit." Storm looked over at Aunt Maile. "You hurt, too?"

Aunt Maile winced. "Damned horse clipped my knee against a tree when he bolted."

"Oh, no." Her words were still slurred, but the nausea was retreating.

"I'll be okay."

"Where's Uncle Keone?" Storm asked.

"He's following in the horse trailer."

Some memories began to return. Storm recalled falling off the horse and Poppy taking off with Luke. The rest was still a muddle. "Where's Luke?"

"Another ambulance. With Tanner." Aunt Maile's voice sounded sad.

"What's wrong?" Storm turned her head suddenly and her gurney took a few whirls. The tech warned her to take it easy.

"Tanner got shot. He was protecting Luke."

"Oh, no." Storm blinked hard. "How is he?"

"Don't know yet." Aunt Maile's voice was low. "Looked pretty bad."

Now Storm was beginning to remember. "It was Dusty, wasn't it?"

"Yes."

"He grabbed me."

Several moments passed and no one said anything. Storm recalled his smell from the dream. The odor still lingered, as if it clung to her clothing. She wanted to gag.

"Where is he? What happened?"

"He's dead." Aunt Maile's voice broke.

A silence fell in the swaying chamber, broken only by the crackling of a voice on the radio. The tech spoke into the receiver on her shoulder. "Stable. Tender over her clavicle, the bone end is tenting the skin. Mental status improving." She fiddled with the IV.

Storm dozed off again.

This time, when Storm turned her head, the tech didn't stop her. Tears wet the sides of Aunt Maile's face. Her voice was so low, Storm had to strain to hear.

"I never thought Dusty would turn into a killer. There was no need."

Storm's brain felt like it was stuck in road tar. Part of it was shock, she knew. "The letter Jenny mailed from Brock," she said. "I think he was protecting Makani."

"Maybe," Aunt Maile said.

"I wonder if Jenny warned him, or threatened him. Delia told me they'd been lovers."

"That poor woman."

"I know." Storm thought about the other damaged souls, all of them associated with the fire. "Connor called the police, didn't he?"

"And I doubted that young man."

"Me, too. Everyone did." Storm thought for a minute. "But why didn't he warn us when he saw us on the road? Before we rode into the valley?"

"Detective Niwa said Connor saw Dusty coming out of Hawai'i EcoTours when he drove in. Skelly was upset, but wouldn't say why. Connor knew it had to do with Dusty, and worried that Dusty was on his way to Halawa. That's why he called the police."

Storm thought about what her aunt said. "Detective Niwa said Poele figured out the murder weapon. But I don't understand why he went after us in the forest."

"He thought the police suspected Connor. But he also knew the sculpture got broken when it was in his possession, not Connor's. It took Poele a while to realize his nightly drinking would make it easy to take it from his living room and bring it back without his noticing."

"You talked to Poele?" Storm asked.

"For a minute or two. He helped get you out of the woods after Nishijima shot Dusty."

"I must have blacked out. All I remember is Dusty limping down the path."

"Forgetting might be a good thing."

Chapter Forty-three

The smell came to Storm in dreams. Along with it, she would feel a sensation of overwhelming sadness, so oppressive that she couldn't move. She couldn't even struggle. Her bed was turning into an adversary; she dreaded the night.

Storm and Aunt Maile stayed one night in Moloka'i Hospital to make sure they were stabilized before they flew to O'ahu for surgery on Storm's collarbone. Aunt Maile needed to see a specialist for her knee.

Storm had no problem remembering that trip, despite the painkillers Dr. Goldbaum administered. What she didn't remember was the story she read in the Honolulu paper once she got home. Dusty Rodriguez had used her for a shield in his shoot-out with the police.

She threw down the paper and barely made it to the bathroom. Fifteen minutes after she tossed her Cheerios, Hamlin called. "Storm, could I come over?"

"Yes, I'd love to see you," she said, and sent a frantic glance toward Aunt Maile, who was nursing a cup of coffee at Storm's kitchen table.

Aunt Maile looked older than she had a week ago, and the look she gave Storm was sad. "I'll go in the other room."

Ten minutes later, Hamlin knocked at the door and Aunt Maile unhooked her cane from the back of her chair, took a section of the paper, and limped to the living room.

Hamlin's arm was still in a sling, but he gave Storm a warm hug. "I'm glad you're home."

"Me too." There was an awkward pause. "You want some coffee?"

"Sure, thanks." She handed him a mug, but instead of drinking, he drew a breath as if he were going to dive under water. "Storm, I'm having trouble with things."

"I know."

"I worry about you." He sat for a minute, and turned the coffee cup in his hands without drinking. "And it's hurting me, too."

"I never wanted you to get hurt."

"I know. I also hate it when you're in danger."

Storm swallowed hard. "I don't think I can change."

"I don't want you to." Hamlin met her eyes for the first time since he'd arrived. He gave her a small, but warm, smile. "I have to think about whether this is working for me."

"You want me to move out of the office?"

"No!" He shook his head vehemently. "Look, I've got to go to the mainland for a client. It'll take a couple of weeks, and I'll take another week to visit my mother and sister."

"You need to get away?"

He shrugged. "I need to reflect, and it'll help if I'm in a different place. You know, to get a perspective."

"Yeah, I know." Storm wasn't at all sure she knew. A kind of numbness had come over her, and a great weight seemed to have settled on her chest.

Hamlin stood and walked over to her. He gently kissed the top of her head and let himself out the door.

A moment later, Aunt Maile came back into the kitchen and took Storm into her arms. She held her for a long time.

Aunt Maile spent a week with Storm. They were the walking wounded, and they comforted each other. Aunt Maile was burdened with the knowledge that someone she'd thought was a decent, if not perfect, human being could have been so savage. Storm tried to reassure her, though she had no answers. Storm found deep solace in Maile's company, and the time they spent together was the first time alone they'd had for years.

Storm also drove one-handed to the doctor's for an MRI of Aunt Maile's knee. Uncle Keone monitored both of them with almost hourly phone calls from the Big Island, and threatened to come to O'ahu at least twice a day. When the surgeon recommended physical therapy before resorting to surgery on Aunt Maile's knee, he relaxed a little.

But Storm's insomnia worsened. Aunt Maile watched Storm's bedroom light go on at two every night, and finally told her she would have to confront the demons that haunted her. Two days after Aunt Maile returned to the Big Island, Storm sat at the Honolulu Airport, shivering in the cold blast of an air-conditioning vent at the Island Air gate. She waited for the eight o'clock flight to Kaunakakai.

Delia would pick her up. They were going to have breakfast together, because the first funeral was at ten. It would be short. The second was at two, and Delia had warned her there'd be a funeral feast. Storm didn't know how she'd bear it. The nightmare of nearly two weeks ago was creeping back. If only she could wake up.

The flight was quick, and Delia was waiting. Storm's spirits went up several notches just seeing her. They hugged, Storm with her good arm. Delia was careful not to press on the side with the sling.

"How're you feeling?" Delia asked.

"Okay." Storm took in Delia's red, puffy eyes. "Oh hell, about the same as you."

Delia tried to giggle, but it hiccupped into something else and she wiped at an eye. "I look like shit."

"I've never seen you without the eyelashes," Storm said.

Delia really did laugh at that. "How 'bout this shirt?" She pulled at the hospital smock she wore. It was yellow, with blue teddy bears. She also had on sneakers and conservative navy slacks.

"I took a job at the hospital. And I like it. I'm taking some classes."

"Hey, that's great. When you apply to medical school at UH, let me know."

Delia looked at her shyly. "Hey, don't laugh. I have to do a lot of work, but I love the classes and Dr. Goldbaum said he'd help me."

"That would be wonderful," Storm said, and hugged her again.

"How's Hamlin's shoulder?" Delia asked.

"It's okay, but—"

"Damn. I thought that only happened to me."

"Hardly," Storm said, and her voice broke on the last syllable.

"If it weren't nine in the morning, I'd suggest a drink." Delia shook her head. "We'll have one later, and I'm buying."

"Thanks." Storm tried to smile. "And I'll buy when you get to O'ahu. We'll drink to celebrate then."

"It's a deal."

Delia drove an ancient Toyota. Storm could see through rust holes to the road. "Your car?"

"Yup. No more big air-conditioned vans."

"You miss working at the ranch?"

Delia thought for a minute. "I miss the people there. But I couldn't stay after Dusty died. Too many memories."

"What about Makani?"

"He'll probably be at the funeral, but I heard he moved back to Maui. I also heard your uncle is bugging him to move to the Big Island and work on Parker Ranch."

Delia took Storm to a diner in Kaunakakai and both women ordered scrambled eggs, toasted Moloka'i bread, and fried rice. Delia ordered a side of Portuguese sausage and dumped half of it on Storm's plate.

The thought of the funeral was giving her a stomach ache. Storm ate the eggs, but could only pick at the fried rice. Normally she loved fried rice. One nibble of the sausage was enough. Delia wasn't eating much, either.

After the initial pleasantries, the reason for the visit loomed and neither woman knew what to say. Delia broke the silence. "Took long enough for the police to release the bodies."

Storm nodded. "Must have been hard on the families."

"Yeah."

Storm pushed a piece of sausage around on her plate. "So why'd he do it?"

Delia's shoulders hunched. She knew what Storm was asking. "Remember I told you Jenny was manipulative?"

"I knew she was unhappy."

"Yeah, well. The only people she was ever really nice to were Luke and Tia. I think she saw herself in Tia, and didn't want Tia's hopes and dreams to die as hers had. Some letters from Tia turned up in Jenny's house. Tia was planning to come back and see her father. Confront him about blaming her for getting raped." Delia put an entire packet of guava jelly on her toast. "Did you know about that?"

"A bit. Makani alluded to it."

"Jenny probably told him about the letter Brock had given her to mail if anything happened to him." She winced. "You find the right person around here, and they'll give you all the dirt on the old families. Brock knew about the Kekapu family line of fire sorcerers, and he found out Makani had studied the chants with his father."

"But Makani wasn't even at the fire."

"Didn't matter to Dusty. He believed." Delia took a bite of toast. "He'd grown up with the legends, and he knew Makani's dad had powers."

"Why didn't he go to a lawyer and ask some questions? Why'd he…?"

"Get so crazy?" Delia finished.

"Yeah."

Delia stared out the window of the café as if insight came down on beams of sunlight. "He knew he failed Tia. Hell, Jenny reminded him. Makani was like his son, and his second chance. He was going to protect him."

"He must have really hated the Lius," Storm said. "I mean, he bashed Brock's head in."

"What I don't get is how Brock ended up in the woods. I thought Hamlin had a receipt he'd signed for a kayak rental."

"I asked Detective Niwa about that. It's one of the few conversations from the hospital I remember. Dusty helped Brock Liu load his SUV at the Ranch, right? Skelly said Brock never showed up at Hawai'i EcoTours that morning. He was supposed to pick up a kayak and paddle a few miles east to the area around Kalaeloa Lighthouse. I guess the Liu family has land there."

"Do the police think Dusty followed him from the ranch?"

"That's the theory. But no one at the Ranch said Dusty seemed upset or preoccupied."

"I wonder if the confrontation didn't just get out of his control."

"You think that's what happened to Jenny, too?"

Delia thought for a moment. "Jenny probably reminded him of his past failures."

"So he clobbered her?"

"He'd twisted events in his mind until he snapped. Her cruel tongue just pushed him over the edge."

"There's another thing I'm curious about. Has anyone figured out how Dusty got hold of the statue? It was in the trunk of Connor's car, wasn't it?"

Delia looked sad. "Connor was too disorganized to notice if it was there or not, and he never locks the car. It would have been easy to take and put back."

"Such a waste." Storm pushed her plate away.

"You got that right, sister." Delia shoved the last of her toast in her mouth and looked at her watch. "We should go."

Dread sat on Storm's shoulders. She could hardly breathe.

Delia watched her, concerned. "We'll sit at the back where you can get out."

"Okay." Her voice was a whisper.

When the two walked into the narthex of the small, airy church, Storm got a whiff of the smell from her dream. It disappeared as quickly as it came, almost like a subconscious message, or memory.

A few people stood around, some of them softly talking, most quiet. Most were making their way to the pews. No one seemed to notice her, though one or two nodded a greeting to Delia.

Delia took her arm. "The two back pews are already filled. Looks like others have the same plan." She looked around, then pointed. "There's room on the left there."

Storm saw Detective Niwa and his wife and a number of people from the ranch. Poele sat in a corner near the front, his swollen eyes straight ahead. Makani sat beside him, and Storm saw his shoulders tremble. She had a sense of déjà vu, which haunted her. Poele always had an aura of discontent, but she'd never seen Makani cry. Had she?

She tried to listen to the minister, who did his best to make some sense of Dusty's death. He alluded to the devastating loss of Dusty's daughter and grandson, then emphasized Dusty's devotion to his family and his commitment to his friends.

Except for allowing the police to think one of those friends committed murder, Storm thought. When Poele stumbled up to join Makani, Skelly, Connor, and two other men as a pall bearer, Storm gave him a lot of credit. He looked as if he didn't have the energy to walk, and she felt a lot the same way. She couldn't have done it if she'd been in Poele's shoes. Skelly looked a wreck, and Connor appeared sadder, calmer, and thinner.

Storm and Delia left the church with the rest of the guests. They held each other's arms like they were ninety-year-old grannies, but they looked in better shape than the young woman who leaned into her husband, sobbing as if she couldn't go on.

It was obvious neither she nor her husband lived on Moloka'i. He was pale and stood out in a dark business suit. The rest of the men wore aloha shirts and slacks. The weeping woman's simple, long-sleeved black dress was also a contrast to local dress.

Storm tried not to stare at the man in the suit. He looked familiar. It was hard to see the woman, because she wiped tears from under large, dark glasses. Two young children stood by, pained by their mother's torment.

Detective Niwa walked up to Storm and Delia. A pretty, dark-haired woman held his hand protectively. "Storm, I don't think you've met my wife. This is Caroline."

Storm held out her hand, but Caroline reached out with both arms and drew her into a gentle hug. "Thank you again for helping David." She gave Storm a rueful smile. "Sorry I was a little grumpy on the phone."

"I understand," Storm said.

Niwa looked shell-shocked. "I still can't get a grip on this. I grew up with Dusty. We played football together in high school."

"What was he like?" asked Delia.

"A ladies' man." A smile shone through the sadness in Niwa's eyes. "Had more girlfriends than the rest of us put together."

He sighed and turned toward the parking lot. "We better go. Got to do something before the next one."

He split off. Storm and Delia made their way to the old Toyota.

"The next one." Storm sounded woeful. "Poor Luke."

"Yeah. We'd better get going, too. It's a long drive."

"It's appropriate, though. Tanner would like it," Storm said, though she dreaded the drive.

The last trip to and from Halawa was still fresh in her mind. She'd been in a haze of pain and shock. She'd been dimly aware that Tanner and Luke were in the ambulance in front of hers, and she and Aunt Maile found out after their arrival at Moloka'i Hospital that Tanner died en route. He'd stepped in front of a bullet meant for Luke and it had ripped through a major artery. Despite the valiant efforts of the emergency techs, he'd bled to death.

To Storm's surprise, the drive was filled with simple pleasures that helped lift her low spirits. Sunlight danced across azure waters. Palm fronds murmured their blessings and the beaches radiated warmth. Delia told funny stories about the hospital and the people she met there.

Parked cars lined the road, more than a quarter mile from the end. Delia looked down at Storm's sandals. "Those are pretty. But can you walk in them?"

Storm left them in the car. She could walk in them, but the heels would sink in the sand. And she liked the feel of sand on her feet.

Bob Crowder and the Richards brothers had set up a bank of tables that were filling up with food. Piles of kalua pork, *lau lau*, *lomi* salmon, poi, salted and fresh fish, poke, and more desserts than one would find in the average bakery. A group of local musicians had used the boat house's generator to set up microphones and amplifiers and were strumming ukulele and guitars.

When the two women got down to the water, an outrigger canoe approached the beach. The mainland people in the dark clothes were in the canoe with Luke, Poele, Makani, and the couple's son. The local guys hopped out to pull the canoe onto some old tires on the sand, then helped the couple out of the boat.

When they got out, Storm saw that even the mainlanders were barefoot. They weren't unfamiliar with local custom. A Hawaiian would never wear shoes in an outrigger canoe. The man, who tenderly held his wife's arm, led her to chairs set up near the buffet table. Luke and the boy followed, while the boy's sister ran to greet them.

It was then that Storm knew where she'd seen the man in the dark suit. He and the woman were in her dream. That's where she'd seen Makani cry and Poele numb with sorrow. The dream had mixed up bits and pieces, but they were all there. Like a puzzle, they began to fit together into a picture.

Storm walked over to the couple. The woman had removed her dark glasses. Her eyes were red and swollen, but so were a lot of people's. She smiled and put out her hand. Storm was struck by her large, hazel eyes. Sad eyes, older than the smooth skin of her face. They were Dusty's eyes.

"I'm Tia Davidson. This is my husband, Michael."

"I'm Storm Kayama. I went to school with Tanner."

"You know who I am, don't you?" Her voice trembled a little, and her husband put his arm around her.

"You don't have to go into that, dear."

Tia turned to him. "Yes, I do. Michael, could you take Tommy and Jesse to get some punch? I'll be with you in a few minutes."

Tia struggled for a moment with emotions that threatened to overcome her. "I could have prevented all this." Her shaking hand swept toward Luke and her son.

"Not necessarily," Storm said. "It must have been awful for you. How could you have known?"

"Luke found the postcard I sent Jenny. He wrote and told me the whole story." Tia looked away, out to the ocean. Her eyes were filled with self-reproach. "I was self-centered, angry, and young. And I held onto my anger for way too long. If I'd confronted him earlier, this wouldn't have happened."

"Who knows? Me, I always speak up at the wrong times." The pain on Tia's face touched Storm. "Women are taught to placate, and when a situation gets out of control, we feel responsible. But you can't control another person's actions."

Tia dug one foot into the sand and blinked rapidly. Storm ached for the woman's pain.

At that moment, Luke rushed up and threw his arms around Storm. He was thinner, if that was possible, but he looked happy at that moment. David and Caroline Niwa and their daughter followed close behind. Niwa and Haley were drinking a lurid pink liquid in paper cups, which Storm guessed might be fruit punch. Caroline carried two glasses of white wine. She handed one to Storm.

"They told me you were hurt when you fell off the horse." Luke eyed the sling.

"I'll be as good as new in a couple more weeks." She grinned at him. "I'm really glad to see you."

Tia gave Storm a brave smile, blew a little kiss, and went off to find her husband and children. She dragged her toes through the sand as if she relished the feel of sand between them. Like a local girl.

The Niwas watched Luke carefully, but Haley gave him a hard punch on the arm. "Want to go toss?"

"Yeah."

"Hey, Luke," Storm said. "If you ever want to visit O'ahu, you've got a place to stay."

He gave Storm a solemn nod and went after Haley.

Storm watched him run off. When he was out of earshot, she asked, "Did Makani really start the fire?"

Niwa shook his head. "There have been some interesting developments since you left. A few days after the incident back here in the valley, Lambert Poele came into the station. This was an honorable act, because ten years ago, when he told the police he suspected Alika Liu, we ignored him—mostly because old man Liu leaned heavily on the chief and local politicians to indict Poele." Niwa took a sip of the pink stuff in his glass and grimaced. "We got back in touch with Devon Liu. This time, he told us he'd made a terrible mistake."

Storm and Caroline stared at him. "Which mistake was that?" Storm finally asked.

"That's all he would say." Niwa looked out at the ocean. He was still pale and he looked much sadder than the Niwa of five days ago.

"What are you going to do?" Caroline asked.

"Nothing. We don't have any proof, and word came in this morning he was admitted to the hospital last night with a stroke."

No one said anything for a long moment. "What did you tell Luke?" Storm asked.

Caroline spoke first. "That both his parents loved him very much. We'll explain things slowly, as he asks. He's a very smart kid."

"I got that impression."

"He's living with us," Niwa said. "We're applying for permanent custody, then we're going to see if he'd like us to adopt him."

"Tanner would like that."

"I hope so." Niwa eyed his wife's glass of wine.

She moved the glass out of his reach, and addressed Storm. "He's got a lot of aunties and uncles here. Skelly's taken him out in the kayaks."

"A holistic medicine manufacturer is making a bid on Tanner's seaweed extraction technique. Tanner kept excellent records." Niwa dumped the punch onto the sand. It left a pink blotch.

"He used to take meticulous class notes, too." Storm took another sip of wine. Not bad for coming out of a box.

"We're going to set up a college fund for Luke," Caroline said.

"If you ever need me, I'm here for him." Storm's stomach growled. She was hungry for the first time in weeks. "Let's go get something to eat."

Dave Niwa looked delighted at that suggestion, and Caroline rolled her eyes.

Glossary

When the missionaries came to the islands around 1820, the Hawaiian language was completely oral. The Christian newcomers began to record the language and teach the Hawaiian natives to read and write. Anyone who lives in the islands for a period of time picks up common non-English words, and to leave them out of a story that takes place in the islands would undermine the portrayal of life here.

There are 12 Roman letters in the Hawaiian alphabet, plus two diacritical marks, the *kahakō*, a line over a vowel, and the *ʻokina*, which looks like a backwards apostrophe and signals a glottal stop in the pronunciation. The ʻokina is often considered a letter, as a word with an ʻokina can have an entirely different meaning than the same spelling without it.

Here are definitions of words used in *Fire Prayer*. Many of them are used in everyday conversation by people in Hawaiʻi.

ahi—yellow fin tuna

ahupuaʻa—wedge-shaped chunks of land controlled by Hawaiian chiefs, which theoretically had their points in the mountains and their bases in the sea outside the barrier reef

ʻāina—land, earth

akamai—smart

akua—devil, spirit, ghost, often sent on an evil mission

'alae —mud hen

ali'i—chief, chiefess, ruler, royal monarch

'a'ole—never, to be none, to have none

'aumakua—family totem or personal gods, deified ancestors who assume the shape of plants and animals

'awa—the plant *Piper methysticum.* The leaves are brewed in a tea as a treatment for insomnia.

'awapuhi, or *'awapuhi kuahiwi*—wild ginger, *Zingiber zerumbet.* A commonly used fragrant plant used for shampoos, anti-inflammatories, ringworm, and other uses.

chiisai chimpo—Japanese slang term used to describe the lack of size of a male's genitalia

char siu bao—Chinese dumpling, either baked or steamed, with meat (usually red pork) filling. Also called *manapua.*

Hā'awe i ke kua' hi'i i kea lo—said of a woman who carries a load on her back and a baby in her arms.

hala—a large wide-branched tree, characterized by aerial roots. *Pandanus tectorius,* also known as screw pine.

hanai—adoption, Hawaiian style

haole—white person

hōlona—novice, a beginner

hula kahiko—the ancient hula, as opposed to modern hula, or *hula 'auana.*

huhu—mad, angry

kahuna—teacher, minister, expert in any profession. Plural is kāhuna; the letter "s" does not exist in the Hawaiian alphabet.

kahuna ho'o ulu lā hui—specialist in increasing population, or getting women pregnant

kahuna lā'au lapa'au —a traditional Hawaiian healer, who uses native plants, herbs, and prayer

kalo—taro plant

kalua pork—salted, smoked pork, cooked until it falls apart. A local treat, often done in an imu, the traditional underground oven.

kī—ti, or the *Cordyline fruticosa* plant

koali, or *koali 'awa*—Morning glory, or *Ipomoea indica*

kolohe—mischievous, naughty

kuleana—business, field of expertise

lau lau—salt butterfish, beef, chicken or pork wrapped in taro or ti leaves and then steamed, a local delicacy. *Ono*-licious!

li hing—salty, sugary powder for flavoring fresh and dried fruits, usually reddish in color. Contains different seasonings and flavors.

limu—edible seaweed used in a number of dishes

lolo—crazy

lomi—rubbed, crushed, or squeezed. Also massaged.

mana—power

manapua—same as char siu bao. Also *ono*-licious!

mo'o—lizard, sometimes a malevolent presence in Hawaiian legends. Unless the mo'o happens to be your 'aumakua, that is.

ono—pidgin (Hawaiian?) for good, or delicious

ono—large mackerel-type fish, also known as skipjack or wahoo. *Acanthocybium solandri*

'opihi—*Cellana exarata* and others, Hawaiian limpet snail, a delicacy that makes its home on rocks at the ocean's edge

paniolo—Hawaiian cowboy

poha—the cape gooseberry, *Physalis peruviana*, a South American perennial herb in the tomato family.

poke—a dish with raw fish, seaweed, and kukui nut. Used as hors d'oeuvres.

pono—goodness, morality. Right, correct

pua'a—pig

pueo—Hawaiian short-eared owl

ule—penis

To receive a free catalog of Poisoned Pen Press titles, please contact us in one of the following ways:

Phone: 1-800-421-3976
Facsimile: 1-480-949-1707
Email: info@poisonedpenpress.com
Website: www.poisonedpenpress.com

Poisoned Pen Press
6962 E. First Ave. Ste. 103
Scottsdale, AZ 85251